"I DREAMED OF MAKING LOVE TO YOU UNDER THE OPEN SKY," HE SAID HUSKILY. "IN A PLACE JUST LIKE THIS.

Lisa, I've thought of you too many times not to know what I want to do with you, what pleasure you could give me, how I could fill you with fire."

Michael rose and gazed into her eyes. "You've told me about Jay. I know he's a lucky man. But he's not all that smart."

"Why's that?" Lisa murmured.

"If I were Jay, I would never have let you out of my sight long enough to come to a place like this."

"And why do you say that?" she breathed as his hands moved lower, urging her against his strength.

"Because I'm here, and I'm going to do everything in my power to make you forget him."

"Michael," she whispered. Then his lips were on hers, and she was moaning with pleasure, wonder, amazement that he could reach her like this, fill her with such a burning desire. . . .

WHERE THERE'S SMOKE . . .

Nell Kincaid

A CANDLELIGHT ECSTASY SUPREME

Published by
Dell Publishing Co., Inc.
1 Dag Hammarskjold Plaza
New York, New York 10017

Dell ® TM 681510, Dell Publishing Co., Inc.
Candlelight Ecstasy Supreme is a trademark of
Dell Publishing Co., Inc.
Candlelight Ecstasy Romance®, 1,203,540, is a registered
trademark of Dell Publishing Co., Inc.

ISBN: 0–440–19417–2

Printed in the United States of America
First printing—February 1984

To Our Readers:

Candlelight Ecstasy is delighted to announce the start of a brand new series—Ecstasy Supremes! Now you can enjoy a romance series unlike all the others—longer and more exciting, filled with more passion, adventure, and intrigue. The stories you've been waiting for.

In months to come we look forward to presenting books by many of your favorite authors and the very finest work from new authors of romantic fiction as well. As always, we are striving to present the unique absorbing love stories that you enjoy most—the very best love has to offer.

Breathtaking and unforgettable, Ecstasy Supremes will follow in the great romantic tradition you've come to expect *only* from Candlelight Ecstasy.

Your suggestions and comments are always welcome. Please let us hear from you.

Sincerely,

The Editors
Candlelight Romances
1 Dag Hammarskjold Plaza
New York, New York 10017

CHAPTER ONE

Lisa Bennett shifted into third and pulled out onto a straight, clear stretch of highway. It was a perfect day to leave New York City behind, to cruise along the open road under the warm spring sun.

She had come from land like this, land that looked remarkably similar though it was hundreds of miles away. Her goal had always been to live and work in one city and one city alone—New York—but whenever she actually left the city and came to anything that looked like her native Iowa she had such sharp pangs of homesickness that she wondered how she had ever left.

Her childhood hadn't been easy in terms of the family's economics. Her father had lost everything the family had worked for for generations with one bad crop and one summer's drought. Lisa had always felt totally secure before then, looking upon the farm's giant harvesters and tractors as nice, weighty signs that nothing would ever change, that the land

and her family would always be there. And then she had discovered her family didn't even own most of the equipment. The bank did, and when her father was forced to sell off what he did own to raise what money he could, the Bennetts were left with nothing.

Now, as she looked at the gentle rolling hills and the broad, endless vistas of amazingly flat land, she knew she had reached the black-dirt region of New York State, that strange pocket of land that perfectly mirrored the fields and farms of her home state. She pulled to the side of the road and got out of her car. As she stood at the side of the road in the gentle warm breeze and looked out over the land, a small cloud of unhappiness closed over her heart as she remembered how much she had loved walking down the long rows of corn in the hot sun with her father, racing ahead of the massive harvesters with their menacing-looking arms, inhaling the corn-sweet air and feeling the world was hers.

The world she had chosen to leave that land for was a good one in terms of certain things: She was a highly paid businesswoman who lived in one of the prettiest areas of the city; she had made friends over the years; and she had held a series of increasingly interesting jobs. But at times like this, as she looked out over the open fields spread out beneath the clear blue sky, she sometimes wondered whether the trade-off had been worth it. Her eyes didn't even get to see this far in the city; everywhere she looked, her view was blocked by buildings. And she felt a freeing of her spirit now, a spirit she had buried over the years.

After a few more breaths of the sultry air, she got back into her car and found her way back to the

Thruway which would take her to the Shawangunk Mountains, where the Eastern Mountain Inn was nestled along the cliffs' upper ridges. And there she was supposed to meet another reminder of her past, this time in the form of a man named Michael Jamison.

She shook her head as she thought of all she had read about the manager of the Eastern Mountain Inn in the last two days. Jamison had had to carry on an extensive correspondence with officers of Eastland Industries, owners of the inn. And judging by the tone and infrequency of his responses, Lisa felt he would have been much happier having nothing whatsoever to do with Eastland. Granted, nobody at Eastland had the slightest idea how to run a hotel. The inn was a relic from the old days at Eastland, when the company's founder, Scribner Hollingworth, had bought the inn for sentimental reasons. Now Jamison had to report to Richard Hollingworth, Scribner's elder son. And the tone in their written exchanges was less than cordial.

And more than anything in the world, as Lisa had reviewed Richard Hollingworth's files, she had felt that Michael Jamison's attitudes bore an uncanny resemblance to those of her ex-husband, Keith. Whenever Hollingworth had asked for a reply in writing, his file showed that Jamison had telephoned instead, stubbornly refusing to follow orders. When Hollingworth asked a question about the running of the inn—a question that may or may not have been innocent—Michael Jamison's responses often bordered on rudeness. But most of all, like Lisa's ex-husband, Michael Jamison, at least at the beginning, had been full of idealistic and romantic suggestions

11

that were totally unrealistic. In one letter he had asked Eastland to allocate a large sum of money to restore a decrepit, historic barn for no purpose other than a decorative one. In another, he had delayed work on a building because a wren had just made her nest in eaves that would have been disturbed. And whenever he was turned down, he sounded childishly angry, with a "to hell with you" attitude more appropriate to playgrounds than business.

Which was one reason Lisa was on her way up to the inn. As the new operations manager at Eastland Industries/Domestic Division, her first duty was to evaluate Michael Jamison's operation from top to bottom—everything from his account books to the guests' reactions to the inn. And judging from the letters, she knew there was a lot of room for improvement in Michael Jamison's management style.

Tim Hershey ran up the path toward his boss, who was just about to disappear into the woods until God only knew what time. He was always planning hikes, ignoring at least a few things that were more important—like the layoffs.

"Michael! Wait up!"

Tim broke into a run as his boss slowed and then turned. Hell, you could never keep up with him unless you ran. Not that he was even that outrageously tall—just about five eleven. But when he got outside, he moved like the wind.

Tim had often wondered if Michael was part Kazakh Russian. The name, of course, didn't suggest it, but he had a certain look; as an art student, Tim noticed these things: high cheekbones, dark skin,

12

hair that was pitch black. Word was that Michael had been a banker down in the city and that he didn't like to talk about it, so no one did, at least to his face. But behind his back there was a ton of speculation, especially among the female employees: Why had he left his job and the city? Had there been a scandal? Where was he from?

And it wasn't that he was remote. Hell, Tim had never worked for such a nice guy in his entire life. But there were just some things you didn't ask, especially if you liked someone and wanted to respect his privacy.

Tim ran up to where Michael was waiting. "What's up?" Michael asked, turning and continuing the walk.

"Uh, I was wondering if you had had a chance to figure out . . ." Tim's voice trailed off. He hated bugging Michael, but the situation had been up in the air for weeks now. ". . . about my job," Tim finally finished. "If the layoffs are going to be stayed in any way."

Michael's jaw tightened. "I wish I could say yes," he answered, slowing his pace. "Karen has decided to go back to school full-time and work there, so her layoff won't hurt her." He sighed. "I just don't know about yours. Eastland has really been coming down hard."

Michael shook his head. Tim was such a damn nice kid. They all were. Mostly from the State University at New Paltz, or recent graduates, they had all managed to find niches for themselves at the inn, juggling their schedules as well as they could with their classes. He had hired them all as "general help"; that was the way he liked to do things. At the

13

interviews he had always gotten some sense of whatever talent or interest they had, and had then let them run with it. Tim happened to be a great guide for hikes, good at fixing things around the inn and settling guests in. Sometimes he even drew portraits on the hikes—of a couple as they sat at the edge of a waterfall, of a young woman lying in the sun, two children playing by a stream. The guests went wild over this. But how did you get this across to someone like Richard Hollingworth, who wanted you to lay the kid off because he had worked there for four years and was now too "expensive"? How did you explain that you couldn't measure the amount of goodwill and better business generated by the kind of work a kid like Tim did?

"All I can tell you, Tim, is that I'll do my best with your case. There's a woman coming up from Eastland today, and I might be able to talk to her about it."

"From Eastland? What for?"

Michael gave a humorless chuckle. "She's an operations manager, which I think is a new title for that old, laudable occupation called 'efficiency expert.'"

Tim smiled. "Really! Do you think she really is? I mean that she could know what she's talking about?"

Michael shrugged. "I doubt it. I don't know all that much about her, but I do know that she's never run a hotel in her life." As he spoke, he reminded himself that *he* never had either, until he had abruptly left banking and turned his whole life around. But he had never taken it upon himself to advise other people, to presume he knew more than they did

14

about their own businesses. Which was apparently a large part of this Lisa Bennett's job. And a friend at Eastland—old George Castleton, who was probably ready to head for the hills now that Richard Hollingworth had stepped into his father's shoes—had told him that this Bennett woman was going to be "advising" not only him, but all the division managers at Eastland. This blindness to what was really going on in any given business was what had driven him out of banking. A company began to go downhill, and immediately someone would be sent in to "punch it up," someone who usually didn't have any experience in that field.

Michael realized it was later than he had thought, and turned back with Tim toward the lodge. This Lisa Bennett would be there soon, and, much as part of him resisted the idea, he wanted to be there to greet her when she arrived. Though he had no intention of trying to curry favor, he knew it was important to try to curb his natural impulses, which were to be hostile and ignore the woman completely. Clearly, that would get him nowhere. He had to walk some sort of middle ground.

Lisa's car took the turns of the road easily, though it was becoming increasingly steep, and the occasional patches of gravel made the road's surface dangerously bumpy. She made a mental note—see what can be done about road—but her attention soon shifted once again to her surroundings. The trees on either side of the road were mostly pine and spruce, with low outcroppings of mountain ash and laurel signaling that the road was gaining in altitude. As the car climbed higher and higher, the air grew cooler and clearer, and Lisa realized with a pang of surprise that she hadn't been out in the country, in the woods or on a mountaintop, for nearly a year.

Partly because she was lost in thought but mostly because the sign for the inn was faded and tiny, Lisa nearly missed it, and passed the entrance before she fully realized what it was. She headed up the road until she found a widened spot for making U-turns, and turned around so she was facing in the right direction. Then, just as she was about to pull out, a car hurtled down the mountain and whizzed by. Lisa was suddenly upset and angry. She had just missed being hit broadside because the damn sign for the inn was so small that only a person on foot could see it. What in hell had Michael Jamison been thinking of?

And she was no less angry after she had pulled into the gravel driveway and her wheels were nearly knocked out of alignment by the deep potholes that scarred almost every foot of the road.

She barely noticed the rambling log and stone inn that looked as if it had been added on to several times over the past hundred years or so as she stormed in and marched up to the registration desk.

A young man smiled a greeting. "Hi. Can I help you?"

"Yes," Lisa spat out. "For one thing, I have a reservation. Lisa Bennett is my name." The man started to say "Okay," but Lisa interrupted him. "And I'd like to know, just out of curiosity, how you expect anyone to find this place."

"There's a sign—"

"That sign is about two inches long," Lisa interrupted. "And I nearly got killed because I almost drove right past it looking for this place."

"Is there a problem?" came a voice from behind where Lisa stood.

She turned. "I—" But her voice left her as she looked at the man standing in front of her. She had seen him before—for the first time a month ago, and then again in her dreams.

She had been at a party, one she hadn't even particularly wanted to go to. She and her then boyfriend, Jay, had just made up after an argument about a man Lisa worked with. Jay had been harboring suspicions of jealousy for weeks and had finally broken down and confronted Lisa. After her initial defensiveness, she had found she was actually touched by his concern. Agreeing to go to Jay's friend's party, where she knew no one, had been one way of conciliating Jay. And then she had seen a man across the room, the same one who was facing her now.

He had been dressed more casually than others at the party, in an open-necked gray-green cotton shirt and black jeans. He looked clearly out of place, a man whose deep tan had obviously come from long months in the sun rather than quick trips to resorts or tanning parlors. He was talking at a rather intimate closeness to a woman teetering drunkenly on very high heels, but a moment after Lisa saw him, he looked past his partner, and his near-black eyes met Lisa's with a shock of desire.

She had been aware of his every movement after that, his every burst of laughter. She could feel his every glance without even looking. He seemed to be as aware of her as she was of him, meeting her eyes every time she looked at him. But she made no move to approach—she was well aware, too, of Jay's

17

watchful eye—and this handsome stranger seemed to understand, and follow her lead.

Now he stood before her, his gaze a peculiar mixture of aggression and pleasure, and she couldn't help staring open-mouthed and surprised. He was in khaki shorts and a black T-shirt, and he was carrying a bunch of croquet mallets and wickets.

"You said something about a sign?" he asked. His voice was as pleasantly rough as she imagined his dark-shaded jaw was.

"Yes," she answered. "It's about two inches across. I don't know how anyone ever finds this place."

"Most people don't," he said, walking past her and hoisting the mallets and wickets onto the counter. "These can all use work," he said to the boy behind the desk. Then he turned, brushed off his hands, and crossed his arms. "You're not by any chance Lisa Bennett?"

"Yes, I am." So he had asked after her at the party. Or he was—

"Michael Jamison," he said, extending his hand.

As she shook his hand—warm and strong, a grip she suddenly wanted to escape—he smiled. "As soon as I said we're hard to find, I had the feeling I shouldn't have. Well, we might as well get you settled in. Are your bags in the car?"

"Uh, yes." It was so strange to be talking to this man she had thought she'd never see again. . . .

"Tim?" Michael said, and the young man behind the counter left to get Lisa's bags.

In the back of her mind Lisa phrased a professional question: Was Tim really Jamison's only lobby help? But somehow she just couldn't ask right now.

She still couldn't believe Michael Jamison was the man at the party. She looked up at him, fleetingly only, for the moment their eyes met, the gaze was too strong. Did he remember? She had been sure it wasn't one-sided.

Michael said nothing to Lisa as he waited for Tim to return. He was still in a mild state of shock. Lisa Bennett was the woman at the party. The Woman. She had appeared as such a creature of mystery that night—draped in red silk, obviously attached to the man at her side but just as obviously eager at some level to break away. With legs that went on forever, a mouth he hadn't been able to put out of his mind, lush, deep auburn hair, and amazing gray eyes that had said so much to him and then had taken it back. She had been a contradiction that night, a mysterious dream-woman he'd thought he'd never see again.

And here she was. The Eastland efficiency expert.

When Tim returned with the bags, Michael took them and led Lisa out the lodge and into the woods, where her cabin was. "I thought we'd put you in one of the cabins rather than the main lodge," he said, striding along at a pace Lisa could barely keep up with. She was five feet four to his large, muscular frame, and the bags she had brought—embarrassingly heavy because she hadn't been able to decide what to bring—didn't seem to faze him in the least. "Not that I'm trying to soften your impressions," he said provocatively, "but it really is much nicer out here in the woods."

And it was lovely, she had to admit. At each step the scent of pine needles and fresh, moist earth reached her senses, and the warm sun dappling

19

through the low-hanging boughs transported her to another time and place—when she had been back home, young and happy and unaware. She had run from just this sort of loveliness, run in order to make her way in the world and not let what had happened to her father ever happen to her. But when she had run from it, she had lost something, a part of her heart, a joy over being out in the wild that she had set aside and nearly forgotten.

And she had to admire how wild Michael Jamison had let the land become. Though this was clearly land that was occupied and used often, with a cabin nestled here or there almost always in view, the woods around them were clearly flourishing, uninhibited by human interference. Birds sang their morning songs and swooped down from massive pines to collect unseen treasures; mountain laurel and rhododendron blossomed pink and white along the paths.

And aside from Michael, there wasn't a human being in sight. "Where is everybody?" Lisa asked.

A corner of his mouth turned up. "You've read our reports. Isn't that why you're here?"

Her eyes widened. "Come on! I realize the lodge's attendance is down, but there has to be someone here!"

He laughed. "A grand total of fifty at the moment, yes. But most of them are probably swimming. Or getting ready for the hike I'm going to lead in about half an hour."

"You seem to do everything around here," she observed. "Checking out the sports equipment, taking guests to their rooms, leading hikes—"

"And you wonder how that leaves me any time for what you probably call 'management.' "

She glanced up at him. It was hard to tell whether there was any humor in those dark eyes. "What I and everyone else calls management. It isn't an abstract concept, you know. It's a very specific way of handling one's business, and part of it involves delegating."

"Ah. I see. Delegating to whom? Do you know how many kids you people have forced me to lay off in the past six months?"

"And do you know what your monthly balance sheets look like? We're not running a charitable organization, you know." Her voice rang out sharply and sent a bird sailing into the trees, and for a moment she wondered how she could be discussing something as prosaic as balance sheets in such a lovely place. And she realized all at once that perhaps something similar had happened to Michael Jamison over the years. Here in these magnificent mountains it had to be easy to forget there was a real world in which bills had to be paid and budgets had to be balanced and profits had to be made.

Michael stopped walking and turned to her. "Does this look like the Hilton, Miss Bennett? There never have been crowds here and there never will be. The draw of the inn is its natural beauty—the way the log and stone buildings all blend into the landscape, the way you can do everything or nothing at all, the fact that you can walk along miles of mountain trails and never see another human being. The moment you change that—the *moment*, Miss Bennett—the inn's entire reason for being is gone." He sighed. "Anyway, we're here," he said crossly, turning and walk-

21

ing toward the small log cabin they had stopped in front of.

She followed and stood behind him as he unlocked the wooden door. He looked angry even from the back, his shoulders tensed and raised as if ready for a fight, and when the door stuck and he had to push and lift it, his movements were abrupt and impatient. How different he was from the relaxed and engaging man she had fantasized about.

But when she stepped into the cabin, she forgot about his anger for a moment. The cabin was charming. Though some of the furnishings—the frayed Navajo rugs, the worn tweed chairs, the whisper-thin bandanna-cloth curtains billowing by the three sets of windows—were slightly the worse for wear, they all fit in perfectly with the atmosphere Michael was apparently trying to create. They let you know warmly and clearly you were in a place where you could relax, put your feet up, and forget about the world. And the bed was extraordinary—a rough-hewn four-poster, handmade out of logs, with smaller, curved branches forming a criss-cross headboard and footboard. And spread across the bed was a lovely old patchwork quilt.

"Aren't you afraid your guests will steal things like this?" Lisa asked, running her hand over the quilt. "This would sell for hundreds of dollars in the city."

"Would you suggest I chain it to the bed?" he asked dryly.

"I'd suggest you switch to standard hotel blankets. What happens when a guest walks off with one of these?"

22

"That guest wouldn't be allowed back," he said, opening the one unopened window and letting in more of the cool forest air. "But so far," he added, leaning against the sill and stretching his long, tanned legs out, "it hasn't happened. And I see more clearly than ever that you really don't understand the nature of the inn. The people who come here are not thieves, Miss Bennett. The too-high price unfortunately excludes most people from even considering a stay here, and those who do manage to come—well, I'm sure one day someone will walk off with something. But it hasn't happened yet, because everyone who comes wants to come back. Stealing would be like stealing from someone's home. They know it's not like lifting a Holiday Inn ashtray or a towel that says Best Western Hotels."

"Which doesn't help *their* balance sheets either."

"You're not serious," he said quietly, rising and walking over to where she stood by the bed.

"Yes, I was," she answered. "Why?"

She was close to him now and picked up his masculine scent—a mixture of sweat, sun, and forest. She admired his beautifully strong forearms, tanned and sleek with silky dark hair, and his lean, muscled thighs, taut and hard from work.

"I can't believe you're that unromantic," he said softly, reaching out and brushing a strand of auburn hair back from her face. *Lord,* he thought—*her skin is so smooth.* "Do you really see that quilt just as something that could be stolen? Or people taking souvenirs as a bunch of debits on a balance sheet?"

"Oh, come on," she said, turning away. She hoisted her suitcase onto the rack at the end of the bed

23

and looked at Michael Jamison with skepticism. "If you're going to sing that same tune the whole time I'm here, Mr. Jamison, neither of us is going to be able to help the other in the slightest."

"I don't understand."

"Look. It's very easy for you to make your voice go all soft and talk about the romance of this inn and the forest, but unless you begin facing some cold, hard facts, you're going to lose the whole thing."

All the color drained out of his face. "What are you saying?" he murmured. "What do you know about it?"

"Nothing in particular," she answered. "But you don't have to be Einstein to see the handwriting on the wall, which is that Eastland—like any company in the world—isn't going to let the inn continue as it is. In other words, they're not going to let you run it as you've been running it, because you've been losing money."

"*I* haven't been losing money. Look, damn it, they may call you an efficiency expert, or an operations manager, and you may call yourself the same thing, but from what I've heard, you've never run a hotel in your life—and no one at Eastland has either."

"And in the time you've run it, Mr. Jamison, the inn has turned from a black entry in the budget to a red one."

"Have you ever heard of a slump, Miss Bennett? I used to be in precisely the position Eastland is in now. I was a loan officer at one of the largest banks in New York, overseeing loans and ultimately entire businesses we had capitalized. You learn a lot when you lend that kind of money. And one thing I learned

24

was that you have to be willing to take risks, to roll with the punches, and you have to recognize that there are going to be dry periods."

She looked into his dark eyes. He sounded so sure of himself when he spoke like that—and very convincing too. But she knew that in this particular case he was wrong. "Look. Maybe we'd better . . . I don't know. You said you have to lead a hike in half an hour, and—"

"Twenty minutes," he said, looking at his watch and then into her eyes. "You're right," he murmured, and then smiled. "Actually, I wish we didn't have to discuss any of this ever again."

"Why?"

"Because when I saw you for the first time, in a sea of faces at a party I was cursing until you walked through the door, I never thought we'd end up talking business." He stepped forward. "You do remember?"

She smiled. "Oh, yes. I was wondering if you did."

He tilted his head. "Was there a particular reason you spoke to everyone there but me?"

She laughed. "I didn't talk to everyone. Just a few people."

"It seemed like everyone."

"Well—" She hesitated under the warmth of his gaze. "I was with someone. It just didn't seem right."

"Ah. Serious boyfriend, then?"

"Yes," she answered, wondering why she had just told a lie. Yes, Jay had been a serious boyfriend, but they had since decided to stop seeing each other. He had talked about marriage and had finally been the one who had said the relationship was over unless there was going to be some kind of commitment in

25

the future, something Lisa had avoided. She often missed him. She was sure he missed her. And she wouldn't have been surprised if he called her up any day now. In the meantime, she had to respect his feelings; she didn't want to hurt him.

Yet, she wasn't sure that Jay had anything to do with the reason she had stretched the truth with Michael. As she looked into his dark eyes, she realized she had preferred him as a fantasy: she could control him when he existed only in her mind, when he was merely a dream-figure experienced from a distance. Now, that distance was suddenly essential.

"Well," he said. "That's too bad. For me, anyway. He's a lucky guy. Jay, isn't it?" He smiled. "Don't look so surprised. Didn't you think I asked some questions after you left? But I couldn't find out anything about you except that you were Lisa who worked for a real estate firm in the city. What happened with that?"

She shrugged. "I heard about the opening at Eastland. And it sounded like a good way for me to broaden my experience. I think I got the job because I've had a lot of real estate experience, but soon I'll be dealing with all the Eastland subsidiaries."

He looked into her eyes and said nothing. She was so different from the fantasy he had created. He had been sure this management thing was something she had fallen into completely unwillingly, out of pure and simple economic necessity. He had thought she dabbled in it so she could pursue some private passion she hadn't yet succeeded in—painting, writing, music perhaps. But instead she turned out to be as firmly and resolutely interested in the ins and outs of

26

the business world as any of the men he had encountered in all his years as a loan officer.

"Well, I think I'll just start getting settled in," she said. "And if you could have one of your people show me where your books are while you're on your hike, that would be great."

"All right," he said. "My office is on the second floor of the main lodge. I could show you now, actually." His voice trailed off, and when he spoke again, it was softly, musingly. "Funny," he said. "I hadn't imagined that when Lisa Bennett came up from New York, I'd wish she were going on the hike with me instead of looking over our books." He smiled. "I had pictured some old crone who'd be perfectly at home with stacks of accounting books and legal pads. But you know what?"

"What?"

"You look like you could use a hike, or a walk in the fresh air."

"Thanks a lot!"

"Relax, relax. All I meant is that you look a little pale."

"In contrast to your Mr. Universe tan, I suppose?"

He laughed. "Mr. Universe?" He looked down at an arm muscle and then winked at Lisa. "Gee, I'd thought I needed to work out for at least another month before I could be called that! But seriously, how about it? I'll bet you haven't ever seen land like this in your life. We've got three-hundred-sixty-five-degree views from the top of the mountain. There are amazing waterfalls, you'll probably see at least a dozen deer, and by the end of the hike you'll be saying what everyone else who comes up here says—

27

how can we live down in the city when it's so beautiful up here?"

"Oh, you don't have to convince me on that count. I come from a small town in Iowa, from generations of farmers, and I'm the first person in my family who ever visited New York, much less decided to stay. I happen to be crazy about the city, but that doesn't mean I've abandoned my love of the country."

He smiled. "Then come. We can even talk business if you want to appease what I'm sure is a conscience that works overtime." He paused. "As it seemed to be doing the night of the party," he added softly.

For a moment they looked into each other's eyes in silence, each remembering that night that had engendered so many thoughts and dreams. He was close enough to touch her, close enough to kiss her if he just leaned forward, and for a few seconds all Lisa could think of was how much she wanted to feel those lips melt her own, how much she wanted to feel his burning touch as he brought her against his hard body with all the passion that was in his eyes. "I'll come," she said softly. "I think I'd really like to."

He inhaled slowly and deeply. *One more step,* he told himself. He had held back from kissing her. She had told him in no uncertain terms that she was involved with someone else. And though with her eyes she had given him the opposite message, something in him had said stop. Don't come on like gangbusters after she tells you something like that.

He'd take her on the hike, get to know her, and, hell, maybe he wouldn't even like her. In a sense she was almost an enemy, someone definitely from the "other side" as far as business was concerned. If only she didn't have those damn gray eyes. If only he hadn't dreamed about her.

'I'll meet you back at the main lodge," she said softly, as if reluctant to interrupt his thoughts.

"Great. See you back there."

For another moment he hesitated. She looked so gentle, so ready to be kissed. But no—it was too soon. If he liked her, there would be plenty of time. . . .

CHAPTER TWO

As Lisa set off down the path toward the main lodge, she marveled at how right Michael Jamison had been about her overactive conscience. She had just arrived; there was no reason she had to begin working the minute she got there; yet she still felt guilty for taking the hike instead of cracking open those account books.

She hated this part of herself. Of course, she had to grudgingly respect it, for without it she wouldn't have gained the financial freedom she had, something that led to many other kinds of freedom as well. But she resented her obsession with work, for she felt as if the quality weren't really her own; it had been born when her family had lost the farm, and sometimes it seemed almost like a curse, like an outside force that drove her life every moment of the day. And oddly enough, it had made her set aside a part of her life that she truly loved.

Michael had been right when he had said this land

was beautiful. She smiled. When had he changed from Mr. Jamison to Michael in her mind? Perhaps, she thought, when he had looked as if he were about to kiss her. . . .

She shook the thought from her mind. Lord, couldn't she meet any man without sizing him up? It seemed that no matter what man she met, he became an instant challenge, someone she had to see if she could attract—and then accept or reject on her terms. It was such a set pattern. When she had first spotted Michael and been attracted to him, she had been with Jay; when she had first met Jay, she had been with another man. There were so many instances—

"Ready?"

Lisa nearly jumped. Michael seemed to have appeared out of nowhere. But then she saw that about ten women and seven or eight men had assembled in front of the lodge, and Michael had obviously come from where Tim and another young man were standing and going through box lunches.

Lisa smiled at Michael. "Sure I'm ready. You're looking at the most broken-in hiking shoes on the East Coast."

"Oh, I don't know. These could rival any," he said, holding up a foot clad in very worn shoes indeed.

"Are you trying to get me to look at your shoes or your legs?" she quipped.

He looked at her in mock disappointment. "What! Only a few minutes ago you called me Mr. Universe."

"I said you had a Mr. Universe *tan,*" she corrected

31

him. "You know how those guys get all tanned and oiled when they're in competition."

He was fighting a smile. "You sound like quite a devotee. Maybe I've misread you again."

"Why?"

"You were beginning to strike me as hopelessly mired in the ins and outs of management strategy and planning. But someone who spends her idle hours admiring men's tanned and oiled bodies—"

"Whose tanned and oiled bodies?" Tim asked as he came strolling up.

"Men's," Michael supplied. "Lisa here is quite a fan."

Tim raised a brow. "Really?"

"Will you two stop?" Lisa laughed.

"All right," Tim said, smiling. "For now, anyway. Michael, everyone seems to be ready. Sure you don't want me to come along?"

Michael smiled. "Definitely not. The people on this hike are going to receive my undivided attention." He winked. "No help is needed or wanted."

As Lisa listened to the exchange and saw the way some of the women were looking at Michael, she decided he probably spent more than a little of his time flirting with the inn's female guests. And he had to have a lot of opportunities. He was extraordinarily handsome, the kind of man some women considered too perfect-looking. With his lean, sinewy frame, obviously in wonderful condition, and his near-black eyes, jet-black hair, and full, sensuous mouth, he was almost too perfect. He was the kind of man you noticed the minute you walked into a room, the kind who dominated any group of people.

But Lisa felt he was saved from the curse of seeming too perfect by his manner, by a sense of humor about himself that seemed to say, What's all the fuss about?

They set off along a narrow, rocky path that circled behind the main lodge of the inn, and soon Lisa began to unwind as the smell of the ferns and spruce reached her, as the sun grabbed every chance it could get to warm her back as she moved between the trees.

Soon the group divided into twos and threes and fours of conversation, and Lisa walked on ahead with Michael. For a while they walked in silence, each just enjoying the beauty of the long, cool stretch of sun-dappled woods.

But when they came out into an open meadow, he leaned over and pointed to the edge of the field, where another thick forest began. "Do you see where I'm pointing?" he asked quietly, so quietly she could barely hear him.

"Yes. Why?"

"It's a deep, dark secret." He smiled. "And please, I've told only two people who have come here."

"Told what?"

His smile broadened. "In there is the most beautiful, private, quiet, utterly magnificent swimming hole I have ever come across in my life. Complete with one sunny shore, deer drinking at its edge, and the cloak of total privacy."

"Really!" She loved the way he looked at that moment. She couldn't quite put her finger on why there was something so seductive about him, but she felt it had to do with his eyes and smile more than anything else. There was such a deep intelligence in his eyes, and a readiness to laugh and smile fully and completely, and apparently never falsely. It seemed as if so many people she met these days, especially those in business, were so quick to smile, but the moment you turned away, or they thought you had, the smile was gone. More than anything, though, his eyes caught her every time she looked at him. They were very expressive, very forceful. And then, of course, there was the way he moved. With his narrow hips and long, lean thighs, she didn't see how he could be anything other than graceful, but his movements were sinuous as well, catlike and confident.

She looked into the trees where he had pointed. There was no sign that anything but more woods lay beyond the thick stand of trees at the edge of the meadow. For a quick, heated moment, a thought flashed in her mind—of Michael's lips upon hers, of his leathery low voice murmuring that he wanted her, of her breath catching as she said "I want you too" and they embraced, naked, in the water. And she felt exactly as she had at the party—filled with a desire stronger than any she had ever felt for Jay, for anyone she had ever been with. "Is that an invitation?" she asked.

He smiled. "Sure. Why not? And just to please you, we'll bring along some ledgers, all right?"

She laughed. "Will you stop with that ledger business? I'm not on the job twenty-four hours a day. I'm not now, for instance."

"Ah. But behind those incredible gray eyes I think I see constant questioning. For instance, when I told you about the swimming hole, you were probably weighing the relative pros and cons of keeping it secret or making it public." He winked. "I could hear the old adding machine calculating possible profits even as we spoke."

"On the contrary," she said, smiling. "First of all, if I did have that sort of mind, I wouldn't want it referred to as an adding machine. The latest microchip minicomputer at the very least, please. But I promise you I wasn't thinking about anything you'd ever mistake for mathematical calculations."

He raised a brow. "Sounds interesting. Any chance of letting me in on those thoughts?"

"Nope."

He smiled. "Nonnegotiable?"

"Nonnegotiable."

"Are you this rigid in business?"

"Absolutely."

He shook his head. "Then I'm going to have to butter you up as much as I possibly can, or try to stall your mission at the very least."

She smiled, but then her smile faded. "Are you really nervous, Michael? I mean about my being here to look you and the inn over? Because if you are, I wish you wouldn't think of it as if it's an adversarial relationship. I really am here to help you—"

"—the fox said to the chickens," he finished. "Yes, I've heard *that* before," he added skeptically. "Usually from my own lips, a month before the bank was going to foreclose on some poor shmo who didn't have the connections or the smarts to stall us off until his bad luck passed over. And you know what's amazing about banks? Something that most people don't even know?"

"No, what?" she asked.

"People think, especially in places like New York City, that a bank has rules that can't be broken. From everything as small as thinking a check has to take a certain number of days to clear to thinking that if you default on a loan or a mortgage, the bank is automatically going to come and take away your business or house or whatever. Of course they do, more often than not. But for certain people those rules are bent and bent often. However—don't for a minute think that the bank is ever going to do anything out of altruism, even if it bends the rules for you. It's just looking out for its investment. And I know Eastland is the same, only worse."

"As far as I'm concerned, nothing could be worse," she said tightly. For as Michael had spoken, he had brought back memories of her family's battles with the bank.

"Why do you say that?" he asked. "It should be obvious that I'm no great fan of the system. I got out, after all, and I gave up a very lucrative living when I did so. But I'm not sure Eastland is any better. They're looking for the best return on their investment just as the banks do."

"And there's nothing wrong with that," she put in. "That's what business is all about. But I happen to have a particular and very deep hatred of banks for a very simple reason. They ruined my family's life. And all because of a loan I know we could have paid off eventually if they had just let us." She told him about the farm and how the bank had taken it away, how her family's entire way of life had been destroyed because of one institution's—or perhaps one man's—decision. "And now," she finished, "now when you say it doesn't have to happen that way if you have connections, that just makes me furious. The only connections my father ever had were with grain dealers and fertilizer companies and cooperative extension agents."

36

"Look," he said gently, slowing and taking her by the elbow. "That's a terrible story, and I'm sorry about it. I had no way of knowing. And I agree with you. It's all very unfair."

"Well, what are you trying to do then? Make me feel as if I'm some sort of bank official coming to pull the rug out from under you? I'm—"

"Of course not," he cut in. "If I thought your being here had anything to do with taking the inn away from me, I wouldn't be taking you along on this hike and I would probably barely speak to you. But I do think there's another aspect of the analogy that's very apt. You said you're here to help me. And I happen to know that . . . well, to put it as honestly as I can, I'm not going to want your help. And I'm sorry that's the case."

She sighed. "Do you know Richard Hollingworth well, Michael?"

He laughed humorlessly. "I ought to. He's my ex-brother-in-law."

"What?"

He looked at her curiously. "That's right. You just started at Eastland when? A month ago?"

"No, a week ago. Hmm, your brother-in-law . . ."

"Ex," he supplied.

"Okay, ex-brother-in-law. Then why do I have to point out how wrong you are? He's just been installed as CEO at Eastland, and he strikes me as very pragmatic. He said I could have a very free hand in suggesting and implementing changes at the inn. That doesn't sound like a man who's going to wait for the winds to shift on their own."

For a few moments Michael was silent, lost in

thought. They were crossing into thick woods again, and Michael absently called out the entrance to a cave called Indian's End and then seemed to retreat into his own world again. The retreat was annoyingly reminiscent of the kind her ex-husband used to make at the most infuriating of times. He'd seem to go off into a world of his own when they were in the middle of an argument—usually one about money. When she'd comment or question him, he'd say, "I'm thinking, I'm thinking," and then he'd come up with a totally outlandish and impractical scheme. He had been that way since she had first met him, and probably still was. And now Michael seemed strangely similar.

"I think I know Richard pretty well," Michael suddenly said. "And I'm sure I know him better than you do, Lisa. Not to get into too many stories from the past, but he does think he's a lot smarter than he is." Michael glanced back at the rest of the group, some of whom were ably following what had turned into a fairly athletic pace. But others looked as if they were just managing to keep up. The ground was rocky, Lisa observed. "Let's wait up for the rest of them," Michael said. "I forgot all about them."

A few minutes later they had all agreed to wait to eat lunch until they got to Highland Point, and when Michael and Lisa set off again, they weren't separate enough from the rest of the group that Michael felt comfortable continuing the discussion. Damn, he wanted to be alone with Lisa. But he had to watch himself. She was so much like his ex-wife, Candace, in so many ways—sure of herself, unavailable, perhaps unattainable. And someone he was attracted to more as a conquest, maybe, than anything else.

Hadn't it, after all, been that way with Candace? He had come to love her; there was no doubt about that. But his initial attraction to her had been pure and simple, based not one bit on her personality: she was a gorgeous blonde, had a lifelong listing in the *Social Register,* and was the kind of person he had never known until he had gone to college.

Even now, years later, he was surprised to find he still hadn't shaken off those old habits. Any woman, particularly an attractive one, who seemed unavailable for any reason, was an instant challenge. And Lisa Bennett fell into this category for a hell of a lot of great reasons. She was pretty in a sexy, sensuous kind of way, with incredible eyes, beautiful hair, and legs that didn't quit; and she was planning to lock horns with him, something that always turned peculiarly sexual and exciting when the person going up against him was a woman.

He could feel her presence as she walked along beside him; he knew how she looked without even looking—her hair blowing softly in the breeze, slim, shapely legs carrying her gracefully along, a look of mystery in those lovely gray eyes. And he knew how she would feel in his arms.

"We're coming to Sam's Pass," he called out to the rest of the group. "And there's the bridge I was telling you about in the announcement last night." He glanced at Lisa. "It's not a big deal, really, but I wanted to be sure people knew we'd be crossing a very narrow, fairly high bridge on this hike. Right up there," he said, pointing through the dark pines and spruces. Lisa couldn't see anything but a big gap in the trees.

"How narrow?" she asked.

39

"Why?"

"Oh, well, nothing . . ." she answered falteringly.

He smiled. "Don't tell me you of all people aren't going to want to cross. I wanted to be sure we didn't get anyone who was afraid of heights."

"Oh." *Damn,* she thought. For as the path darkened and they once more entered a thin strip of woods, she saw the bridge. It was incredibly narrow —just wide enough for one person, she estimated— stretched across a wide abyss like the kind of bridges you saw in Sunday-afternoon jungle movies. Only this wasn't a movie. She was going to have to cross the spindly looking thing, with its thread-narrow "railings" and its walkway held up by absolutely unseen and unimaginable forces.

"Are you afraid of heights?" Michael asked gently.

"Well, yes," she said, looking up at him. "I wish I could pretend I wasn't. It's actually my one concrete fear, but I . . . I've never been able to conquer it."

He smiled. "Don't be embarrassed. I happen to be afraid of airplanes."

They were now just a few feet from where the bridge started, and Lisa got her first glimpse of the rushing waters about fifty feet below, and she felt sick with fear, dizzy with a nausea that spread through her whole body.

"How do you want to do this?" Michael asked, gently taking her elbow.

She turned away from the river, but the sounds of the water rushing over the rocks below seemed even louder. She felt so irrational, so helpless. And so angry too. It really was her only real fear, and she hated the idea that everyone else was going to cross the bridge with ease, and she alone would—what? She couldn't imagine setting foot on that thing.

There were some oohs and aahs as the rest of the group reached the bridge, and Lisa heard one woman suck in her breath and curse. But with nervous laughter and anxious bravado one by one they set off across the bridge. It swayed dangerously at each step each person took, and Lisa's knees went weak.

Finally, Lisa was left standing on the riverbank alone with Michael, feeling exactly as she had dozens of times in camp when she had been left with a friend, a counselor, or sometimes no one at all on hikes exactly like this one.

"I really feel ridiculous," she said.

"Don't," he murmured. "Just stay here and I'll be right back, okay?"

She smiled. "Don't worry. I'm not going anywhere."

She watched as he walked easily across the bridge, totally unconscious of the dangers it represented to her. He spoke to the rest of the group, pointing through the woods, and a moment later they all set off in the direction he had indicated.

Lisa was mortified. God, how embarrassing! First she had lagged behind. Now, in the unlikely event that anyone had failed to notice she hadn't crossed, Michael was telling everyone and instructing them to go on ahead.

As she watched them walk away, Lisa took a deep breath, steeled herself, and took a step toward the bridge. The height was dizzying.

"Wait!" Michael called from the other side. He ran—she couldn't believe he was actually running!—

across the bridge, which dipped and swung dangerously under his weight.

"Michael!"

He was smiling. "Will you just relax?" he said,
taking her by the shoulders. "What did I ask you to
do when I left? You said you'd wait right here."

"I know. But I feel ridiculous." She looked into his
beautiful dark eyes and was suddenly distracted.
They were so deep, so tender.

He tilted his head and ran his hands down her
arms. "I have the feeling you can do whatever you
want to do, Lisa," he said softly. "I just wanted to
be alone with you for a moment." His hands slid into
hers and clasped them.

She could feel the strength of his thighs as he
brought her close, could feel the warmth of his
desire. She smiled, loving the tension and heat, that
wonderful uncertainty about what would happen
next. "Then you don't think I'm embarrassingly
chicken?"

He looked surprised. "I think you can do anything
from crossing a bridge you just *think* you're afraid of
to seducing every man you meet."

A corner of her mouth turned up. "Am I seducing
you?"

He drew her closer. "Do you really have to ask?"
he whispered. His hands smoothed the curves of her
hips and settled against the warm skin beneath her
shirt, their roughness excitingly scratchy against her
sensitive skin. His touch was warm and gentle, but
insistent, with a persuasiveness that ran deep. As his
fingers gently encircled her waist, they sent their
message in a torrid path to her breasts, and her nipples tingled, taut against the fabric of her shirt.

"I thought *you* were seducing *me*," she murmured as he lowered his head and his lips brushed against hers. She could taste him even though their lips had barely touched, could taste him and sense him and imagine what it would be like to be his, to give herself up to the pleasures of his lips, his hands, his urgent male need.

"I'm trying to," he whispered, and grinned. "I would have tried a month ago if you hadn't seemed to back off when I got close. And I would have given up, except . . ." His voice trailed off.

"Except what?" she asked.

"Except that you seemed to—maybe I was wrong." His hands moved to cup the soft curves of her breasts. She caught her breath and closed her eyes, melting under his touch, wanting him. "You seemed to be sending a very different message with your eyes. Even though you were with your boyfriend."

She opened her eyes and met his deep black gaze. "I always do that," she said softly, her head arching back as his lips descended on the smooth skin of her throat. His cheek was abrasive, but the touch of his warm wet lips was infinitely gentle, deeply exciting. She wanted more.

"You mean you like to flirt," he whispered into her ear, taking a nibble of her lobe.

"Yes," she murmured. "You could say that."

"Doesn't Jay mind?" His lips were just grazing above and below hers, and his breath was warm and sweet against her skin. His fingers worked their magic, circling her breasts, bringing her nipples to peaks of desire.

43

"I suppose he does," she breathed. "But flirting is harmless, isn't it? A little eye contact never hurt."

"I dreamed about you," Michael said huskily. "I dreamed of making love to you under the open sky, in a place just like this, of persuading you very slowly, very deeply, very pleasurably that you were made for me, that I could give you more pleasure than you've ever had in your life." He nuzzled his lips along her neck and downward, and she began melting deep inside as his hard body insisted against hers, and she desperately wanted him to give her the satisfaction he was so sure he could.

"Maybe that sounds arrogant," he said softly. "But I don't really care because I'm that sure, Lisa. I've thought of you too many times not to know what I want to do with you, what pleasure you could give to me, how I could fill you with fire." He gazed into her eyes. "You've told me about Jay, and I know he's a very lucky man. But he's not all that smart."

"Why's that?" she murmured.

He slowly shook his head in wonder. "If I were Jay, I would never have let you out of my sight long enough to come to a place like this."

"And why is that?" she breathed as his hands moved lower, splaying over her hips, urging her against his strength.

"Because *I'm* here, Lisa, and I'm going to do everything in my power to make you forget all about Jay."

"Michael," she whispered. And then his lips were on hers, and in one scintillating moment his tongue came into her mouth, and she moaned with pleasure, wonder, amazement, that he could reach her like this, that he could fill her with such ravaging desire.

44

And she knew he had been right; she knew from the sensuous, suggestive movements of his tongue, knew from the heat that was making her burn inside, knew from the wild pleasure her thoughts were bringing her. For just imagining him inside her, filling her with the fire he had promised, rocking her to the core with his hard strength, made her ache with desire. He was sure he could coax her to the heights of passion, make her flame under his persuasive touch, and she knew he was right and she wanted him. He hadn't even done all that much—and she was undeniably overwhelmed.

But he pulled back, confusion and desire churning in his dark eyes. "I could stay with you forever," he said hoarsely.

She smiled lazily, still in a haze from his kisses, still in awe of how right they were for each other.

"We do have to get going though—"

"Going?" she asked.

He smiled. "Across the bridge. To the picnic."

Damn. She'd forgotten all about it. "Oh, right," she said uncertainly.

He searched her eyes. "It really frightens you, doesn't it? Do you know why?"

She shook her head. "Not only do I not know why, but I've never even come close to getting rid of it either. You're looking at a real ex-tomboy too. I did everything my brothers did on the farm. When it came to work, I could do it all. But when it came to playing, I couldn't climb trees or anything even remotely off the ground."

"Would you like me to carry you across?"

Her stomach jumped at the thought. "Are you

kidding? And have you slip and send me hurtling down to those rocks?"

He smiled.

"And thanks a lot for your understanding!" she cried, glaring at him.

"I'm sorry," he said, still smiling. "Really. It's just . . . Come," he said, taking her hand. "We'll get this over with and never mention it again."

She gripped his hand as tightly as she could and followed him onto the bridge. She felt it sway under her first step, and she froze.

"It's all right," he said softly. "I promise. Let's just keep going."

And step by cautious step, they did. At each lurching swing of the bridge, Lisa felt her stomach drop, but it was all over in a few moments, and then she had fallen into Michael's arms and was hugging him. "Oh, God, I feel so silly but so glad you were here."

He held her close. It was a precious moment for him, one that had stolen up on him unexpectedly. He had sensed a vulnerability, a sensitivity in her, but he hadn't known he'd ever be able to know it or get close to it. She was embarrassed by her fear, not knowing it had made her more accessible. Back there in her cabin he had been afraid, with all her talk of red ink and budgets and plans, that there was no real soul behind those beautiful gray eyes. But her openness, her having let him help her, had changed her from a possibly brittle, probably difficult and beautiful employee of Eastland to a living, breathing woman with feelings and emotions he could touch. She had needed him, if only for a few minutes.

Maybe her stay at the inn wouldn't be half as

46

difficult as he had anticipated. Maybe it wouldn't be difficult at all.

Candace Hollingworth Jamison threw the folder down on the desk and stood up. "I wish you had talked to me first, Richard."

Her brother looked at her without concern. "I'm running this company, Candace, and I'm not going to consult with you and Scott on every minor matter."

"I'm not asking you to consult with me and Scott. I'm asking you to consult with *me*. And I don't consider anything that has to do with the inn to be minor." She walked over to the window and looked down at the streets below. Park Avenue, the whole damn East Side sprawled out for miles. Just beautiful. And Michael wanted to live in the mountains. She spun around and faced Richard. "Tell me about this Lisa Bennett."

Richard shrugged. "What's to tell that you haven't read in the folder? Smith College on a scholarship, Wharton M.B.A. on a fellowship, lots of real estate and hotel experience, first-rate references, a real head on her shoulders. And as down to earth as they come."

"What's that supposed to mean?"

"I mean she's not going to be swayed by that back-to-nature nonsense that seems to have captured your darling ex-husband. She knows how to spot future red ink as well as anyone I've ever seen. Her boss on her last job was very sorry to see her go, as a matter of fact. She had just made recommendations for some very drastic changes. Tough time to find a replacement."

47

"And you think she'll find problems with Michael's operation."

"She'll have to," Richard said, leaning back in his leather chair and swinging his legs up onto the desk.

Candace sighed and sank into a chair. "But she won't make Michael look bad?"

Richard raised a brow. "Look, sister dear. You can't have it both ways. If you want him back in the city in his old banker gear, you've got to be willing to throw some not very flattering light on the old boy. It's the only way—the means to the end. Otherwise you'll have to get used to the fact that he threw you and the life-style you're so very fond of over in favor of this nature-lover routine. Ethan Cobb notwithstanding. Anyway, Candace," he added, looking into her clear blue eyes, "you can always blame the whole sorry mess—which is what it's going to be—on me. I want to sell the inn. I know I can get at least ten million for it and the fact of the matter is that I would proceed no matter how you felt. I want in on that disk-drive company, and I'm not going to let the chance slip by. High-tech moves fast these days, in every way. First issues get snapped up by institutional investors, and products get outdated before they even hit the market. This year I intend to be a victor rather than a victim, Candy, and nothing's going to stop me. Including you."

"I could always tell Father," she said, her childish tone surprising her. But damn it, Richard's title didn't mean everything.

Her brother swung his long legs down from the desk and steepled his fingers on the blotter. "We're on the same side, Candy. Interested in the same things. Why don't we try to keep it that way?"

"I just want Michael to come through this fairly well."

"Fairly well, he will. Unscathed, no. But I think you prefer damaged goods to none at all. And Michael will bounce back just fine if you handle him right. He's not exactly helpless."

She sighed. "I just hope I'm doing the right thing."

He looked up sharply. "You want him back, don't you?"

"Yes. You know that."

"Well, you're not going to get him back with him up there and you down here all the time. It's the best way I can think of."

"Let's hope," she said disconsolately. "Let's hope."

CHAPTER THREE

That night at dinner Lisa found that she kept remembering the afternoon and the kisses she had shared with Michael. At the end of the hike he had asked her to join him for dinner, and she had accepted gladly, partly because she simply enjoyed his company but partly because she was deeply intrigued by this man who was so strangely arousing. Yes, he was very handsome, and it shouldn't have been surprising that he would have such an effect on her. But the attraction had taken a quantum leap once she had actually kissed Michael, for she had never felt so right with anyone in her life.

Now, as she sat across from him in the cool, breezy dining room, a fire flickering in the old stone fireplace in the corner, she looked at him with affection. He was a superb host. In the few minutes they had been in the room, he had stopped by each table to greet the guests, made everyone laugh as he had announced the next day's activities with jokes and general good humor, and transformed the room from a drafty old cavernous dining hall to a warm and friendly, much more intimate room. And he seemed —finally—ready to talk business.

"I know you'll get me sometime," he said with a grin. "I might as well be a willing and perhaps more persuasive victim."

She took a sip of the Beaujolais he had ordered. It was delicious, full-bodied and just the right temperature. "I wish you would stop assuming you'll be some sort of victim. I've told you before that I'm just here to help you."

He raised a brow. "And I've told you—Well, we've been through this already. I know what that sort of 'help' usually involves. And I know Richard Hollingworth. He sent you up here because he wants changes made. 'Improvements,' he'll call them."

"He didn't give me any guidance at all, actually. He just said go up and do your stuff."

"It will come sometime. As I told you, I know him well." He paused. "Do you know Candace, by the way?"

She shook her head. "No. I've seen her name on the company letterhead, but I've never seen her." She paused. "When did you two get divorced?"

"Well, the divorce came through three months ago. But we had been separated for well over a year. The Hollingworths are a difficult family, Lisa, and when you marry one, in a sense you marry all of them. I hadn't counted on that, and after a while I discovered it wasn't the sort of life I wanted."

"I've heard about families like that. Dynasties, I guess. But I've never understood how that sort of thing could actually destroy a marriage. I mean, you don't have to tell me . . . it's certainly none of my business."

"Don't be ridiculous," he said softly. "I'd like it to be your business." He took a sip of wine, hesitated, and took another sip. "I suppose one of the roots of the problem was that Candace and I wanted different things. She had married a banker—me, when I was a very different man, someone who lived on Park and Sixty-fifth, belonged to the New York Athletic Club and the University Club, ate at Le Cirque and La Grenouille. When I fell in love with her, I really courted her"—he smiled at the memory—"because I knew exactly the sorts of things she loved, and I loved her. I was living exactly the type of life she had always lived, and the kind she wanted to continue." He sighed. "When the change came, it came gradually," he said, "without my even realizing it. I suddenly . . ." But his voice trailed off as a young woman came and took their orders and then left again.

"Anyway," he continued, "it's odd that what happened to your family was exactly the sort of problem that drove me from banking. We weren't exactly lending to farmers—at times I headed up business *and* real estate loans. But the whole thing got to me little by little. And the turning point, oddly enough, happened when I was with Candace, right here at the inn."

"What happened?" Lisa asked.

He looked around at the high, vaulted ceilings, and Lisa's eyes followed his gaze as he took in the rest of the room. "I suppose I fell in love with this place, with the mountains and the streams and these rickety old buildings. I couldn't believe that Eastland owned the inn and Candace and I had never come here before. When we got back to New York, something just snapped in me. I was fed up with my job, with New York, fed up with every aspect of the life we had been leading. I was making more money than I knew what to do with, but I wasn't happy. With life in the city or any other part of my life, really."

"Do you come from around here?"

He smiled. "No, from Boston as a matter of fact. I had always led a strictly urban existence. But not the kind Candace grew up in. You might say I was originally from the wrong side of the tracks. I probably seemed like an exotic species to someone like Candace. Anyway, when the change came, I guess Candace and I both thought it would be temporary. We arranged with Scribner, Candace's father, for me to run the inn, and Candace and I just assumed we would live part-time in the country and part-time in the city. Neither of us ever thought of the move as the end of the marriage. But we just grew apart. We found we didn't need each other, and we didn't want the same things, the same experiences, anymore. There was no more sharing." He took another sip of wine and looked into Lisa's eyes. "Then Candace took up with an old friend of ours—Ethan Cobb—and that was that."

"Gee. I'm sorry," Lisa said quietly.

He shrugged. "It was bound to happen. We were moving in two different directions. I don't know—maybe I wouldn't have been that accepting if we hadn't already made the split. It was sadder to realize we didn't need each other anymore." He reached forward and covered her hand with his. "You, on the other hand," he said with a curve of his lips.

She smiled. "I what?"

"You appear to be very much of the anything-goes school of thought. Jay must have a lot of patience."

His hand was sending a warmth through her fingers that kindled vivid memories of their kiss. "If you think what I do is so terrible, why are you encouraging me?" she asked, tracing light circles across his palm with her thumb. "Hmm?"

"I'm not Jay," he answered softly. "And I haven't been able to put this morning out of my mind."

"Well, I was pretty distracted myself. After we got back and you showed me where the books were, I really—I didn't get all that much done."

He smiled and squeezed her hand. For a moment she was caught in his dark gaze, captured by the pull of his handsome smile. But she mistrusted something in that smile. She didn't feel they were on opposite sides in a battle, but he kept insisting they were. Was he trying to distract her from what he saw as her mission?

Their food came, and she tried to steer the conversation to topics she considered neutral. But everything she and Michael said was charged with meanings that complicated matters. And Lisa found that she was growing fonder of Michael by the minute.

When dinner was over, Michael took Lisa outside. As they walked down a tree-lined path that was bathed in the blue-white glow of the moon, Lisa could see how this land had exerted such a powerful influence on Michael. At every step and through every sense, Lisa was filled with the loveliness of the forest at night. The ground beneath her, covered with pine needles and ferns, was soft, giving, fragrant, and the rhythmic chirping of the crickets was hypnotic and calming. And the smell—fresh, vivid, alive with promise—awakened her as if from a deep sleep. Michael took her hand and they walked, silent under the moon, out into a clearing. And then, as Michael led her forward, she gasped in surprise. For the glimmering lights of the valley below were spread out like a blanket of glistening stars, as if reflecting the sky above in a small but bright pool of light.

"Pretty, isn't it," he said, drawing her close as he slung an arm around her shoulder. "We might not be alone, by the way," he murmured, "since I know this is a favorite spot for guests. But I thought you'd like to see it."

She looked up at him, his face beautifully illuminated by the moonlight. "But?" she repeated, smiling. "You mean that we're not supposed to go anywhere if we're not going to be alone?"

"Maybe," he said, taking her in his arms. He brought her close, his lean form pressing against her softness. "I think it's obvious that I like being alone with you. And it seems equally obvious that, Jay or no Jay, you're glad you're here."

She gazed into his eyes. "I lied about Jay," she said quietly.

"What do you mean?"

"It's over between us. It has been for weeks."

"Why did you say you were still seeing him?" he asked softly, brushing a strand of hair from her eyes.

"Oh, it just seemed safer," she murmured.

He searched her eyes. "What happened between the two of you? Why did it end?"

"Oh, well, I think what you said before about your marriage with Candace—when you said you wanted different things—that was the problem between me and Jay, too, only at a different level. He wanted a commitment—marriage, actually. And I wasn't ready. And he was very jealous, which put a real strain on us because of my work. At that time I was spending ten to twelve hours a day at a construction site in the city, with a lot of very good-looking, very forward men. And it drove him crazy. Especially because in a certain sense his suspicions were right."

"Really?"

"Well, he'd come to the site unannounced. He worked in the area, and he'd come to pick me up, and on some evenings I was working very closely with some pretty attractive guys. We were all adult enough to fool around and know that it wasn't necessarily going to lead anywhere, but there was often an attraction no one was about to deny. And it drove Jay crazy. Not to mention the fact that I started seeing him while I was still seeing someone else. He was really paranoid about that. He always said, 'If you cheated on him, someday you'll be cheating on me.'" She shrugged. "I just really didn't feel that the word *cheating* was particularly operative. I wasn't married to him and I wasn't married to the other man."

"And you've never been married?"

"Well, actually I was, years ago." She sighed. "Now I like to take things as they come, and the relationship just didn't mean as much to me as it did to Jay." She hesitated. "I guess that sounds callous. I don't mean it to."

He tilted her chin up with a gentle hand. "It doesn't sound callous. Just honest." He studied her eyes, his own lit like fiery opals in the moonlight. "But tell me something." He ran his warm hand down the cool skin of her neck, along the sensitive edge of her collarbone, and then he took her in his arms.

Once again his slightest touch, the pressure of his hips against her body, his warm strong hands wrapped around her, was all enough to make her forget everything but the deep pleasure and deeper promise of the moment.

"Tell me why it seems dangerous to be with me," he said huskily, his lips brushing hers. "Why you didn't tell me the truth, Lisa."

His hands encircled her waist, and then he was guiding her down to the ground, to the gentle carpet of grass that was green-soft in the moonlight. "Is it because I want you so much and you can feel it? Tell me why," he urged her.

"Because I want you," she whispered.

He moaned with pleasure as his lips sank into hers, as he laid her back and branded the flesh of her stomach with his fingers.

She had been cool in the night air, but at this first touch of skin against skin she was warm, aching to fall into that rapturous haze he had plummeted her into that morning.

His lips parted hers with an urgency she found thrilling, and when his tongue came into the warmth of her mouth, she moaned and wrapped her arms around his strong back, wanting him closer, wanting him completely. He teased, tasting her deeply, nibbling her lips and then plunging inside, and she hungrily roved her hands over his back, over his hard buttocks, urging him nearer, imagining him deep inside her, overpowering her with blazing pleasure.

He raised his head and looked down at her, and

she could barely see his wonderful face etched darkly in the moonlight. But the lack of light made her more aware of everything else—his male scent, woodsy and arousing, and the roughness of his cheek and hands, the leanness of his body she had sensed when she had first seen him, and the sound—so close—of his breathing, quick and urgent. Here in the forest her senses seemed new, more alive than ever before.

"How do I know this isn't the same thing as your trifling with those men on the construction site?" he breathed.

She smiled. "Trifling?"

He fought a smile. "You know what I mean."

"Well, maybe you don't know that. It is trifling when you've known someone only one day."

"Not with me it isn't," he whispered. "And it hasn't been just a day, Lisa. It's been a month."

She smiled. "Well, a month with a lot of space in it, then."

He said nothing, looking into her lovely gray eyes and trying to read them. He wanted her so much. Didn't she know what she did to him? He had kissed every inch of her in his dreams, made her cry out with the passion he knew was burning inside of her. She had stroked and coaxed him, urged and persuaded with hungry fingers that had aroused him as no others had, and her sweet softness had throbbed in need of his love.

Yet he had to remember those had been dreams. He felt as if he knew her, and he didn't. Not yet. But he was going to make damned sure he did soon. Damned sure.

From far, far away, Michael heard voices and gently pulled back. "I don't know if you care, Lisa, but in about three seconds, we're not going to be alone."

She let her hands slip from his frame and quickly they both scrambled to stand up. "Ah. I think I do care. Professional ethics and all."

He nodded hello at a couple who to Lisa seemed to have appeared out of nowhere, and then he and Lisa began heading back toward the inn. "Is that a problem?" he asked.

"I'll tell you if it is. I don't really know yet," she said quietly. She looked away from his compelling eyes and bit her lip. Damn. She really didn't know, and it wasn't at all appropriate to discuss her doubts. For if there was a reason to mistrust him, he was the one person she couldn't explore her suspicions with.

As they came out into the clearing near the inn, he took her hand and squeezed it. "Come to my cabin?"

She looked into his eyes and nearly melted once again under their dark spell. But the mood had been broken. She had to know him better. It had been only one day. "Not tonight, Michael," she said quietly. "I'll see you in the morning."

"All right. I'll walk you to your cabin."

"That's okay. I think I'd like to take a little walk by myself, actually. Walking through the woods alone at night is something I haven't done in years."

"And you like it?"

She smiled. "I love it. It's something I used to do on dares from my brothers, and it just kind of stuck with me."

His eyes shined with affection. "A woman after my own heart. Then I'll say good night here." He brushed her lips gently with his, held himself back from parting her lips, and drew back, amazed he had succeeded. She was so damned seductive. Almost a tease. "Good night," he whispered, and walked off into the night.

Lisa smiled as she got ready for bed. She was so happy, filled with a carefree lightness that seemed to have no reason, no cause for being. She knew part of it came from being in such a lovely atmosphere. It was as if she had found a part of herself that had been lost for years, and it had changed her mood, her perceptions, even her energy level. And what a coincidence that the man at the party had turned up in her life as Michael Jamison!

He had been hard to resist. But she didn't plan on necessarily resisting forever. She had never fallen into bed with any man at the drop of a hat, but she tended to feel more comfortable with men more quickly than a lot of her friends did. Maybe it had to do with growing up with three brothers, she felt. But whatever the reason, she found that she usually knew almost right away how she felt about a man— she was a good judge of character—and certainly the attraction was either there or it wasn't.

The only unfortunate part was that she could never manage to maintain her interest. And that made her nervous. It was almost as if she had to see if she could "get" them. And once she had, the thrill tended to go. The conquering heroine, perhaps.

And this bothered her deeply. Her relationships tended to fizzle like so many spent firecrackers, and there never seemed to be anything she could do to revive them.

Yet sometimes, as she looked back on her own marriage and thought about those of her friends, she figured she wasn't missing all that much. She enjoyed her life; she enjoyed the relationships she had while they lasted. And she felt that when the time was right, when she was ready, if ever, things would fall into place. In the meantime she wasn't going to think of every man she met as possible marriage material.

She slid into bed and drew the curtains back from the windows. It was lovely the way the bed was right beneath. The cool night air wafted in and filled the room with its pine freshness, and the forest outside was softly shadowed in the moonlight, dark and mysterious.

A twig snapped outside her window, and Lisa sat up and looked outside. About ten feet away, a shadowy figure she knew was Michael walked past, silent in the night.

"Psst," she called out on impulse.

He stopped in his tracks, and she smiled.

"Some trailsman," she hissed. "Over here."

He was smiling as he walked toward her, and his walk was different, almost a swagger rather than the easy gait he had used before she had called out.

He came up to the window. "What do we have here? A damsel in distress? Damsels aren't supposed to hiss like construction workers, you know."

She laughed. "And hissees aren't supposed to come traipsing over. Or swaggering over. You're obviously not an experienced object of hoots and hisses and other city-street pleasures."

He smiled. "As you obviously are."

"Of course," she said.

He leaned forward and brought his face close to hers.

"You're so beautiful, Lisa. I don't know whether

you even know that. Your eyes, your hair, I don't know what I noticed first about you." For a moment he just gazed into her eyes. "I know what I can't forget about you now, though. The taste of your lips," he whispered. "So sweet, so—" And he brushed his lips against hers, nibbling and gently kissing, tasting and murmuring how much he wanted her.

But then he drew back. "This is not the most comfortable position in the world, you know, great kisses or not."

She smiled. "Maybe I shouldn't have called you over. I just couldn't resist."

"Hmm. But now?"

She laughed. "Now I *can* resist."

"Do you know that you're a temptress?" he whispered huskily. "Difficult to leave, difficult to accept a no from." He frowned. "Who knows?" he asked musingly. "Maybe that's why you were such a find for Eastland. I had heard they were very, very happy with their new operations manager."

"I should slam down the window for that remark," she said softly but half seriously.

He looked surprised. "There's nothing wrong with being pretty, you know. Or sexy. And seductive. And unforgettable. Haunting, even. Bewitching. Mysterious."

She fought a smile. "Now you're looking for trouble."

"Sounds good," he laughed. "Reconsidering your need to sleep?"

"Definitely not."

"Then good night. I hope you're tormented by

unendingly sexy dreams of me while I work into the night."

She laughed. "We'll see. I promise I'll call you if I need you."

"Sure, sure," he said, smiling, and after saying good night, walked off into the moonlit woods.

Ten minutes later Lisa cursed him as she tried futilely to get to sleep. For she was indeed being tormented, haunted by the memory of his lips, his tongue, the hard thighs that had hinted at so much, his need which when unleashed would be explosive. She wanted him; she knew he had somehow reached her more deeply than any man before. But it was too soon to make love. She wanted to know him better, and she wanted to get some of the Eastland issues straightened out without having them complicated by the issues lovemaking would raise. But if and when that time came, she would be ready for him.

The next morning, when Lisa returned to Michael's office to begin her examination of his books in earnest, she found he was already there, ready and waiting on the worn leather couch. His arms were crossed, his lips were in a half smirk, half smile, and he was looking at her with an expression of clear and unadulterated challenge. "Rather late on the job, aren't you? I've been here for hours. I thought all you operations managers were sticklers about time. And I don't maintain timesheets for my employees, by the way, just in case you were looking for them."

She let his last remark pass for the moment. "I do usually eat breakfast, Michael. I thought I'd see you there, actually."

"Me? Are you kidding? When I knew you'd be nosing around here? I told you—"

"I know, I know: You've been here for hours. Well. As long as you're here. I didn't do all that much with the books yesterday, but I did dream about one of the things I wanted to talk to you about, believe it or not."

His brows shot up. "Dream about? You mean you actually dreamed about these damn accounting books?"

She smiled. "Mmm-hmm."

"Not about me and my handsome smile?" He was fighting so hard not to smile that she had to laugh.

"Not at all," she said, lying through her teeth. Most of her dreams had been continuations of the fantasies he had left her with before sleep, and she had awakened full of desire. "Just numbers and more numbers."

"Ah. Too bad. Well, then, I'll make us some coffee and we can get this unpleasantness over with."

She looked at him with annoyance. He seemed so much like Keith. She could remember so many incidents in which Keith had used just that tone and just those words. When she'd insist that they had to start budgeting their money, or she'd ask for his check stubs from their joint account so she could balance the checkbook, or when he would come home and ask if she had any money because he had spent two hundred dollars in a day without knowing how or on what. He had constantly, in more and more ways as each day went by, forced her into the position of being the "responsible" one. *She* was the one who took care of the finances; *she* was the one who paid the bills and deposited all their checks, who planned the budget for each of his increasingly farfetched projects, and watched as each one fell to pieces. And the more she took charge, the more Keith resented her. Yet, as each day passed, he forced her into her role more deeply still. And the conflict had ultimately destroyed their marriage. The very imaginativeness that had first made her fall in love with him drove her away from him in the end. Each time an idea of his failed, he resented her for her success, for the role he began to suspect she had played in his failure. With one venture—a clothing store he hoped to franchise nationwide—he ran out of money six months before Lisa had projected break-even, and he had blamed her for the failure of the entire operation. And when she pointed out that he had spent way beyond the budget, he accused her of being unsupportive.

"Do you take it black?" Michael asked, interrupting her thoughts.

"What? Oh. No, with milk if you have it."

"Coming right up." He stooped and took a container of milk out of a half size refrigerator in the corner of the room. When he straightened, he had a gleam in his eye. "Personal acquisition, by the way."

"What?"

"The refrigerator. I can see that the adding machine in the back of your mind is working again."

You're asking for it, she said silently. "All right, let's get to work," she said as he handed her her coffee. "What I thought about—or dreamed—last night was your advertising program. I see here that you're budgeted for an amount you don't even come close to spending. Why is that?"

He slid onto the bench next to her. The gleam in his eye was sparkling more brightly than ever. "I didn't like the kinds of people the ads were bringing in. And they didn't like the inn. The ads were slowly but surely ruining our reputation."

"I don't understand."

"All right, look. What is your general impression of the inn so far? What is the feel of the place as you see it?"

"Well, very nice. Rustic. Casual."

"Exactly. Old Scribner Hollingworth used to put ads in magazines that brought people who expected something entirely different. They wanted to know where the swimming pool and saunas were, where the hotel valet was, and why they couldn't buy souvenirs." He sighed and took a sip of his coffee. "You know, this area of the country is unique in a very important respect."

"What's that?"

"It's famous for its natural beauty, and it's still relatively unspoiled. Now, I happen to be as wild about places like the Grand Canyon as the next person. Except look what's happened in places like that and Yellowstone Park. You can't drive in or out without being inundated with all kinds of things that remind you—in case you forgot—that you're in a tourist area. That will never happen around here, because it's never been popular to anything close to that extent. But I don't want to have any part of that sort of approach."

"And that explains why you don't advertise? Come on, Michael. You've got a business to run. This isn't a private estate to which you can invite guests of your own choosing."

"If I change it, Lisa, I'll lose the small but steady clientele I do have."

"Did I ask you to change it?" she demanded.

"I recognize your approach," he said carefully.

"I doubt it. I recognize your attitude though. You've had a very obvious chip on your shoulder since I arrived, and that's told me one thing very clearly."

"What's that?" he asked, almost smiling.

"It's not anything to smile about either," she said testily. "I mean it. You see my being here as an annoying little interlude—I don't mean personally, but in terms of both our jobs. From the very beginning you've seen me as an adversary, as someone you have no interest in cooperating with. And that's not going to get you anywhere."

"Then I was right," he said flatly. "I have to do what Richard Hollingworth—via Lisa Bennett—says, and I'm supposed to do it with a smile."

"Oh, you're impossible. God! You're just like—" She stopped, catching herself. No time to bring up her husband. *Ex-husband,* she corrected herself.

"Just like whom?" he asked.

"Never mind."

He searched her face. "You have the most beautiful eyes," he said softly.

She shot him the nastiest glare she could muster. "*Now* do you think so?"

He smiled. "More than ever."

"I think we should get back to work, Michael. Really."

"So you can help me."

"Yes, damn it!"

He shook his head. "Don't you understand, Lisa? I can tell that your whole approach is based on a conception that just doesn't fit the inn. I know the

67

kinds of hotels you've worked on before you got to Eastland, and—"

"How do you know that?" she interrupted.

"I have friends at Eastland who know your background," he said simply. "Anyway. You've worked on hotel chains and apartment complexes. What knowledge does that give you to pass judgment and dole out advice for this sort of place?"

"What knowledge did you get from banking?" she snapped. "What knowledge does any businessman or woman bring to a new company in a different field? Concepts and ideas and management styles that work in any field. And you don't need to have gotten a degree in hotel management to see that you need to change some of your ways. And at a certain point, Michael, you're going to have to listen to me or lose the whole operation."

"Then I was right."

"It's just common sense."

He stroked his chin, and she remembered—without wanting to—the wonderful scratchy feel of it against her own skin. "All right," he said quietly. "Let's hear what you have to say."

"Good. You might even like some of it."

His eyes sparkled. "I'm sure I will. I like the person who'll be saying it," he said softly, gently stroking her cheek.

She covered his hand and put it back on the table. "You're not going to distract me, Michael, no matter how hard you try."

For a moment the look in his eyes was so soft and gentle that she was totally lost, without will or discipline.

But then she caught herself. She straightened up,

took a sip of her coffee, and slowly launched into a series of criticisms and suggestions that surprised her, for she hadn't realized she had so many ideas. But once she began talking, one idea led to another. The only frustrating part was Michael's attitude. He seemed receptive enough to the idea that he could advertise in a different sort of magazine from the ones Scribner Hollingworth had wanted him to. But when Lisa asked him about the dropoff in attendance over the past six months, he was defensive and uninterested in what she had to say.

He took a sip of coffee and looked at Lisa with an odd sparkle in his dark eyes. "I'm surprised you would ask a question whose answer is so obvious," he challenged.

She sighed. So he was back to that attitude again. "What's the obvious answer?" she asked.

"New York City is eighty-five miles away, but your weather isn't all that different. Haven't you noticed it's rained for the past fifteen weekends, something like a hundred-year record? And that the amount of snow that fell this winter wasn't even enough to drag a child's sled through, much less to support skiing or snowshoeing or sleighriding? This is an outdoor resort, Lisa, in case you hadn't noticed. Winter, spring, summer, and fall."

"Tell it to Richard Hollingworth."

"What?"

"Tell it to Richard Hollingworth! If you're going to take that kind of attitude, Michael, I really can't help you. Don't you see? I know about the weather. I'm sure it did have something to do with the dropoffs. But you can't put the blame on it and you know that as well as I do." She paused. "I don't know—maybe this sounds silly. But why not try putting yourself in the position you used to be in? I mean, you know that as a loan officer or whatever you were, you would never have considered someone a good business risk if they blamed things like the weather when their business began to go bad. Maybe if you did that you'd come up with some ideas."

"Damn it, Lisa, I left all that behind."

"Left what behind?" she demanded. "Good business sense? Come on. Wake up, Michael! Look, how about this? Offer something like a rainy-day weekend, in spring, summer, and fall—a cut-rate to encourage people to come up in bad weather. People could have gourmet picnics in their rooms and that sort of thing. And you could have snowless weekends or whatever in winter. I think that sort of pricing could really bring people in, Michael. *I'd* come."

He raised a brow. "That isn't a bad idea," he said carefully. "It really isn't."

"Well, thank you very much. Now maybe you'll begin to listen to me."

And in fact, they listened to each other over the next few days. Lisa learned from him and he learned from her, and gradually they came up with plans that almost satisfied each of them. Lisa saw that many of Michael's problems with the inn stemmed from cutbacks that Richard Hollingworth had forced him to make, and she promised to try to stem the tide. And she convinced Michael that this would be possible only if he agreed to certain plans for the future. Her report to Richard Hollingworth could be very, very positive if she felt deep down that Michael would turn what new financial allocations she could get into some of the plans she had outlined.

One night, a week after Lisa had first arrived, she and Michael were eating dinner under the stars on the lovely flagstone terrace off the main lodge's restaurant. As she looked at his face, lit by the flickering candlelight and the glow of the moon and the stars, she hoped her struggles with him were going to end soon. For what seemed like an infinite number of days, she had fought her attraction to him.

She remembered one night—two nights before— when they had stayed up until two, going over plans and budgets in his office until neither she nor he could stay awake. It wasn't so much the lateness of the hour as the fact that they had switched from coffee to wine at around nine, and had mixed work with drinking, laughter, and long, heated gazes as the night wore on.

When Lisa was in the middle of explaining why he had to cut the nightly dinner menu by 75 percent, he began smiling.

"What's so funny?" she asked, taking a sip of wine.

"I'd say ridiculous, actually" he murmured. "That I'm here drinking my favorite red wine in the world with a woman who is very rapidly becoming my favorite woman in the world. And we're talking about menus."

She smiled, but her smile faded as he reached out and cupped her face in his hands. "I mean it," he said softly.

She loved the way his eyes looked at that moment —dark and warm, caring and concerned, deep with the passion she knew he possessed. "And in a way I wish you were somewhere other than here."

"Why?"

"Because I wouldn't be constantly tempted. I can't stand people who can't take no for an answer—men and women both—but when I'm constantly with you, it's so difficult."

She smiled. "Don't you think it's difficult for me too? I've just—I've changed lately though. I like to keep things light and all that, but I have to follow my feelings too."

"Don't apologize," he murmured. "It's okay."

"Oh, Michael," she said, and she leaned forward and kissed him in a kiss that grew instantly deeper as their tongues entwined in pleasure. She didn't want to tease him; she didn't want to tempt him; but it was so difficult to stay away when he was so near, when she had been aware all night long of his closeness, the desire just beneath the surface of every glance, every pause, every movement. And she liked him so much.

She drew back before it could go too far.

"I think I know what you're thinking," he said softly.

"What?"

"That it's easier not to be together at all than to pull back."

She smiled. "Well, yes, it was along those general lines."

"I want to tell you something," he said, taking a strand of her dark auburn hair between his fingers. "I'm here for you when you want me. I want you to be sure. I don't want to be another Jay, or any of the other men you've known. I don't know exactly what happened with any of them, but I don't want to be somebody you rush into a relationship with on the rebound. So don't forget, I don't want you apologizing about waiting."

She had smiled again, and they had spent the rest of their time together that night in a closeness that was wonderful, each very aware of what the other was thinking. She felt he genuinely meant what he had said; it wasn't a line designed to make her like him. And it had had the added benefit of making them work better together as well.

And now, over dinner, as she looked into those eyes that were as dark as the night, she hoped the wait was almost over. In a way, she felt she was being a little bit arbitrary. All the work was done; she was very, very fond of Michael; there was nothing tangible to hold them back. But in the back of her mind a voice warned that it made a lot more sense to see Michael Jamison on her terms, in a simpler situation than the one they were now in. And from some of the things he had told her about Richard Hollingworth, a gut instinct whispered she'd do well to keep the relationship totally aboveboard for now. She didn't want gossip or rumors to taint what she felt was going to be an excellent report.

After dinner, as they walked along the moonlit path that led to the cliffside lookout point Michael had shown her that first night, Michael slung his arm around her waist and drew her close. "I'll miss you when you're gone," he said softly.

She smiled. "I'll miss you too."

He hugged her and said nothing, for he had suddenly remembered he had felt exactly this way, used

73

the very same words, years before with Candace, when they had first met. That had been in Palm Beach, when he was on vacation and had gone to a charity ball Candace had hosted. They were nearly inseparable for the next week, and he had always felt that if she had come from a different social class, they might have even have gotten married that quickly. Hell, they were in love. But she had needed a proper courtship, and he had waited and gone through the required motions.

He thought about the telephone conversation he had had with her just this afternoon. Strange. He could almost think she wanted him back. It seemed damned unlikely though. She had thrown him over —not the other way around.

"I might be coming down to the city, actually," he said as they reached the log fence that edged the cliff.

"Oh, really? When?"

"Well, Candace wanted me to come to a charity thing she's been organizing for months. It's called Playtime, a day-care organization I've been involved with for years. I haven't been active in it lately except by giving money, but if she can't get another escort, I'll be going to their annual ball."

"I see," Lisa said, not too happily. She knew that as he had presented the story, it was unimportant, insignificant. But her stomach had tightened anyway, and she felt as if she were only half there as she said, "I hadn't realized you two still saw each other."

"We didn't until recently. We had dinner a few weeks ago, though, and then she called today about the Playtime affair. Other than that, though, it hasn't been that often."

She looked up at him, trying to read the expression in his handsome profile. But no clues were there. He just looked dreamy, as dreamy and uncertain as his voice had been.

And an inner voice of her own told her she'd never forget this night, that in a few weeks she'd remember his words and cry.

CHAPTER FOUR

Lisa sank into her chair at her Eastland office and spun around so she could look at the view of Park Avenue. She needed something to distract her. She had just handed in what she felt was an incisive profile of the inn; it was full of truly constructive criticism, both of Michael and Eastland management, with a solution to virtually every problem she had targeted. Yet she couldn't shake the nagging, uneasy feeling that had closed over her like a shroud the night before.

Michael had been very affectionate, not at all distracted by thoughts of Candace the way she was. But the introduction of someone new—someone she had written off as definitely a part of the past and the past only—made Lisa realize how deeply she cared for Michael, and how much she wanted him to care for her. And she knew how people from the past could sneak into the present with unexpected force and passion.

76

It was only six months ago that she and Keith had seen each other again, and it was a memory that still made her uncomfortable. He had called her up—as he often did even now—and she had assumed that he wanted money, as he usually did. But she had assumed wrong. He was happy and flush with success from a new venture of his, and he wanted to take her out to dinner, talk about old times and to show a little appreciation, as he put it, for the help she had given him since the separation. She didn't like to be reminded of the fact she had lent him money since the divorce—it was an attempt, she knew, at expiation of a guilt she felt was wrong. *You have nothing to feel guilty about,* she had told herself at the end of the marriage, but deep down she didn't really believe her words, and she lent him money to try to wash away her feelings. And, she realized now, probably to maintain the hold she had on Keith. After all, she had to have gotten some inner pleasure or good feeling if she had maintained that balance of power all those years, and if she was still doing it, it obviously did something for her.

But six months ago it looked as if all that had changed. Keith was clearly on his feet, secure and optimistic—without being wildly so—and very, very sexy-sounding on the phone. And out of a rush of nostalgia and a twinge of attraction she only half acknowledged, Lisa said yes.

The evening was charged with a suppressed excitement that was impossible to ignore. Lisa was shocked at Keith's appearance. He looked better than she had seen him in years. And he seemed as taken with her as he had been before they had married. They ate dinner at a cozy, firelit restaurant they

77

had gone to dozens of times before, and afterward, when Keith invited her for a drink at his apartment, it seemed like the most natural thing in the world, as if no time at all had passed and they were still in the first months of discovery of each other. Once at his apartment, they came together quickly, passionately, completely, more intimately than they ever had before. Lisa didn't question it; she couldn't. Her whole body and soul were united with Keith's in an experience that could neither be questioned nor stopped.

Afterward, though, as they lay in the quiet of his apartment, smoking cigarettes in the darkness and looking up at the ceiling, she realized she hadn't given a bit of thought to what she had done. Would they get together again? Did she want that? Did he? And in moments she knew the answer, just by looking around the room and remembering. She knew that the lovemaking had been an interlude, deep and important, but something that could never happen again.

A painting on one wall made her remember a fight they had had, one of many in which he hadn't wanted her to go out with some friends—girlfriends, no less—because he had thought they'd "run into trouble." When she had pointed out for the thousandth time that she was out on her own all day anyway, and that if she wanted to "run into trouble" she had plenty of chances, he grew angrier still, launching into a jealous tirade that ended only because Lisa had stormed out of the apartment and slammed the door. Later that night, as they always eventually did, they made love, dissolving each other's anger in passion that was made up if not of love, of at least a desire for love. But the good times had never outweighed the bad. Their relationship had been chipped away in too many areas. And she didn't want to begin trying to repair it, an attempt she knew would fail.

Now, though, as she looked back on that night of six months before, she was frightened. For she knew that no matter how many reasons there were for staying away from Keith, and no matter how many reasons there would be for staying away from him in the future, there was a deep well of passion that no amount of reason or logic could obliterate. They had been married; they had loved each other; they had shared things with each other and no one else. That would never change. There would always, she was sure, be a residue of passion, a spark that could burst into flame under the right circumstances.

And she was certain this was true of Michael and Candace as well.

The intercom on Lisa's desk buzzed, and she pressed down the flashing red button and spoke. "Yes, Grace."

"Do you have a few minutes, Lisa?"

"Sure. Come on in." Lisa smiled. Grace had finally called her Lisa, something Lisa had been trying to get her to do since she had first arrived two weeks ago. Grace was in her early forties, a woman from the old school as far as her secretarial duties were concerned. She had never worked for a woman before, had always been asked to handle all sorts of personal duties for her male bosses, and had been treated in ways that Lisa couldn't stand, having endured many herself. And she was determined to change as many of the negative aspects of Grace's job as she could.

Grace knocked, stepped in, and sat down by Lisa's desk. She looked apprehensive, her blue eyes fearful and evasive as Lisa looked at her.

"What's wrong?" Lisa asked. "You look terrible."

Grace looked down at her lap and pulled at a ring on her right hand. Then she sighed and looked into Lisa's eyes. "I was just talking with Tracy Arness—you know, Mr. Hollingworth's new secretary. Well, she's a temp, actually."

"Oh, yes," Lisa said. "The one with the streak in her hair."

Grace looked as if she had a bad taste in her mouth. "Yes, and on such lovely hair." She sighed again. "I'm awfully sorry to be the bearer of bad news, Lisa, but I understand that Mr. Hollingworth has read your report, and according to Tracy, he was livid. I thought you'd want to know."

Lisa's stomach tightened. "Livid?" she said quietly. "Why?"

Grace raised a brow. "I wish I knew. I typed the report and I honestly thought it was excellent." She smiled. "And I've typed an awful lot of them over the years."

Lisa bit her lip. What was wrong with the report? It was her first report, the first concrete evidence of her abilities. And Richard Hollingworth was livid.

The phone rang, and Grace leaped to answer it. "Miss Bennett's office. . . . Yes, Tracy, one moment please." She put Hollingworth's secretary on hold and looked at Lisa. "Mr. Hollingworth wants to see you at four."

Lisa swallowed and nodded. "All right," she said hollowly. "Tell her I'll be there."

A few moments later, after Grace had hung up and

left the office, Lisa leaned forward and put her head in her hands. For the second time in as many days, she felt a deep sense of dread.

Richard Hollingworth's office was everything Lisa had expected, though she had never seen it before. He had interviewed her in the board room, and had had little to do with her since she had been hired. But she could have guessed accurately, from his demeanor, what his office was like. Cool, clean lines matched the cool, clean lines of his clothes; the smoked-glass tables echoed the sunglasses he wore 90 percent of the time, even in the office; and even the leather of the sofa and low-slung chairs perfectly matched the dark-gray leather of his slim attaché case.

He wasn't in the office when Lisa was shown in, even though she was right on time.

Lisa was left alone then, and she restlessly looked out his window, sat down, got up and examined an abstract painting on the wall, and sat down again before Richard Hollingworth finally came in. And she was certain, as he breezily apologized and took his place behind the desk, that he had wanted only to make an entrance, to create the impression of an unendingly busy man who barely had time to attend even the meetings he himself had scheduled.

Unfortunately, he was an attractive man, and Lisa was distracted from her annoyance by his sharp, incredibly pale blue eyes. He was deeply tanned, with an angular, almost-thin face, and straight, sandy hair. His clothes were unadventurous choices: a white shirt with striped tie beneath a dark, well-cut but nondescript suit, and Lisa was surprised that a man so young—he couldn't have been more than thirty—felt the need or desire to dress so conservatively when he was already at the top.

But when he slid her report out from a folder, she immediately forgot about what he looked like and what he was wearing.

"I read your report," he said quietly, fingering the papers as if they were faintly distasteful. His keen eyes met hers. "I'm sorry you spent so much time up at the inn for no purpose."

She swallowed, her throat suddenly bone dry. "I'm afraid I don't understand," she managed to say as calmly as she could.

He sighed and steepled his fingers. "You came to me on very high recommendation, Miss Bennett. I understand that we lured you to Eastland just as nineteen employees were about to be dismissed as a result of recommendations on your last job."

Her heart skipped a beat. She hated the memory, hated the thought that she had been responsible for that. She hadn't meant for her report to be interpreted as it had been; but what was even more shameful to her was the fact that she didn't come out and *say* her recommendations had been misinterpreted. When Richard Hollingworth had first interviewed her for the Eastland position and she had told him about her job, she could tell he was very, very impressed with what he saw as her hard-headedness, her cool toughness, and she had let the impression stand uncorrected, knowing it would help her. Even now she didn't correct him.

"I had understood too," he continued, fiddling with the papers, "that you had a clear grasp of just what it is that an operations manager does."

"I had thought so," she said.

He sighed. "I've read your report three times, Miss Bennett." He winced. "Would you excuse me for a minute?"

"Of course."

He pressed a button on his desk and barked loudly into a speaker, "I thought you were bringing me those aspirin!"

"Yes, sir! I was just—I'll be right there," came a harried, high-pitched voice from the speaker, and a moment later his secretary came bursting through the doors. "I'm sorry, Mr. Hollingworth. I couldn't find the kind you wanted down at the drugstore in the lobby, and I had to go—"

"Never mind," he said irritably. "Are they safety sealed?"

"Yes, sir."

"Then just give me the bottle, please, and bring me some coffee."

"Yes, sir." The young woman handed him the bottle as if afraid he would snap her hand off, and then ran quietly out of the office.

"Sorry," Hollingworth said, resting his elbows on the desk and holding his temples. "My head is killing me. I feel as if a knife is going right through from one temple to the other."

Lisa winced. "And you're taking your aspirin with *coffee*?"

He looked alarmed. "What's the matter with that?" he asked nervously. "They say coffee helps headaches."

"Well, some," she offered, "but water would be better for your stomach. Aspirin's bad enough, if you take a lot of it, without adding the acidity of coffee."

He blinked. "Great. Now I'm on my way to getting an ulcer."

"Are you?"

"I don't know," he exploded, holding his stomach. "This is all just great." He clenched his fist. "I was on a prescription drug for these headaches but they were ruining my judgment, not to mention my memory. I cut them out cold turkey. But this—this is impossible. And now you're telling me I'm getting an ulcer?" He buzzed the intercom, waited, buzzed again, got no answer, and slammed a hand on the desk. "Damn it, where is that girl?"

"Getting coffee, I imagine," Lisa said. "If you'd like me to come back at another time, Mr. Hollingworth—"

He shook his head. "Richard, please. And no. This is far too important." He closed his eyes and clenched his jaw, then looked at Lisa with fear clearly shining from his pale blue eyes. "I drink five to six cups of coffee a day. Do you think I should cut down?"

"Yes, I do," Lisa said, mystified by the role he was placing her in, and by his behavior as well. He was chief executive officer of Eastland Industries, a man who should have been more concerned with profits and losses than ulcers, aspirin, and an employee's opinions about his health habits. "I really wouldn't be at all surprised if the coffee were giving you the headaches. It can, you know."

"Great," he said, reaching for a cigarette and lighting it. "Don't tell me about these, Lisa. I know about these." He exhaled a big cloud of smoke and leaned back in his chair. "You must have some vices yourself."

She met his gaze. It was difficult to tell if the words had been meant provocatively. Normally she would have made her conversation at least slightly suggestive with a man who looked like Richard Hollingworth. He was undeniably handsome, and Lisa had found that flirting never hurt in almost any situation. But she kept thinking about Michael. She missed him. And for the first time in her life, a man was able to hold her interest even when she was away from him.

"Hmm?" Hollingworth prodded her, raising a brow. "I've heard a lot about you, Lisa. They don't come as tough as you without letting off steam somehow, in some area."

Now there was no mistaking his tone. She had liked him better when he was an unknown but hostile force. "I manage," she said noncommittally, and was relieved when a gentle knock sounded tentatively at the door, and Richard's secretary gingerly stepped in.

"Here's your coffee, sir." She nervously set it down on the desk and stood there uncertainly, like a young dog waiting to be hit by her master.

"All right, thank you. And no calls."

"Yes, sir," she said quietly, and she raced from the room.

He shook his head after she had left. "Damn temps. They're either like scared rabbits or paid gossips. That one out there is both. Don't ever tell her anything you don't want the whole building to know." His gaze penetrated hers. "If you have any secrets, that is," he said smoothly.

"If I did, I would hardly tell someone I barely know," she said evenly.

He dragged on his cigarette without shifting his gaze from hers. The buzzer on the desk rang, and he looked at it with astonishing anger. He slammed the button. "What *is* it?" he demanded. "I said no calls."

"It's your father," the tiny voice said.

"Oh. Well, put him on then. . . . Yes, Father. . . . No, it hasn't been—I'm doing the best—All right. . . . Yes, I promise. . . ." He grabbed his cigarette and dragged deeply on it. "Yes. . . . All right. . . . Right. . . . All right. . . . Good-bye." He hung up and stubbed his cigarette out. Then he reached for the aspirin, shook out four, swigged them down with his coffee, and looked up at Lisa. "All right, let's get down to business. What we have here, as the saying goes, is a failure to communicate, Lisa. Now, if I had wanted a series of recommendations for improvements we could make to the inn, I could have asked Michael Jamison himself to write them up." He leaned back in his chair and sighed. "Your function—your purpose in being here, Lisa, was to point out the problems *inherent* in the inn's functioning—to outline the reasons it's been steadily losing money over the past eighteen months."

"Without suggesting solutions?"

He sighed and closed his eyes, and she could see that his jaw was clenching and unclenching, either from tension or pain or both. When he opened his eyes, they were cold and ungiving. "There are solutions other than pouring additional funds into the place. You must realize, Lisa, that the inn is only one small part of a very large conglomerate. There is no way we're going to begin making the kind of allocations you recommended in your report."

"But you know as well as I do that more often than

not, you have to spend money in order to make money. You'll see at least a dozen places in my report in which it's clearly just a matter of money, plain and simple. For instance, with the proposed layoffs—"

"We are *not* interested in that sort of item," he cut in. "In fact, I was very surprised when I read that section of your report, Lisa. *Very* surprised. You sounded more like a bleeding-heart union leader than the new operations manager of Eastland Domestic."

"I've always based my recommendations on what I see as the truth, Richard—as the best means for a company to grow and prosper. And the situation at the inn is clearer than any I've ever encountered."

"Clearer than the numbers? They speak for themselves, don't they? I had thought you would give us a report that would complement the numbers, not the sort of idealistic claptrap I've heard from Jamison since I became CEO. Do you understand me? The inn is losing money and *it will continue to lose money.*"

She not only understood; she was deeply disappointed. She remembered a certain phrase he had used when he had first asked her to evaluate the inn—*it doesn't look at all promising.* Now she saw what he wanted, what he had always wanted: He wasn't interested in positive suggestions or plans; he obviously had his own negative ideas about the inn, and he wanted her to justify them through a supposedly "objective" report. And she was 99 percent certain she didn't have any choice in the matter. He had termed her honest report unacceptable. Would anything short of what he wanted ever be seen by anyone else? He could just hand back whatever she wrote if he didn't like it.

"If I understand you correctly," she began slowly, "then—"

"Say no more," he said softly, smiling gently. "I think you already do understand." He rose and came around to her side of the desk, swung a hip onto the edge, and looked down at her. "You look too pretty and too smart and too savvy to have me explain anything to you—anything I wouldn't want repeated, that is." He inhaled deeply, as if taking her to him with his gaze and his breath alone. "I think we might both benefit, though, if we knew each other a bit better. Now that you're back in the big bad city, how about dinner tonight?"

She looked at him carefully and thought fast. She didn't like Richard Hollingworth, and she certainly didn't trust him. She didn't want to have dinner with him; the only question was how much that would mean to him. But as she reminded herself how good-looking he was, she realized it had to be an insignificant matter. He probably went out with a different woman every night of the week.

She rose and said, "I'm sorry, I'm not free. Perhaps another time."

He reached out and gently encircled one of her wrists. "What if I need more help with a headache? Who's going to stop me from taking aspirin with coffee again?"

"Oh, I'm sure you can find any number of willing helpers," she said, freeing herself from his grasp. Though it had been gentle, there was something very unsettling about it.

His lips tightened. "All right. But I expect you to

make the new report top priority. Don't rush it, Lisa; it's got to be right this time. But get it done."

"I'll do that," she said tonelessly, but moments later, as she walked out of his office and down the beige-carpeted hallway back to her own office, she wondered how she could do what Richard Hollingworth had asked. And how she could go against him.

She had seen this happen before so many times that she had often questioned whether or not she wanted to stay in her field. Once management decided that part of its operation had to go, they could juggle the numbers so anyone in a decision-making position would unquestioningly vote to divest. Lisa had learned a long time ago that numbers do lie when the person arranging them has clear and definite intentions. And in the case of the inn, no one had to touch the figures; they spoke for themselves. What Richard Hollingworth wanted from her was one interpretation and one interpretation only—that the losses from the inn would continue to grow. No plans, no suggestions, no alternatives, were welcome or needed. Which meant that he ultimately wanted to convince someone else that Eastland should sell the inn.

She had to tell Michael. At least she wanted to. But would it jeopardize her position with Eastland?

It was only a few days ago that she had felt she couldn't trust Michael completely. He had acted as if he wanted something from her, as if he had wanted to influence her. She knew him much better now. But could she trust him to that extent? Telling him of her suspicions was a serious matter, something she could perhaps get fired for if anyone discovered it. Yet, how could she not tell him? She cared for him too much to just sit back and . . . and what? For she couldn't imagine even writing the kind of report Richard had ordered, much less sitting back and watching the hatchets start to fall.

When she got back to her office, she called the inn, and her heart wrenched as she recognized Tim's voice. He was such a nice kid. And he would probably be among the first to go.

A few minutes later Michael got on, sounding out of breath but happy to hear from her. "Hey, Lisa," he said softly. "What's up? How's it going down there?"

"Not well, Michael. Listen. I have to talk to you, and I really can't do it over the phone. When were you planning to come down?"

"Well, not till the night of the ball. But I'll come tonight if you want."

"Great. That's . . . that would be really good."

They made arrangements to meet at her apartment around seven, and then hung up.

Lisa spent the rest of the afternoon going over her report and trying to figure out what changes she was going to make, but she was too distracted to do much more than stare at the words. There were so many people whose lives would be hurt if Richard's plan went through. Young people like Tim and his friends would bounce back; but what about Murph, the old man who had been caretaker of the inn for over fifty years? Where would he go? What would his life be like even if he did manage to find a place to live? He had made a home for himself near the inn's vegetable gardens, out of what had once, long ago, been a chicken brooder. He had no family as far as anyone knew, had kept to himself, tended the garden and the grounds quietly and efficiently for all those years. And it made Lisa ill to realize she was in a position almost exactly like that of the loan officer who had forced her father to sell off the farm. She remembered one phrase the man had used over and over again; she had been too young to understand much else: "I'm so sorry," he kept saying. "If I could do anything I would, but you see, it's the bank. It's not me." Lisa had made those words—*the bank*—into a powerful image in her mind, a massive building that rumbled forward like a tank, crushing and capturing whatever it wanted. And for years, even after she had learned the bank wasn't a physical entity but really a group of men, she still didn't know the real truth. The real truth was that, just like Eastland Industries, the bank had been simply a group of men, a group of individuals who had perhaps wanted the same thing, or perhaps had been swayed by one persuasive man with motives and reasons known only to him. And now, with Eastland, she was going to be the one who provided Richard with the ammunition he needed to convince whomever he needed to convince that it was time to sell the Eastern Mountain Inn.

When Michael rang her bell a little before seven, she put down the wine she had been drinking and ran to the door.

The moment she saw Michael and his wonderful dark eyes, she felt better. She would tell him and he'd help her figure out a solution. "I'm so glad you're here," she said as he stepped in and took her in his arms.

He kissed her gently and smiled. "Me too. Mmm. Bordeaux?"

She smiled. "Guess again."

He kissed her more deeply then, coaxing her tongue with his, drawing her against his lean frame with a hunger she loved. She just couldn't get over how she was instantly enveloped in heat when he touched her, kissed her, held her.

"I could do that forever," he whispered.

"Me too," she murmured. "Come on in." She led him into her living room, flooded now with light from the sinking sun, and sat down on the couch.

"Tell me what happened," he said softly.

She poured some wine for him and more for herself, and took a sip before speaking. "Tell me about Eastland," she said. "I know it's a privately held corporation—I assume that means it's owned by the Hollingworths. Anyone else?"

He frowned. "What's going on?"

"Just tell me first," she said.

He leaned back and stretched an arm across the pillows of the sofa. "Well, it's owned jointly by Scribner, Candace, Rich, and the youngest brother, Scott. When Scribner's wife died seven years ago, the shares were reorganized. Now Scribner owns just twenty-five percent of the shares. And his children each own twenty-five percent, but it's not as equitable a distribution as that sounds."

"Why?"

"Well, Scribner is strictly of the old school." Michael smiled. "Those kids are terrified of him too. But it's sad, because his twenty-five percent doesn't go very far when the three kids are allied. Richard is really running the show."

"I see," she said quietly.

He reached out and touched her cheek. "Now, why don't you tell me what this is about."

She looked into his eyes. "Oh, in a minute. Tell me about Candace, Michael. Is she active in the business?"

"She goes through phases of wild activity, throwing herself into one or another of Eastland's divisions with an unbridled passion that usually lasts about a month. And then she's back to her charity activities." He took a sip of wine. "I don't want to make her sound like a dilettante though. She's a really fine person. And the only reason she doesn't fit in anywhere at Eastland is that deep down she doesn't think she's allowed to, or supposed to. Her father and his wife, Vanessa, taught Candace from the very beginning that the only proper area in which a well-bred lady could work was charity. Which can be very hard work, actually. Right now, though, she's working very, very closely with Richard and doing pretty well. I just wonder how long she'll keep at it. She seems dissatisfied with everything she does, always wanting more but never knowing where to look."

"I see," Lisa said. She wasn't thrilled with this massive understanding that was pouring forth from Michael. She hadn't asked for a treatise, after all. "Well. What about Scott?"

"Oh, Scott was wise enough to steer clear of Eastland altogether. And when I say wise, I mean in the gut way. Scott has common sense. No business acumen, unfortunately, but he's probably better off with what he's got."

"What does he do?"

"He owns a couple of pharmacies. Now, why don't

you tell me what all these questions are about?"

She sighed. If she was going to tell him, now was as good a time as any. "Oh, Michael, it's just . . . it's so awful." She looked into his eyes. "But you've got to promise me . . ." Her voice trailed off. Could she trust him? It was one thing—and a bad one—to tell her suspicions to someone else; but telling Michael was extremely serious. She had to trust him though. She felt almost sure she could. "You've got to promise me you won't breathe a word of this to anyone."

"All right," he said quietly.

She took another sip of wine and then set her glass down on the table. "I think that Eastland is planning to sell the inn."

"What?"

"I'm almost sure, Michael. It's following all the patterns I've seen before—right on track, right on schedule."

"Tell me why you think that," he said.

She gave her reasons, and tried to convey the sense of inflexibility that Richard had exhibited. "He won't accept any report other than the one he wants," she said. "It's as simple as that. He made it more than clear, Michael."

. At first he didn't say anything. She was sure he was so shocked, so disappointed, that it was difficult for him to speak.

"I'm really sorry," she said.

He shook his head. "Lisa, I don't think you have to be. I don't think you're right."

"What? Michael, I know I am. I was there. Maybe I'm not conveying it very well, but—"

94

"You're conveying it perfectly," he said. "I can just see Richard giving you all that nonsense. But you're not interpreting it correctly, Lisa. Don't look so shocked. I know Richard Hollingworth very, very well. I can imagine the time you had with him. But believe me, if what you said were true, I would know it."

"How?" she demanded.

"Candace would have told me."

"Candace?" She sighed. "Oh, that's just great. I can't believe your naiveté, Michael. Why would Candace tell you, when you've just told me she owns twenty-five percent of the shares of Eastland stock and she's intimately involved with the company right now?"

"Because she's my wi—my ex-wife," he snapped.

"Yes, your *ex*-wife."

He studied her eyes. "Ah. And you think the ex means there's no communication? No honesty? Lisa, I don't know what your divorce was like, but you can't assume everyone's is the same. Candace and I have an excellent relationship."

"So you've been telling me," she bit out. "Look. Why don't you just leave."

"What? Why?"

"I don't feel like talking to you or seeing you or looking at you, Michael. Not right now. I've just told you something I shouldn't have even told you, and now you don't even believe me."

He searched her eyes. "All right," he said quietly, standing up. "I'll talk to you . . . whenever. But let me tell you, Lisa, if you plan to go back up to the inn, I won't be there for a few days."

"Why not?"

"Well, the charity ball is in two nights, and it's silly for me to go back at this point."

"When did you decide that? I had thought—"

"Just now," he said tightly. "If that's all right with you, of course."

"It's just fine," she snapped. "That's just great."

He sighed, looking into her eyes. "All right. I'm leaving."

A few moments later, as he stepped out into the warm night air and headed up Third Avenue, he wondered whether he had been wrong about Lisa, blinded by her loveliness. She had been totally undone by the fact that he hadn't believed her. Furious, as if all that was between them depended on that, and had been destroyed. Hell, what was so incredibly important? He knew Richard. He probably hadn't liked her report; he'd been unclear, as he always was, and he felt no qualms about having her start all over again, because he never had qualms about other people's work. He wasn't being put out, so what did it matter? The main point, though, was that Lisa's theory couldn't be true, because if it were, Candace would have told him. And if Richard were working on his own, what did anyone have to worry about? The guy was much too neurotic; he had no follow-through; he never would and he never had.

A pretty, dark-haired girl smiled at Michael as he crossed Third, and he thought about Lisa's eyes. Her damn gray eyes. The question, really, was what she meant to him. He had cared for her so much up at the inn.

But down here in the city, even seeing her for a few

minutes, it all seemed different. She seemed different, annoyed or driven by something he didn't like, something he didn't understand. More like Candace, actually. And Candace, strangely enough, was being as sweet these days as she had been when he had first met her. Odd how things could switch. Had he been wrong about Lisa? He had liked her so much. . . .

CHAPTER FIVE

That night Lisa was too caught in her anger to do anything but stew and sulk. How could Michael have reacted as he had? How could he not have believed her? And worse yet, how could he have said that Candace would have told him about it if it were true? That just made the blow doubly stinging.

And, at the time, she had accepted the fact that he was staying in the city because of the charity ball. She had always felt that Michael devoted too much time to the inn anyway, delegating too little and taking too much responsibility for minor details that could easily be handled by someone else. But that didn't mean that he had to stay in the city just when she was supposed to be revising her report up at the inn!

Of course, she didn't need him that much for her coming work. But she wanted his support; she had no idea how she was going to write the kind of thing

Richard wanted. How could Michael not be there when she needed him?

And why didn't he feel he needed her? At the beginning she had worried that he was using her in some way, and was suspicious of him for that reason. Now, when to a certain extent he did need her, he was acting as if she were totally unimportant. Part of her was tempted to do exactly what Richard seemed to want: to rip the inn's future—and Michael's—to shreds. But she couldn't bear the thought. She loved the inn, and she was much too fond of Michael. Damn. What would she do?

The next morning she went into the office early. Whatever initial writing she was going to do could be done there just as easily as in her apartment, and though at other companies she had had almost total freedom, she sensed it would be good to make an appearance.

And she had been right. For when she arrived she found a note on her desk from Richard: "Come see me when you get in, please. Richard."

She locked her purse in her drawer and set off down the hall for his office, letting in a tiny ray of hope that said Richard had changed his mind. But she didn't allow too much hope to bloom. She had been around far too long to expect that sort of positive change to occur.

When she walked into Richard's office, he jumped up from behind his desk. "Lisa! Good to see you!"

"Good morning," she said a bit more temperately. "What did you want to see me about?"

"Sit down," he said, gesturing at a chair.

As she sat he leaned against the desk so he was, as

99

far as she was concerned, uncomfortably close. "I understand that Michael is here in the city and isn't going back up to the inn just yet."

"Oh?" There was no need, she figured, to tell all.

"Mmm. My sister saw him last night, and he's going to the Playtime ball on Friday night, something that's always been very big with our family. Which means that if you had any plans to reinterview Michael, they'll have to wait."

"Yes, well, I can work around that," she said quietly, her mind on Michael. So he had seen Candace last night. . . .

Richard smiled. "I'm sure you can. That's not why I called you in here. You see, the Playtime ball is something that all Eastland executives traditionally attend. And I had forgotten that you were hired after all the invitations had been sent out. So I'm extending my personal invitation to you now. I realize it's short notice—Friday is only a few days away—but it should be fun, actually."

Well! she thought. *The famous ball I've been hearing so much about.*

"It's not quite a command performance," Richard said hastily, apparently interpreting her hesitation as negative. "But I *would* like you to come, as my guest. It will be held at the Houghton-Edgeworth, and it should be quite nice. It always is."

She smiled. Whenever she had read about these charity balls in *The New York Times,* they had sounded like events out of another era, when glamor was everything and people put aside all their worries of the day for one evening. They usually took place at hotels like the Waldorf, the Helmsley Palace, even the Metropolitan Museum. And the names of those attending were always the same, always famous. And she had always wondered what it would be like to actually go to one.

"I'd like that," she said. "It sounds like fun."

"Great. Then I'll pick you up at seven."

"Oh, I hadn't realized," she began clumsily.

He smiled, not unpleasantly. "'As my guest' means as my guest, Lisa. It seems that some sort of temporary and thank God minor curse has befallen the Hollingworths. Both Candace's and my escorts have fallen mysteriously ill. That's not to say, of course, that you're a second choice. I simply didn't know you until three weeks ago. Anyway, I'll pick you up at seven," he said, standing up and walking around his desk. "Give me your address, Lisa."

Just as she was about to, the intercom buzzed, and his secretary—a new one since yesterday, said, "A Dr. Bradford is on the phone."

"Put him through," Richard demanded, and signaled for Lisa to wait. "Hi, Doctor, thanks for calling back. . . . They're in already? . . . Really? . . . Well, are they reliable?" He frowned and stroked his chin. "Okay, so what next? . . . He's good? What hospital is he affiliated with? . . . Okay." He wrote something down. "Right. Got it. Will do, and talk to you soon." He hung up, looked at what he had written, and then looked at Lisa. "All right, give me your address, Lisa."

She did, and then said, "Are you all right, Richard? I mean, is everything all right?"

"Sure, sure. Let's hope so, anyway." Fear flashed in his pale blue eyes and Lisa's heart went out to him. Clearly he was plagued by an anxiety that couldn't easily be assuaged. And at times like this she actually

liked him: he didn't seem like some heartless bureau-
crat out for the bottom line with no thought to other
people; he seemed human, and almost likeable. "So
I'll see you then. In the meantime, Lisa, you'll go
over the materials on the Priority Two list we dis-
cussed last week, right?"

"Okay, fine," she said. "See you Friday if not
before then, and I hope you feel better, Richard."

"Thanks," he said glumly. "So do I."

The work that Richard had asked Lisa to begin
took her mind off Michael to some extent. The other
divisions of Eastland Industries were, at least for the
moment, run by strangers whose faces she didn't
know. And they were all at least marginally profita-
ble for the moment, too, which meant that her job
would be a simple matter of honing and refining
rather than drastic reorganizing, or worse.

Lisa thought about Michael often, though, whenever she wasn't deeply involved in reading the files.
She remembered his wonderful smile, his promise to
show her the secret swimming hole, his deeply arousing kiss that made her want him so much. She
remembered the argument from last night, and she
wondered how she would react when she saw him
again. For no matter how strong her anger and re-
sentment were, she knew they were no match for the
passion, and the desire that was unleashed at Michael's touch. Well, she'd have a chance to find out,
she figured, on the night of the ball when he was with
Candace, and she was with Richard, of all unlikely
people.

On Friday night Lisa had very mixed feelings as
she got ready for the ball. Until now she had half

expected, in the back of her mind, that she would have spoken to Michael by this time. She had thought she'd call him, or better still, that he'd call her. But pride and anger had kept her from picking up the phone. And she could only guess that lack of interest had held him back. Either that or offense, as she *had* asked him to leave. And now she'd have to see him with his ex-wife—the woman she was sure was up to something, even if Michael didn't realize it. He was so damned unaware at times!

Despite her dread of the evening, though, Lisa managed to dress well for the occasion in a floor-length silvery beige silk gown. Her hair was swept in a graceful French knot, with dark auburn tendrils framing her face. The lavender eye shadow enhanced her gray eyes, and her makeup brought out the rose-colored tone in her pale cheeks. Maybe, she realized as she waited for Richard, she had dressed well because of her feelings.

Richard appeared at her door right on time, and he looked handsomer than she had ever seen him, in a dark tuxedo with a simple white shirt that made his tan look deeper and his pale eyes a beautiful sky blue. Why he thought he was plagued with illness was a mystery to Lisa. He looked as healthy as anyone she had ever seen. But even now, as she greeted him and he waited as she put her shawl on, she could see the tension in his face. He was obviously preoccupied.

He seemed to barely notice her surprise as she saw the limousine they were going to the hotel in. It was a stretch limo, and inside there was a full bar, a telephone, and a color TV.

"Is this yours?" Lisa asked, knowing that most stretch limos in the city were rented.

"Mmm," he answered without interest. "It's Father's really, but he's been using his Mercedes, so he's lent me this. It's rather nice, actually, because I can get a fair amount of work done on the way to and from the office."

"That's great," Lisa said. "A lot better than taking the bus, anyway."

"Is that what you do?"

"Mmm, or I walk."

"Well. We'll see what we can do about that," he said softly, laying a hand on her knee.

She knew she shouldn't have been surprised, but she was, and she must have shown it, for he said, "Oh, come on, Lisa. Don't look so shocked. Unless your knee is that much of an erogenous zone." He paused. "It is, isn't it?" he asked silkily.

She took his hand and put it back on his own knee. "If you're ever going to find out, Richard, I guarantee it will be in my own time and at my own speed."

"I wouldn't play high and mighty with me if I were you," he said quietly.

"I can do whatever I want. We're not in the office. Even if we were, I'd do what I wanted, Richard."

He leaned back and said nothing. "I'm sorry. I didn't mean that 'high and mighty' nonsense. I just . . ." His voice trailed off, and she sighed.

"Just forget it," she said disconsolately. "Let's just have a good time." Which, given the way things were going and the way she expected them to continue, didn't seem likely.

The decor of the ballroom at the hotel was lovely —all gold and white, with a high, domed ceiling, flowers everywhere, and the gentle strains of a waltz coming from an orchestra in the corner. All the guests dressed as if they had just stepped out of a fairy tale. And the food—beautifully prepared roasts and cheeses and fruits—looked delicious.

But then she saw Michael over at the other end of the room. He was dressed in a classic tux, which shocked her. She wouldn't have thought he'd ever wear such a conventional outfit. He was, as were most other people, drinking champagne out of a long-stemmed glass. And on his arm, clasping him as if she'd never let go, was a woman Lisa knew was Candace.

Lisa swallowed and stared, feeling infuriatingly as if she were thirteen and at her first eighth-grade dance. Candace was beautiful, and worse still, un-conventionally so, which somehow made her beauty that much deeper and more startling. Tall and with a mane of wavy blond hair and wide-set blue eyes, she could have been a model, but a nose with a small bump at the bridge would probably have made that unlikely. Yet, her beauty was strengthened by this irregularity, something Lisa knew by instinct must have appealed to Michael long, long ago. And there was no reason to assume it didn't still appeal to him. He seemed perfectly happy with Candace clutching him as if he were some sort of nearly detached part of her own body. He stood talking with a similarly tuxedoed man, smiling and laughing alternately with him and then with Candace. A clearly happy man. Yes, clearly happy.

"Oh, there's Candace," Richard exclaimed at the precise moment that Lisa had decided she didn't particularly feel like bumping into Candace and Michael.

But it was too late. Richard was already moving through the crowd, and it was better to follow than to hang back and have him say "Oh, Lisa must be here somewhere," or something worse.

Lisa hadn't realized how emotional she'd feel seeing Michael. She had never made love with him, yet she had so many times in her fantasies that she almost thought she really had. She had shared something with him. And now, seeing him with Candace was painful, more painful than she had thought it would be, more painful than she felt it should have been.

In his eyes as she approached, she saw surprise and then an emotion she couldn't read. In Candace's pale blue eyes, mirrors of her brother's, she saw only curiosity—a bland, mild curiosity that made her want to say to Candace, *I know Michael better than you think. I know you better than you think. And I know what you're trying to do.* It was just infuriating that Candace probably viewed her as someone who had no connection to Michael.

Lisa barely heard the introductions Richard was making. She was looking into Michael's eyes, wondering whether what she thought she saw was really there. He seemed surprised, even hurt. Confused.

"And you two know each other, of course," Richard was saying.

"Yes, yes, of course," Lisa said.

There was a short, awkward silence that seemed to go on forever.

"You ought to go say hello to Slate Carlton, Richard," Candace finally said.

Lisa could feel Michael looking at her curiously,

106

searching her eyes and face for something he needed to know.

"Oh, he can go to hell," Richard said irritably.

"Why? What happened?" Candace asked.

Lisa glanced at Michael. He clearly hadn't heard a word either Candace or Richard had said. His eyes were dark and sad.

"Well, he may be a fine securities analyst," Richard was saying, "but don't ever go to him for any other kind of advice."

"What are you talking about?"

He hesitated and glanced at Michael. "Another time, Candace."

She glared at him. "Tell me," she said forcefully. As the older sibling, she clearly exerted a good deal of influence over her brother.

"Oh, he told me about an allergist who in my opinion shouldn't have a license to practice medicine."

Candace shook her head. "The time you spend on doctors, Richard. Honestly."

"Did I force you to talk about this, Candace? You asked—twice—and I told you." He sighed and looked guiltily at Lisa. "An old and boring family squabble. Candace thinks I spend too much time worrying about my health and I think she spends too much time worrying about the business. For which she has as little acumen, most of the time, as I have answers to my medical problems."

"Oh, go to hell," Candace said, taking Michael's arm. She turned and looked into her ex-husband's eyes. "I'd rather dance than listen to any more of this nonsense," she said, and after Michael gave one last unreadable look at Lisa, the once-married couple glided onto the dance floor, leaving Lisa and Richard alone.

"Sorry," he said easily. "She can be difficult at times, especially when she's with Michael. She gets very, very skittish."

"Ah," Lisa said, distracted by the sight of Michael and Candace gracefully moving across the dance floor with the ease of two people who had been together for years.

When she turned back to Richard, he was looking at her closely, curiously.

"What's wrong?" she asked, uncomfortable under his scrutiny.

He said nothing, apparently trying to glean some sort of information from her eyes. Then he shook his head. "Nothing," he said quietly. "I was just thinking."

Lisa was curious, but not overly so, for not too much later she saw Michael and Candace leave, hand in hand, and a lump came into her throat as she realized she might have lost Michael forever.

She knew their leaving didn't mean all that much; Michael was just the type to make an appearance at a function like this and then leave on impulse, obligation or no obligation. But she didn't like any of what she had seen before the departure either. Michael and Candace had been smooth together both on and off the dance floor, meshing in a way that bespoke something Lisa didn't want to think about. Once again she was reminded of that night with Keith; it had been so unexpected, so intense. Were Michael and Candace about to share the same kind of passion?

The evening dragged on, with Lisa and Richard

alternately dancing and talking to people Lisa found were much more interesting to read about than to actually meet. Lady Sylvia Hargreaves-Hill, a woman who was mentioned nearly every other day in the society columns, joined Richard in an interminable discussion about headaches, and Princess Wilhelmina Von Reichenburger seemed interested only in talking about her children's hatred of their new boarding school.

Richard was perfectly pleasant and polite to Lisa, with no more knee-grabbing or leers. But Lisa hardly cared. She couldn't stop thinking about Michael. She had been angry at him that night, but she hadn't meant to be the catalyst that would drive him back into the arms of his ex-wife.

Just as Richard and Lisa were finally leaving, Lisa saw a beautiful blond young woman come rushing through the crowd with her gaze intent and steady on Richard. Richard seemed not to see her, and Lisa was about to tap his arm and tell him someone was obviously looking for him when the young woman, breathless, reached him. "Richard, I'm here."

He turned and looked at her as if she were dirt, which Lisa thought was horrible in itself. But since the young woman was among the prettiest of all the guests at the ball, it seemed very strange as well.

Richard turned then to Lisa and said, "Would you excuse us for a moment?" He didn't wait for a reply, but instead moved off quickly into the crowd with the young blonde. But before he was out of Lisa's earshot she heard him demand, "How did *you* get in?"

The two disappeared into the crush, and Lisa lost sight of them for the next few minutes. When Richard returned, he was pale and alone. "Let's go," he said gruffly.

He was silent nearly the whole way home, which was fine with Lisa, aside from the fact that her curiosity about the young woman and Richard's rudeness hadn't been satisfied. But she was relieved that he was angry and sullen. That meant there would probably be less of a struggle at the end of the evening.

And indeed, when the limo pulled up in front of Lisa's building and the chauffeur got out and opened the door, Richard turned to her and said he had an excruciating headache. "So I'll say good night here if you don't mind," he added.

"Well, I hope you feel better," she said with easily summoned concern now that she knew she wouldn't have to fight him off. "You should get some sleep."

"Mmm. I've been at the office by seven every morning," he said abstractedly, more to himself than to her. "Well, good night, Lisa, and thank you for coming."

"You're welcome," she said, and a moment later smiled as she said good night to her doorman. Thank God the evening had ended so easily. She could feel a headache of her own coming on from tension and too much champagne, and all she wanted to do was flop into bed and blot the image of Michael and Candace from her mind.

She let herself into her apartment, dragged herself into the bedroom, and went over to the answering machine, whose lit red light showed she had gotten at least one message. She rewound the tape to the beginning and sat to listen with a sigh of apprehension. Lately she had been so busy—first with her old job, then with the new—that she had fallen out of touch with many of her friends. Most of them understood; they had all been through similar periods themselves; but even so, she couldn't shake her feelings of guilt. And her family, whom she cared about more than anyone in the world, really couldn't understand why she didn't call or write at least once a week, a situation that only added to their suspicions of New York City as a powerful place that could turn even the sweetest person into an aggressive conniver in no time. She did have to call them; it had been weeks.

The first message, in fact, was from her mother, and the second from her brother, who was planning to come east in a few weeks. There was a third from one of her closest friends, unexpectedly in town for the week. Lisa was cheered by all three messages, but when the tape beeped and signaled there were no more to come, her heart sank. For secretly she had been hoping Michael would call.

Michael looked around the room he had spent so many years in. It was beautifully decorated—professionally, too, for Candace wouldn't have considered anything else—all in beige, with thick, plush carpeting, soft sofas with even softer cushions, a few great Impressionist paintings—many belonging to Scribner Hollingworth—which were all that Michael really missed. Everything was spotless, gleaming, as if someone had run through only moments earlier, dusting and polishing and burnishing every inlaid cherry table and rosewood cabinet and every chair in the room. Candace had added a few things, of course, since the separation. She had finally bought the

Steinway grand she had always wanted, and there was a large new collection of crystal figurines. The apartment looked more feminine, too, with large dramatic sprays of irises and tiger lilies in giant crystal vases, some sort of floral scent that was perhaps real, perhaps artificially helped. But as Michael looked around he remembered the apartment had never been all that masculine to begin with. Candace, whether consciously or unconsciously Michael didn't know, had had the decorator model the apartment after the Hollingworth's town house almost to a T. Michael had never really disliked the grand old prewar Park Avenue apartment; the furnishings were too beautiful for that. But now he realized how stifled his tastes had been during the marriage. He was a lot happier in the inn's more masculine atmosphere.

Candace came gliding into the room, and the floral scent grew deeper. So it had been perfume, and she had just put more on.

"Well," she said, smiling and sitting down on the couch. She had brushed her hair, he noticed. Or no, that wasn't it; she had let it down. "It was nice going back to Le Cirque. Like old times, really," she said softly. "How about some brandy?"

"Sounds nice."

She began to rise, but he waved her back down. "That's okay," he said. "I'll get it." He went over to the bar, still as well-stocked as ever, and poured out two generous snifters of Courvoisier. It was strange to be at the bar, familiar and wrong at the same time, as if he were dreaming something that didn't quite fit, like swimming through clouds or talking to characters out of a movie. So much time had passed, and the smallest gesture in this apartment he had lived in for years felt suddenly unreal, imprecise.

And Candace. Damn, she was beautiful, more so than when he had first met her. She was more self-assured, less edgy, less insistent.

He sat down beside her and handed her her glass, and she raised it in toast. "To Playtime," she said softly, gazing at him with pale blue eyes he remembered well, "for bringing us back together."

He drank, letting the warm sweetness pass down his throat and spread melting heat through his body, and then he put his glass down.

Candace did as he had, and stretched her arm across the back of the sofa. Then she reached up and gently tugged at his hair. "That's getting a little long, you know. You should start going back to Rex."

He smiled. "I never went to him, remember? I do just fine myself with a pair of sharp scissors and a good mirror."

She looked at him skeptically. "You can get away with it now, darling, but in a few years you'll be glad you pampered yourself—getting the right cuts and using the right shampoos." She paused, gazing into his eyes again. "Of course, it's turned out you're one of those lucky men," she murmured.

He smiled. "What lucky men?"

"Those damn lucky men who seem to get better and better looking as the years go by."

He reached for his brandy, conscious that her hand was still at his shoulder, conscious too that Candace was damned seductive and getting more so by the moment.

"Michael," she said softly.

He swallowed his brandy and turned to her,

vaguely aware that the liqueur had given a buzz to all the champagne he had drunk at the party and the wine he had drunk at dinner afterward.

"Michael, I miss you," she murmured, stopping then and closing her eyes. When she opened them, they were brimming with tears. "I really, really miss you. I hadn't planned—" She reached for her brandy and drank a long sip. "I hadn't planned to—oh, I don't know, to make some kind of declaration, as if . . ." Her voice trailed off, and he pulled her to him, letting her nestle against his shoulder as he stroked her hair.

She wanted him back. The sweetness of her perfume rose from her hair and made him feel drunk with pleasure as his hand absently ran down her back over the gentle contours of her shoulders, down the familiar spine.

And then he thought of Lisa. She had asked him to leave her apartment, hadn't called him since, had turned up tonight with Richard. He didn't need her feelings spelled out any more clearly than that.

But damn it, why? He had been certain they shared something deep, instinctively certain from the moment he had first been alone with her. It went beyond conquest too. Sure she was virtually unavailable. But hell, he knew he'd want her even more once he—

"Michael?" Candace raised her head and looked into his eyes. "I, uh, don't feel well," she said shakily. "I really—oh, God."

"It's all right," he said gently. "Where do you want to go, Candy? To the bathroom? The bedroom to lie down?"

She shook her head, her face suddenly a ghastly

114

pale mask. "The bathroom. Definitely. Ugh," she groaned as he helped her up. "I'm really sorry. I feel so silly."

"Will you stop it? Come on. This is Michael you're talking to. Just—just try to think of something nice, something calm."

A few minutes later he was helping her into bed, whispering over her moans that she'd be all right. She lay curled like a child, and he sat next to her and held a cool cloth to her forehead above her eyes, shut tight against a feeling he knew well. He had gone through more nights like this than he cared to count —mostly when he had been tense and had drunk much more than he realized, when he had been so wound up he'd forgotten to eat. And now that he thought about it, he realized Candace had barely touched her food at Le Cirque. They had talked and laughed and reminisced, but she had drunk more than he and eaten only a few bites of her fish, only a bit of her salad.

And he was sure now that her desire to get back together had been nothing more than a drunken wish, a rush of sentimentality he, too, had been caught up in. She hadn't seemed drunk, but then she rarely had, in all the time he had known her. Tomorrow she'd wake up and be embarrassed but much wiser; in the meantime, the best thing for her was sleep. And when he looked down to tell her that, he saw that she had already taken the advice. He brushed a blond lock of hair back from her cheek, whispered good night, and went back to the living room to make sure everything was okay to leave. He blew out the candles, took the glasses to the kitchen, turned out the lights, and left quietly.

115

He walked out onto Park Avenue and began heading uptown. It was a beautiful night—cool, breezy, the kind that made him like New York in small doses. But he was suddenly feeling wretched. He was crossing Seventy-ninth Street—where Lisa lived, but farther east. Damn it. Was Richard with her now? He looked at his watch—it was nearly midnight—and the thought that Lisa might be with Richard made him break out into a sweat.

He had made a mistake, a damn big mistake by walking out with Candace tonight, by leaving without talking to Lisa; but he had hated to see her with Richard, and he had hated the way she was glowing with—what was it?—maybe happiness, maybe excitement. She had looked totally pleased with all that was going on, as if she weren't the slightest bit bothered that what they had had—what he *thought* they had had—was over.

And what the hell did her connection with Richard mean in terms of the inn? He knew Richard didn't have the kind of power Lisa thought he had, but still, wasn't it an unhealthy alliance? What was she trying to do? What would she do in the future?

Before, she had seemed so distraught about what Richard had asked; tonight, she seemed like a different woman.

She had told him of her troubles with Jay, of what she saw as her fickleness, a deep character flaw. He had laughed it off, too captivated by her loveliness to pay much attention. But damn it, maybe she was right. Maybe it was time to fight for her, time to try to change her.

He turned up Eighty-third Street and walked over to Third. Martell's, a bar he had gone to often in his banking days, was still open, and he walked in almost automatically, as if it were ten years ago and just any Friday night. It was packed with men and women crowded around the bar, and the smoky humidity that came from all those bodies and drinks and cigarettes brought back a lot of memories for Michael— memories he would rather have left behind.

Damn it, tonight was one of those unfair nights when he had realized something and realized it too late. He ordered a Scotch, drank it right down, ordered another and drank it right down, and then walked to the phone booth, looked up Lisa's address, and strode out. He didn't care if it was late.

By the time he got to her building, the cool night air had made his thinking a bit clearer, as did the doorman, who was clearly disapproving of an unexpected guest for Miss Bennett at such a late hour. He rang her up and spoke so quietly, with such obvious disdain in his glances at Michael, that Michael began to wonder if he looked all right. A very dark, thick, five o'clock shadow always appeared on his face every day, and by early morning, as tonight, he more than needed a shave. Or maybe—that was probably it—he smelled drunk. Someone had spilled a martini on his tux jacket in the bar, and the smell of the gin was suddenly blasting from him as if he were a distillery working at full tilt.

"Name?" the doorman drawled.

"Uh, Michael Jamison."

The doorman turned away as if from a bad smell, and Michael smiled. "It's a Mr. Jamison," the man sniffed. There was a pause. Then: "You may go up," he said with surprise. "It's the ninth floor, apartment B."

117

"Thank you," Michael said, and walked in feeling as if he had just passed a government inspection.

He barely noticed the lobby as he walked through. It was luxurious, with oriental rugs, chandeliers, plants, and paintings everywhere. He was still wondering whether he had done the right thing in coming. It was late—after one—and how many days had it been since they had even spoken to each other alone?

The elevator man gave him the same ungracious once-over as the doorman had, and he was beginning to wonder if there weren't still something wrong when the doors opened and he was let out at the ninth floor. Too late to turn back, too late to change anything. The elevator man waited for him to ring the bell—one of two on the floor—and left only when Lisa finally opened the door.

"This is a surprise," she said carefully, looking at him with those gray eyes he loved.

Loved. *Oh, Lord,* he thought.

She was wearing a pale gray silk robe belted at the waist, and he could see the soft outlines of her body beneath every graceful curve of fabric.

"Were you asleep?" he asked. "I'm sorry, Lisa. I didn't think all of this through completely."

"Well, I was just going to bed," she said tonelessly, but she apparently expected him to stay, for she turned away, and he followed her. They walked to a sunken living room that looked remarkably like a toned-down, slightly smaller version of Candace's, with mostly beige furniture and lots of small but nice antiques—a working woman's version of luxury.

Lisa padded over to a small bar improvised on an antique walnut tea table, and poured a glass of brandy for herself. "You smell as if you've drunk all the liquor in New York," she called over her shoulder. "But you don't quite look it, so what'll you have?"

He smiled and came over to her. "Someone spilled gin all over this tux," he said.

She looked up at him with sparkling eyes. "Mmm. A likely story."

His smile faded. "Do you think I'm here because I'm drunk?" he asked quietly. He stepped forward and took her shoulders in his hands. "Is that what you think, Lisa?"

"What about Candace?" she asked, her voice nearly a whisper.

"What about her? We had dinner, I took her home, and I left." He paused. "What about Richard?"

She half smiled. "Oh, about the same. Except we had dinner at the ball." She looked into his eyes. "I should still be angry, you know. I want to still be angry."

He slowly shook his head, his beautiful dark eyes never leaving hers. "No," he said softly. "Don't be, Lisa. Don't be." He took a deep breath and tightened his grip on her shoulders. "By the time I got here I had lost half my nerve. I didn't know what had gotten into me. But the answer is right in front of me. In your eyes. And your lips," he said softly, "in a voice that's whisper-soft and tells me what's past is past."

She was silent, strangely affected by his words. For with Michael standing before her, suddenly she felt the past was past. She had been comparing him in so many ways to Keith. And why? They were two different men, with different needs and personalities, different hopes and plans, different hearts and minds. She had once loved Keith. Was there a chance she could love Michael now?

"I want you to tell me something," he said softly, his voice commanding yet gentle at the same time. "Maybe I have no right to ask, Lisa, but I'm going to anyway."

"Okay," she said quietly, beginning to dread what was coming.

"I want you to tell me if you're interested in Richard Hollingworth."

She began to smile.

"I'm serious," he said.

She hesitated. "All right, no. I don't think so. He's very good-looking, but he's a little odder than . . . I don't know. I just think he's odd."

He studied her eyes. "Lisa, I don't want the inn business to come between us," he said softly. "When I'm not with you, you're all I think of; when I'm with you I just want to take you in my arms, to make love with you."

For a moment she gazed at him, drinking in the pleasure his words had just given her, wondering if they were really true. And then she took the leap, knowing that she could try to make them true even if they weren't, that she had to trust her instincts, give some credit to the deep inner voice that said, *This man is like no other man you've ever met. You've known that since you first saw him.* And she knew all she could do was trust.

She raised her eyes to his. "I've thought about you too. A lot."

He held her face between his hands and kissed her

gently, then more deeply as they came together with an excitement neither could hold back. She had wanted him since she had first seen him, more so after she had first kissed him. She had wanted him in every way she could have him, had wanted his love and passion and affection.

In his dreams he had done all she had wanted and fantasized about in real life. He had given and taken pleasure as never before, merged in blazing unions that were explosively satisfying. In the weeks he had actually known her, there had been times he had had to drop what he was doing, so consumed had he been by her image, by the thought of her lips sinking against his, trailing down his chest, kissing his aroused form. He had been trapped by his thoughts, caught in images that refused to go away unless he gave himself some of the pleasure he wanted from her. But it was Lisa he wanted, not fantasies, not dreams. And now, could she be his?

His tongue urged her to say yes, told her deeply of the need he felt, of the rapture he could give her. She moaned as her tongue met his, wrapped her arms around his neck, and brought him close.

When he felt the softness of her body against him, desire flooded through him, and he pulled her buttocks close, holding her against him.

Lisa parted her thighs, aching for him, awash with a desire that was fierce, throbbing. She pulled away from the kiss and looked up into his beautiful dark eyes. "Come," she whispered, and she took his hand.

She led him to her bedroom and turned to face him. "I don't see any reason to play games," she murmured, her voice thick with desire. "I've never

. . . I've never felt what I feel with you, Michael, just from a kiss. And I—I want you."

"Lisa," he said hoarsely. "I want you too."

Despite her declaration, he was gentle, undressing her carefully, almost adoringly. When she lay naked before him, his eyes darkened with pleasure, and she warmed under his gaze, provocatively stretching as his eyes took in her breasts and the curve of her hips.

He was wildly aroused, and he tore off his clothes fiercely, never letting his gaze leave her naked form. And then he stood before her, magnificent and lean, handsomer and sexier than she had ever let herself imagine. His body was dark, tanned and covered with fine dark hair, and his hips were narrow, his thighs colt-lean and strong-looking. And his desire was urgent, ready.

"I've never wanted anyone in my life as much as I want you," he said hoarsely, climbing onto the bed. "Are you—are you taken care of? Prepared, I mean?"

"Yes, yes," she said, reaching for him.

She wanted to explore his whole body, to pleasure in his taut male nipples and lean hips, his buttocks and strong thighs. But she wanted him quickly, fiercely, as she had imagined so many times, and she reached for his hard strength.

"My God," he moaned, as her fingers teased. "Lisa—"

"I want you," she whispered.

"Lisa." He found her throbbing desire and possessed it with a hand, grasping her deeply, searingly.

"Take me," she whispered. "Fill me with fire. Give me all that you promised, Michael."

He held her from beneath and with a magnificent

thrust made them one, made them both cry out with rapturous pleasure. He coaxed and stroked her, whispered words of love that made her burn with pleasure, glow with fire. She moved with him, nipped at him, grasped his buttocks and made him cry out with pleasure, and somewhere, far in the back of her mind, delighted that she had been so right. Never had she felt this enflaming passion, never had she felt so close to any man; and she hardly knew Michael—not as she had known others. But he moved and urged and whispered as if they had been made for each other, and her last thought before consciousness left her was that they had been made for each other, in some deep and mystical and primitive way. And then she was lost to a burst of pleasure that blazed in him, too, and together they soared to the heights of passion, shimmering into pure pleasure, pure bliss.

Lisa wasn't even aware of how much time had passed when she finally moved again, when she raised her head and he shifted off her. They were both covered with a damp sheen, sated, exhausted.

He gathered her up in his arms and kissed the top of her head, and then he shook his head. "Amazing."

"What?"

"How right one can be. I knew about you so instinctively."

She smiled, nuzzling against his chest and snuggling so her body was perfectly molded to his. He stroked her back with his wonderful warm hands and ran his fingers through her hair.

She shifted and looked into his dark eyes, eyes that seemed to be shining with love and deep, deep affection.

"I've never felt so right about anything in my life,"

he said, smiling. "I've always trusted my instincts and I've usually been right, but with you, Lisa—" He sighed. "Hell, even my dreams didn't compare."

She laughed happily, more relaxed than she had felt in years. "I feel the same way," she said softly.

He studied her eyes. "You're going to have to change your ways now though. You know that."

She propped herself up on one elbow and ran a teasing finger down along his chest, circling each nipple and then moving on. "Oh, really? What ways are those?"

"I'm serious," he insisted. "What made you go to the ball with Richard anyway?"

She let her hand rest on the flat of his stomach. "Oh, I don't know. I've never been to anything like that and I thought it might be fun, and it really was the diplomatic thing to do. Plus," she said, gazing into his eyes, "I knew you'd be there with Candace, and I just wanted to get a look at her, to see what was going on."

He smiled. "Between the two of us?"

"Mmm-hmm."

"Well. I hereby"—he kissed her on the forehead—"give you my solemn"—on the mouth—"promise"—at the pulsepoint of her neck—"that you are the only"—at the valley between her breasts—"woman in my life." He drew his head back and gazed at her with eyes that were dark and stormy. "I mean it, Lisa. This is too good to disrupt with third or fourth parties." He smiled. "I still can't believe that the woman I dreamed of all those nights—that you're all I had dreamed and more."

"Did you really dream of me?" she asked softly.

"Did I ever. Haven't you ever looked at yourself in that dress you wore that night?"

She smiled. "Well, yes."

"From now on, you wear that sort of thing only when I say you can wear it."

"Sure. Of course," she said playfully. "Anything you say."

"I mean it, Lisa."

"Are you kidding? Come on, Michael."

He searched her eyes. "I know you, Lisa. I've seen you when you didn't even know I was looking. When you were at that party a month ago, you were still with Jay. I wouldn't want you looking at another man the way you looked at me that night."

"Are you serious?" She stared. "Michael, what's the harm in flirting? In an innocent or not-so-innocent stare?"

"I just don't see why it's necessary, that's all. Why a person would need that kind of outside stimulation if he or she were really happy in a relationship."

"I think you're being naive," she said.

"Am I?" His dark gaze captured hers, and she was suddenly self-conscious.

"Look, I don't want to fight," she said quietly. "Not now, on our first night together." But she had questions. Why was Michael such a combination of men from her past? First he had reminded her of Keith. Now he was being like Jay. Damn it, why were things getting complicated already, so quickly?

"I can think of two or three things to do that would be a lot more fun than arguing," he whispered with a smile, and he drew her into his arms, gazing into her eyes with such obvious affection that she had to put aside what he had said before. And soon he

125

was making love with her in a slightly different way —less urgently, more slowly, wonderfully sweet and deeply exciting. Already he was beginning to know her body—to know what touch could make her tremble, which kisses made her moan, and she could feel how much he loved his discoveries, how urgently he responded to her own exploration of his wants and needs. And suddenly, when his persuasive fingers had awakened her with deep hunger and she moaned against his neck, gently biting, pulling Michael close, he rolled over and masterfully made them one. Fierce warmth became urgent pleasure that burned, and with each stroke, each dizzying thrust, he brought her closer, higher, heightening her pleasure until she thought she would burst, filling her with uncontrollable passion that suddenly coursed and merged into a trembling release.

And then slowly, with sighs of pleasure, gentle murmurs, and caresses, they came back to a place that was just tender love, sated breathing, gentle holding.

Lisa felt she had never been happier, never been as contented as she was at that moment just feeling Michael in her arms—damp from lovemaking, completely relaxed, obviously satisfied.

Then she began to dimly recall the discussion they had had before making love. She had felt immediately defensive, instantly sure she was about to be called on the carpet, that her "flaw" would be the cause of long and bitter arguments. Yet now, as she basked in the afterglow of their lovemaking, her body in a state of wonderful relaxation, she couldn't even imagine why the subject would ever come up again.

She loved Michael. She didn't know whether it

was because of the magic she felt with him or whether that was only part of it; she didn't know when it had happened; but she knew, deeply and surely, that she loved this wonderful man lying at her side.

On Richard's orders Lisa had returned to the inn with Michael, and over the next few days her happiness was marred by one thing and one thing only: the revised report she was supposed to write. Richard had called her on the second day she was there and told her to conduct spot interviews with the inn's employees, for inclusion in the report. When she had begun to say that he might be surprised by what those employees had to say, he interrupted her and said, "Just get them for me, Lisa."

She had set about the task in her usual way, which was to let the employees talk about virtually any aspect of the operation they wanted, with just gentle prodding so they stuck to the subject at hand. On other jobs she had often taken pleasure in this part of the evaluation process. It was here that an unfair or irrational boss could be exposed by his employees, often when such a thing hadn't been remotely anticipated or expected by top management.

But as Lisa interviewed each employee of the inn, she heard a few phrases over and over again—that Michael was "the greatest," that the inn was "hurting" because of cutbacks, that none had ever worked for such a "wonderful boss." And she had the sickening sense that Richard had known this, and that all this, too, would damn Michael in some way.

So far Michael had insisted on maintaining his stance about Richard and his request. "He doesn't have that much power, Lisa," he had said. "*If* he's up to anything at all, which he may not be, he's just making a stab at a vague idea." And after several circular discussions and irritating arguments, Lisa and Michael had dropped the subject. But she couldn't put it out of her mind. The report was the reason she was at the inn; it was the linchpin of her job at the moment; it was something that could ultimately affect Michael's life drastically and deeply. And she resented him for what seemed to be a very limited choice on her part; she could either endure his complacent silence or listen to his infuriating words of blind faith about the matter. And she disliked both choices.

But the consolations and distractions were too strong to make Lisa dwell on her problems. Michael, more and more each day, let her into the magnificent way of life and the world he had created for himself, one that was open to guests and all those he cared for. Sometimes alone, sometimes with others, they went trout fishing at dawn, hiking at noon, walking through the moonlight at night.

Lisa was pleased to discover that the excitement that had fired her from her first kiss with Michael was still there—stronger, even, than before. And Michael seemed totally relaxed and carefree, happy she was there and obviously interested in spending as much time with her as he could.

Four days after she had arrived, though, Lisa knew it was time to go back. She had done all the additional research she could possibly justify. But what could she write? She and Michael had tacitly agreed to stop tugging the subject back and forth, but that hadn't made the report go away. She was still faced with a terrible dilemma. And damn it, she had to make Michael face it as well.

After she had packed, she found Michael at the main lodge, greeting some guests who had just arrived. When he saw her, his face lit up, and a few moments later he sat down with her in a cozy corner of the lodge.

"What's up?" he asked, a gleam in his eye. "You look like you have something up your sleeve."

"Well, I'm leaving, actually."

He paled. "Why?"

"Michael, you knew I'd be leaving any day now. I have to get back to the city." She sighed. "The only bad thing is that we really haven't talked about the report."

"We've talked about it as much as it deserves talking about, Lisa," he said, taking her hands in his.

"Are you kidding?" she asked, incredulous. "We've both been avoiding the subject for four days, Michael. We've hardly talked about it at all. And when we have, we haven't decided anything. Like what I'm going to do about it, for example."

"I'd always thought that was up to you," he said calmly.

She stared at him. "It *is* up to me," she cried. "Obviously. But that isn't the point. I need to talk to you about it. I would need to and want to even if it didn't bear on you, Michael. Don't you see that? I don't have any idea what I'm going to do and I need some support. And the fact that I might hurt you in some way by doing the wrong thing just makes it worse."

"You're not going to hurt me," he said. "Believe me."

"But I don't believe you," she argued. "Don't you see that?"

He sighed and brought each hand of hers up to his lips and gently kissed each one. "I see that you're worrying over nothing."

"Oh, Michael! Come on!" she snapped, disengaging her hands from his. "This is my job you're talking about. Not what color lipstick I'm going to wear or what I'm going to have for dinner."

"Don't worry," he said firmly, with a smile. "I know how preoccupied you've been, and I didn't see any need for us to cover the same ground over and over again without having any new information. I don't feel you should worry, but I do know how you've felt lately, so this morning I called Candace."

"You what?"

He looked very pleased with himself. "I called Candace, and she's coming up this morning to discuss the whole thing."

"Michael, what did you tell her?" she asked hopelessly. Didn't he understand anything? How could he have gone right to Candace—Richard's sister—with the story? Then Richard would know she had told Michael what was going on—behavior that was totally unjustified and totally unprofessional.

"Lisa, what's the matter with you? This is Candace we're talking about. Now, I know what you're thinking—that she's Richard's sister and I shouldn't have trusted her. But I did and I do." He sighed. "I did it only to ease your mind. I thought it would help."

"Oh, Michael," she sighed. "God, I can't believe . . ." She shook her head. "I did want your help; I wanted you to be there when I needed you, to talk things through. I didn't want you to go running to your ex-wife to try to get help for me or God knows what." She stood up. "You don't seem to have any idea of the pressure I'm under. Or if you do, you have some very warped ideas about what to do about it." When she saw the look in his eyes as she finished, she could have bitten her tongue. He looked as if she had slapped him, or worse. But she meant what she had said. She did need him; and he had done the worst thing possible.

"Lisa, I'm sorry," he said.

She glared at him. "I just hope you didn't do anything irrevocable—like something that could make me lose my job."

"Lisa, I promise you," he said, standing up and reaching for her. But she backed away. "I promise."

She searched his eyes. "We'll see, Michael. We'll see." And she stalked off, first walking and then running through the woods to her cabin. She had to get away, to get away from this man who seemed so infuriatingly short-sighted. She pulled her suitcase off the bed, slung her purse on her shoulder, grabbed some bills, left a tip on the bureau for the maid, and opened the door.

But Michael was standing there, blocking her way. His dark eyes were fired with emotion, his strong jaw tense and taut. "You're not leaving," he said quietly. "Please, Lisa, not until we talk this thing through."

"It would have been really nice if you had thought about 'talking things through' before you called Candace, Michael. That's what bothers me. Why is it that you seem to be more of a team with Candace than with me?"

"I was trying to help!" he bellowed.

"Well, you made a mistake. And your blindness—your absolute blindness is just—it—" She shook her head. "It just really surprises me, that's all. And it disappoints me."

"Don't go," he murmured, taking her in his arms. He brought her close and tried to kiss her, but she wouldn't part her lips, wouldn't respond at all, and when he saw this he drew back immediately. But he didn't let her out of his grasp.

"Let me go," she said softly. Then louder, "Michael, I mean it."

He looked shocked, hurt. "I hadn't realized," he said softly, and for a moment he seemed unable to speak. "I hadn't realized," he said again, "that you felt so strongly. I'm sorry, Lisa." And he turned and walked away, out between the pine trees without another word, without a backward glance.

She felt dizzy, unable to think, unable to accept what had just happened. She knew she had hurt him deeply, that he didn't understand why what he had done was so wrong. But he had hurt her, too, by trusting more in his ex-wife than in the two of them trying to solve a problem together.

And as she walked out to the car with her bags and threw them in the back seat, she felt shaky, as if she hadn't even begun to understand the import of what had just happened.

She saw old Murph shamble into the main lodge, and she felt a pang of emotion. She was in many ways responsible for his future. She was all alone now, alone with decisions she didn't want to make, memories she didn't want to face. And she couldn't bear it.

As she got into the car, she was so shaky that she

felt it would be unwise to drive. The steering wheel felt hard and unfamiliar, the gas pedal spongy and uncertain. She felt as if she hadn't driven for years, as if the car were some foreign machine she had come into contact with long ago.

But she had to get away. She had to leave and get things straightened out somehow. And so she turned the key, revved the motor, and spun out of the gravel lot without looking back.

Richard Hollingworth stood up from his chair. "Well, Darcy! This certainly is a pleasant surprise!"

The young woman tried to smile, but she didn't quite manage. Her full, pouting lips quivered and then parted, and her big green eyes just stared as if not really seeing. This was a far cry from the lovely young woman who had so far graced two advertisements for Thornton Sportswear for women. But then, she wouldn't have gotten the jobs without Richard's very forthcoming help, and back then she had been absolutely perfect-looking.

"Richard, I just had to talk to you," she said in a small, high voice.

"Sure, honey. I'm glad to see you." *If it weren't for this damn sinus pain,* he thought silently. He managed to drag himself out of his chair and kiss her, but damn—when was the throbbing going to end? He had kissed her and felt nothing—nothing!—because of the damn pain.

"Richie," she said softly, looking up at him with watery green eyes. No amount of pain could keep him from loving those eyes. "Richie," she said again, "I have to tell you something."

She turned away suddenly and began hastily rummaging through her purse for a cigarette, and he smiled. It was the same posture, the same movements she had made when he had first met her. She was so transparent, so naive. He had seen her before she had seen him, on Second Avenue and Fiftieth Street, rummaging for a cigarette just as she was doing now. She had looked like the classic out-of-towner, the classic girl from the Midwest, with clothes that looked as if they had never come in contact with a speck of dirt, and a face so lovely it had stopped him in his tracks. Her jeans had been too long, her blouse hopelessly out of date, and her shoes had heels that were much too high and formal for the outfit. Richard knew these things because they were a hobby of his. And he also knew the sweet hopefulness that lay just beneath the surface of this girl, the eighteen or twenty or twenty-two years of dreams she had been carrying around in her head that had finally propelled her to the city of her dreams. He had met her type in countless numbers in New York and Los Angeles, but he preferred the ones who came to New York. They were more frightened, desperate, quicker to trust. Like corn that's just been picked— sweet, tender, impossible to imitate.

Darcy had grown up quite a bit since then. He had been seeing her off and on for nearly a year now. She was older than she looked—twenty-one or—no, twenty. And she already had more money than she had dared to dream of back home in Iowa, thanks to the modeling jobs he had gotten for her. And she was still properly grateful—but a little too demanding these days as well. When he had told her at the very beginning of the relationship that there was a good chance he'd see other women, she had cried for what seemed like a month.

And now she was upset again, looking up at him with those damned green eyes and exhaling as if she had just learned to smoke.

"Why don't you tell me what's the matter?" he asked quietly, soothingly, taking her hand and leading her to the leather sofa. She usually calmed down instantly when he took on a patient, paternal tone; it was when he became angry that she fell apart completely.

She sat beside him and took what had to be a painfully long drag on her cigarette. Then, with tears welling in her eyes, she looked at him, let the smoke out, and burst into tears.

He took her cigarette, stubbed it out, and put an arm around her. "Honey, tell me what's wrong." He didn't like the way she couldn't get the words out. Usually she was too communicative; but this was worse.

"Richard," she said softly, gazing into his eyes. She swallowed, hesitated, then said again, "Richard, I—I'm pregnant."

He said nothing, looking at her with stony pale blue eyes.

"Richard?" She looked frightened. "Richard, say something."

He stood up, walked over to his desk, and took a cigarette out of the polished brass box his father had given him. He turned around only after he had lit it.

"Richard?"

"Why are you telling me?" he finally said.

"What? Richie, it's yours. Ours."

He blinked. "I don't see how that's possible."

135

"What do you mean, you don't see? What have we been doing for eleven months?"

"You told me you were on the pill."

"I was," she said. "I was. But, um, I stopped."

"You stopped?" he said savagely. "You stopped? What the hell kind of a stupid thing was that to do, Darcy?"

"I saw the news!" she cried. "Come on, Richie, you must've seen the reports too. I didn't want to be putting something in my body that was bad for me—not with my career and everything just starting to take off."

"So you decided to get pregnant instead."

"I didn't de—"

"Damn," he said softly, shaking his head. "You really are something, Darcy." She turned pale as he went on. "Do you honestly expect me to believe it's mine?"

"Richie, what are you saying?"

"And stop calling me Richie," he snapped.

"Richard, then," she said with an edge he had never heard before in her voice. "It *is* yours, Rich—Richard. It's yours," she added shrilly.

He leaned back and looked her square in the eyes. "I still don't know why you expect me to believe that," he said quietly. "I see many reasons you'd like me to, but—"

"I haven't been with anybody else since I *met* you! You *know* that! I had thought . . ." Her voice trailed off.

"You had thought what?"

She swallowed, but the tears came anyway. She spoke between sobs. "I had thought you'd marry me, Rich. That we'd get married. It wouldn't look that

136

bad. The doctor said I'm only five weeks pregnant, so—" She stopped when he shut his eyes. "Richard?"

"Just don't say that word again," he hissed, finally opening his pale blue eyes. "Now, listen to me," he said slowly, "and listen carefully, Darcy, because I'm not going to repeat myself. We are not getting married. We are never getting married, under any circumstances." He went on as her face seemed to crumble before his eyes. "I have no reason to think what you've told me is true; I would have no reason to do what you wanted even if it were true; I have never given you any reason to believe we would become engaged or married." He paused, amazed at how quickly she was falling apart before his eyes. "Now, you are going to leave this office, quietly, and I'll call you at your apartment tonight. I don't want you coming here ever again."

At his last words she seemed to freeze, and when she looked up at him, there was a dark strength in her green eyes he had never noticed before.

"I'm not leaving," she said quietly. "You can't make me."

"I can call Security. Would you like that?"

"You wouldn't," she murmured. "You wouldn't one bit. Go ahead. Call them."

He stood up. Calling Security was out of the question; news of the incident would be all over the office in five minutes, especially with that new temp sitting right outside. No, that was out of the question. "I don't have time for this sort of nonsense," he said flatly, looking down at Darcy with all the authority he could muster. "I have an appointment across town in twenty minutes. You can leave with me now, in which case I'll get you a cab, or you can leave afterward, in which case you're on your own. In either case, I'll call you later tonight, Darcy, and we can talk about this some more if you'd like. But I promise you—nothing is going to change." Without waiting for a response, he strode back to his desk, gathered up the papers he needed, snapped his attaché case shut, and buzzed his secretary on the intercom. "Have my car ready downstairs in five minutes, please," he said, and then looked over at Darcy, who was still sitting on the couch.

Her tear-stained face was immobile, like that of a crushed doll, and for a moment he wondered if it was safe to leave her in the office. But she had had tantrums before; she was harmless; and he couldn't stand to be with her for another minute. Anyway, this was no time for gentle sympathy.

And so, after one further glance Richard left the office with Darcy Bonner sitting silently on his couch and staring into space.

CHAPTER SIX

"I wish I could stay longer," Candace said, smiling at Michael. She raised her wineglass in a toast. "To another visit, I hope. When it's a little cooler." She glanced out the window behind her seat in the corner of the main lodge. It was lovely, with the lilacs still in bloom and the trees lush and full. But it was so damned hot already, and only June!

Michael smiled. "That won't be until the fall. But thanks for coming, Candy. I really couldn't get back to the city today and I wanted to talk to you in person."

"About this strange idea you have," she said, leveling her blue eyes at him.

"Mm. Although I wouldn't necessarily call it strange. Just unlikely, which is what I told Lisa."

"Lisa, yes." She sighed. "And the theory is what? That Richard wants her to make the inn look bad? Why would he want to do something like that?"

"Oh, if he wanted to sell, maybe—to convince you

and Scott and Scribner that Eastland could use its money more profitably in other ways, other areas."

She looked at him skeptically. "Oh, come on. The inn? You know how Daddy feels about this place. He hasn't sold up to now, has he?"

"Obviously not. But Richard could be up to something even you don't know about."

She took another sip of wine and hesitated before speaking again. "I really don't think so," she finally said. "I know everything Richard has his sneaky little paws in. More than I'd like to know, actually. It's amazing how he finds any time to spend on Eastland, considering the number of doctors he sees every week. I wish he'd consider substituting an analyst for at least one of those appointments. I'm sure half of his hypochondria and paranoia comes from pure and simple guilt. With all the scheming he's involved in, he has to feel guilty."

"Then he could be involved in some sort of scheme," Michael said.

She shook her head quickly. "No. Not this time. I'm sure of it. I'll talk to him if you'd like, but this Lisa—what's her name? Bennett?"

"Yes."

"This Lisa Bennett must have misinterpreted. Either that, or it's some internal matter. I can see Richard trying to make the inn look particularly bad on paper for this quarter, so that in a year, say, he can show Daddy how much everything has 'improved.' It's easy to manipulate figures with something like a hotel. But if it's anything at all, I'm sure that's the most it is. And Lisa Bennett could be—well, so eager to please that she's trying to read his mind, to second-guess him." She looked into Michael's eyes. "Do you want me to talk to Richard, darling?"

"No, no. I'd rather you didn't, as a matter of fact. There's no need for him to know any of this, and every reason to keep it just between us."

"Anything you say," she said softly. "Anything you say, darling."

Michael found the next few hours with Candace to be more trying than he would have ever imagined possible. He had work to do; he was busy; but because he had asked her to drive all the way up—and she never used the chauffeur anymore—he felt obligated to spend at least some time with her. And it wasn't so much that what she was doing and saying was annoying for any real reason. He just kept getting irritated, and he didn't even know why.

Candace just looked so damned out of place. He didn't mind her clothes. She had a right to wear whatever she felt like; but she seemed so obviously displeased by everything around her. Flowers he knew she would have bought if they had been properly arranged by Mädderlake on Madison Avenue went unnoticed; the gently warm sun, certainly no hotter than the South of France in June, was "too damned hot," and a gentle rain in the early afternoon was a "thunderstorm." Most of all, though, a tension that he couldn't identify hung in the air like a sickening miasma. He didn't think it was sexual; in fact, she seemed remote, as if she were holding back for some reason. She acted so unhappy that he wondered why she was even bothering to stay; there didn't seem to be any mood, any direction to the afternoon except unpleasant impatience.

Finally he told her he had to get back to work. He didn't want to be rude, but he had spent enough precious time with her.

As he walked Candace to her car, she took his arm. "Uh, about the other night, Michael," she said nervously. "I hope it didn't seem . . ." Her voice trailed off.

"Forget it," he said gently.

She tried to smile. "I must have been wonderfully charming with that feeble declaration followed by that marvelous torrential vomiting." She shivered. "I still wonder about that champagne. Though no one else was ill, I know." She sighed and looked up at him. "Will you really put it out of your mind?"

He smiled. "I had until you brought it up just now, Candy." He marveled at the way he could feel her totally relax. Perhaps all the tension of the day had stemmed from her worries about that night. *Women,* he thought. Impossible to understand.

But Candace wasn't thinking about the night of the ball; she was smiling at the way he had called her Candy, at the fact that he didn't seem to suspect her role in Richard's plans one bit. For a moment she had thought she was overdoing it with all that talk about Richard's scheming little paws. But Michael hadn't even blinked. Poor Michael—in his own way he was certainly an innocent. Damned savvy in business when he wanted to be, but too much of the time, in his personal life, he took people at face value, treated them as if they were as good-hearted as he was. And unfortunately for him, he was dead wrong, at least when it came to dealing with her family.

Knowing she was dangerously upset, Lisa had

142

pulled over before she had gotten on the Thruway, and stopped for coffee and an English muffin. On the whole drive back she forced herself to listen to a radio talk show about finance—safer than listening to her usual country-western music, which would be sure to put Michael right back into her thoughts.

When she got back to the city she put her car in the garage—an indispensable luxury that cost about what she had paid for an apartment when she had first come to New York. Then she showered, changed, and went straight to work. Damn Michael and his problems. She had work to take care of.

Luckily, business involving some of Eastland's other subsidiaries came up, and Lisa managed to put the inn report to the back of her mind as soon as she sat down at her desk. Luckily, too, Richard seemed very, very preoccupied with something else when he had spoken to her that morning. When he had told her about the other matter he wanted her to look into, he had seemed only half there, as if he were deeply worried about something. When she had asked about his health, he seemed uninterested, and she figured he was either worried about something else or was so upset about his health that he couldn't bear to think about it. Either way, though, he seemed to have little interest in her report at the moment, which was just fine with her. She still hadn't decided what to do.

At the end of the day, as she was trying to make her way up Third Avenue through the crowds, she wondered what Michael was doing. Was he looking up at that beautiful sky they had made love beneath? Was he sitting at the cliff's edge, waiting for the sun to set? Was he walking alone through the woods?

Was he with Candace?

This was the day, of course, that Candace was supposed to see him. The thought had popped into Lisa's mind every few minutes all day.

She had known—she had just *known*—that Candace would be trouble. For all of Michael's sophistication and intelligence, he had a few blind spots, and Lisa was certain that Candace fell into the shadows of at least one. He was so trusting, so unsuspecting. And while Candace wasn't necessarily up to any good as far as the inn was concerned, Lisa was almost certain that the woman had set her sights on Michael. And he didn't seem to have any idea that this was true.

Lisa looked around at the sea of people who were walking uptown as she was. There were the women in expensive linen suits, who had finally put comfort before fashion and donned running shoes for the long walk home, while less confident ones teetered painfully up the sidewalk on reed-thin high heels.

And then there were the men. They looked 100 percent more relaxed than the women, turning easily into corner bars and sidewalk restaurants with a casual slap on the back and a "let's have a drink," or perhaps heading home to an empty apartment that felt pleasantly quiet rather than lonely, good rather than bad. In this city where it was such a financial achievement to have an apartment of one's own, half of Lisa's girlfriends spent every night of the week wishing they had company. When they bought magazines, they read articles about men, with details of every aspect of "catching" them, holding on to them, making them happy, consoling themselves

144

when they lost them. And what did the men read? About everything, it seemed, except women.

Many of Lisa's friends had reached the point where they were fed up with men to the extent that they had honestly and sincerely abandoned the plans they had held all their lives—for traditional marriage and children. And Lisa admired their pragmatism, their willingness to abandon all they had once thought in favor of new and radical beliefs. But in the face of her friends' decisions, she had been forced to examine her own feelings, and she didn't really know what they were.

When she had first met Michael, she had been sure of her feelings. Damned sure. She knew that she wasn't cut out for long-term relationships. She knew there was no point in looking at other couples and saying "But they're doing it." She was different. Yet now she wasn't so sure.

She was furious with Michael, hurt by what he had done. But every time she looked back at the time they had spent together, at their lovemaking, at their laughter, a small inner voice asked, *What if it were always going to be like that? Don't you want that kind of life? Don't you want that kind of sharing?* And for a few minutes she'd allow herself the pleasure of fantasizing what life with Michael would be like.

And then, inevitably, the dark side of the dream would appear. Michael was so much like Keith. It was only a matter of time before the deep conflicts that were brewing would erupt. She already found fault with the way he ran his business; those feelings would have to spill over and stain their life together, just as they had with Keith. And what about faithfulness? She still couldn't trust herself to keep the fires kindled, to love Michael as she seemed to love him now. And she did love him; she knew that. She loved his voice, his laugh, his gentle touch, the sparkle in his dark eyes, the spirit that had driven him to lead exactly the kind of life he wanted to lead. When she was in his arms, she felt such overwhelming love, as if the experience were totally new, as if it would last forever.

But deep down she knew it wouldn't. In a few weeks or a few months she would find someone new, just as she always had before. With sadness she would realize the thrill of being with Michael was over; and with regret she would move on.

And what of her strengths? She had always felt that a turning point in their relationship had been her moment of fear, when she had been frightened to cross the bridge at Sam's Pass and Michael had helped her across. She was no longer embarrassed about the incident—she and Michael had come too far for that—but she did feel that he had been most comfortable then. Then and when they were making love. At these times he was wonderfully confident and tender and caring, giving completely of himself because he knew he had so much to give. But what about the situations in which he didn't feel he was in control? Wouldn't he begin resenting her just as Keith had? He had already told her she'd have to "change her ways." She had laughed the comment off with a kiss, but what would ultimately happen?

By the time she reached her neighborhood, she was too exhausted to go shopping for food. There had to be something, she figured, in the freezer or the refrigerator. She said hello to the doorman and walked into the lobby, and she was just walking past

146

a young woman who was slumped on one of the sofas when she heard her name.

She turned. The young woman was looking at her, and as Lisa looked closer, she recognized her as the girl who had approached Richard at the ball, the one he had been so rude to.

"Miss Bennett, can I—can I talk to you?"

Lisa looked at her in confusion. "Do I know you?"

"I think you do," the girl said, standing up. She was surprisingly tall—taller than Lisa had remembered. "I was at that dance, remember?"

"Ah, yes," Lisa said cautiously. "What's your name?"

"Darcy Bonner."

Lisa nodded. "I don't understand though—"

"I have to talk to you," the young woman interrupted. "About Richard."

"Hollingworth?"

"Uh-huh."

Lisa looked around the lobby, feeling oddly as if she were being watched. The whole scene was so surreal; she wasn't used to being confronted by total strangers.

"I don't care where we talk," the girl said. "We can go to a coffee shop if you want."

"Look, I'm awfully tired," Lisa began.

"Please?" The girl looked at her with deep green eyes that were near tears. "I just need your help. I just have to ask you something."

Lisa sighed. "All right," she said resignedly. "You might as well come up to my place. Once I sit down I'm not going to get up, so I don't want to go to a restaurant."

"Fine. And thank you, Miss Bennett."

A few minutes later, when Lisa was opening the door to her apartment, she could feel this young woman's presence behind her as if feeling a strong emotional energy. She had never really believed in or given much thought to the idea of auras, but this young woman seemed to be feeling some emotion so strongly that it was actually palpable. And Lisa realized she wasn't being all that wise letting a total stranger—or near-total stranger—into the apartment. But the young woman knew Richard. And there was something familiar about her as well, something Lisa couldn't quite put her finger on.

"I'm really sorry for barging in," Darcy said as she followed Lisa into the kitchen. "It's just that I thought I could trust you, maybe."

"Why is that?" Lisa asked, putting the kettle on for tea.

" 'Cause I know you're from Iowa. One town away from mine."

Lisa turned and smiled. "You're kidding! Where're you from, Darcy?"

"Crossett."

Lisa shook her head. "I can't believe it. That's just the next town. But tell me. How do you know that's where I'm from?"

"I looked through Richard's files. I know everything about you. That you went to Smith College, that you got a master's degree in business, that your last boss called you 'indispensable.' " She sat down gingerly at the table. "And don't look at me as if I'm some kind of spy, Miss Bennett. Please. I'm really here because I think we can help each other."

Lisa raised a brow. "How is that?"

148

Darcy bit her lip. "Well, um, I don't—I just have to talk to you, Miss Bennett."

"Lisa, please."

"Okay. Lisa." She sighed. "I don't know how to start except to ask you a question."

Lisa looked at her carefully. "All right. I can't guarantee that I'll answer you, but ask away."

Darcy swallowed and looked down into her lap. "I want to know if you're serious about Richard," she said quietly.

Lisa stared. "Richard? Richard Hollingworth?" She almost laughed. "Why do you—tell me what's going on. Why you want to know."

Darcy looked up at Lisa with the widest, clearest green eyes Lisa had ever seen. "Richard thinks I'm stupid," she said quietly, her voice low with anger. "He told me he'd call me tonight, but I know he won't. I know he's not going to call me ever again unless I force him to somehow. He actually tried to kick me out of his office today. He actually threatened to call Security."

This news didn't thrill Lisa. "Why was that?"

"I'm pregnant," she said softly. "I'm pregnant with the son or daughter of Richie Hollingworth. Of Richard Scribner Hollingworth, to be exact. And he never wants to see me again."

Lisa could see Darcy fighting with herself, battling the tears that were ready to spring forth at any moment. "Anyway," Darcy continued in a strangled voice, "I—he finally left me there, at his office. That's when I read your file." She gave a short, unhappy laugh. "I thought about tearing apart his office. I really did. Wouldn't that be something if he came back and found everything in ninety million shreds?

149

But then I thought, no, that's what he'd expect, and he'd just think I was a jerk, plus he'd probably have copies of everything anyway. He has lots of tapes, you know." She put her head in her hands. "I don't even care about his office, about what I—What do I care about his file cabinets and his stupid papers? I can't believe what he did to me." She looked up at Lisa and began to cry. "Do you know that he actually denies—he denies that the baby is his." She shook her head. "That bastard," she sobbed. "I haven't even looked at another man in eleven months and he knows it. He knows it!"

She began to cry so hard that she couldn't speak, and Lisa sat down next to her, unsure of what to do. She wanted to comfort Darcy, but on the other hand she didn't even know her; she still felt a bit odd that this young woman she had never even met was crying her eyes out in her apartment.

Finally Darcy looked up with mascara-smeared eyes. "All I'm asking is that you understand," she said quietly. "I'm really not trying to make trouble. But I don't think it's fair either. And I—I just wish I—oh, I don't know."

"Darcy, do you think I'm going out with Richard Hollingworth?"

The sobbing stopped. "Well, aren't you?"

"No, Darcy. Not at all. He's just my boss—as you know. And I went with him to the ball. You must have seen other Eastland people there too."

She shrugged, wiping her eyes. "Well, sure, but—I don't know, I just figured. Plus Richard said you were his date. He really tried to get rid of me fast, so then I came to the office because he wouldn't even talk to me. We had had a big fight even before he knew about—about what happened."

"Well, believe me, there is nothing going on between us." Lisa stood up and brought the tea to the table, and poured some out for each of them. "Is your family still back in Crossett?"

"Uh-huh," Darcy answered, sniffling.

"Have you told them?"

"Are you kidding? No way. I mean, I know that I have to eventually." She shivered. "I just can't believe this whole thing. I mean, I really loved Richard. I loved him a lot. And I was so dumb to think—" She shook her head. "You know, if I read about a girl like me in a magazine, like in a story or something, or an advice column, I'd think, God, that girl sounds really dumb to think that that rich guy would marry her if she got pregnant with his baby. She's not from the same class or—or anything like that. But you know what? He took me everywhere. I wasn't like one of those girls you read about, where the guy sleeps with her and doesn't want to see her. He took me to all the really nice places in town. Places I had read about." She held her fist against her lips to stop herself from crying again, and at that moment she looked closer to twelve than the twenty or so years old Lisa guessed her to be.

Darcy stared at her tea and picked it up to drink it, and then put it down. "Maybe I shouldn't have this."

"I think you're right," Lisa said. "I completely forgot."

"That's okay. I've got to start concentrating on what I eat and drink and stuff." Darcy said. "And I'm really glad you're not involved with Richard. I mean, I guess there could be others I don't know about." She shrugged. "And in a way maybe it's too bad you're not involved with him, because at least you're nice." She bit her lip and looked into Lisa's eyes. "What do you think I should do?"

Lisa sighed. "Look, Darcy, I don't think you're looking at this in quite the right way. If there are other women involved, that doesn't really affect your situation. Even if you knew who they were, you couldn't just show up at their houses and expect them to stop seeing Richard because you ask them to."

"Well, maybe I wouldn't be so nice. I was nice to you because you're from Jeffreyville. But maybe all I'd have to do would be to show up, and they'd be so upset he was seeing someone else that they'd leave him." She sighed. "I don't know though. Maybe I haven't really thought it through."

"You haven't," Lisa said gently. "The other women aren't the problem, Darcy. That's what you have to see. It's Richard who's the problem."

Darcy frowned.

"Really. I know that isn't very nice to think about, but you're going to have to face it sooner or later."

The phone rang, and Lisa rose to answer it. "I'll be right back," she said, and ran into the bedroom. "Hello?"

"Lisa, it's me. Michael." From the phone and through the window she heard the screech of a car's brakes.

"Where are you?" she asked.

"Downstairs. At the corner. I didn't feel I could come up without calling."

"You were right," she said coolly. "As a matter of fact, I have company."

Silence. Then: "I have to talk to you."

She sighed and closed her eyes. Damn it, why did his voice remind her of other times—wonderful times? "Michael, I just don't feel—"

"Are you on a date?" he interrupted.

"Why?"

"Just tell me. If you are, I'll hang up."

"Actually, Michael, I wish I were alone. I'm really tired, really fed up, and totally uninterested in talking to anyone right now. But this girl is here, and—"

"I'll be right there," he said, and hung up before she could say another word.

Lisa marched back to the kitchen, so furious that for a moment she forgot Darcy was still there. "Listen," she said, "I have some unexpected company coming over."

Darcy jumped up. "Not Richard—?"

"No, no, of course not. Relax. I just didn't want you to be surprised."

Darcy bit her lip. "Well, I guess I should be going anyway." She looked into Lisa's eyes with an expression that was both hopeful and unbearably sad. "Mission accomplished in a way, huh?" She picked up her purse. "Do you mind if I call you, maybe? I mean I still don't know what to do, and you've been so nice . . ."

"That would be fine," Lisa said. "You know how to reach me at Eastland, and—"

The doorbell rang and made Darcy jump, and Lisa again told her to relax and went to answer the door. *And relax yourself,* she said silently. *Darcy isn't the only one who's jumpy.*

153

Lisa wrenched the door open with a force that shocked her.

Michael was standing there looking very serious and very subdued. "I'm sor—"

"You have some nerve," she cut in. "I told you I was busy. What gave you the right to just hang up and come running up here?"

He shook his head. "It was a spur of the moment decision. You said you weren't on a date, that some girl was—" He stopped, and Lisa followed his gaze, turning.

There was Darcy, white as a ghost, her purse slung over her shoulder. "I have to be going," she said quietly as she pushed past Lisa and then Michael.

"Darcy, wait!"

"Forget it!" she called over her shoulder. When she saw that the elevator wasn't coming right away, she looked desperately around, found the red and white EXIT sign for the stairs, raced through the door, and began clattering down the stairs.

"Darcy!" Lisa pushed past Michael, but he grabbed her arm. "Let go of me!" she cried. "She's going to hurt herself!"

She wrenched out of his grasp and raced after Darcy, but by the time she got to the stairwell, she could hear that Darcy was already two or three flights ahead. "Darcy, wait!" she called.

"Forget it! I'll call you if I want to talk to you, Lisa. Just forget it. And don't try to find me!"

Lisa sighed and turned away. Michael was standing in the doorway, and at that moment he was the last person she wanted to see. Darcy had obviously run because of him; she probably knew Michael had once been married to Candace, and probably thought

154

Michael had some unpleasant connection with Richard. For whatever reason, though, she had run when she saw him.

"That's just great," Lisa muttered as she came back toward the apartment. "That girl is really in trouble and she'll probably never come back."

"Well, what did I do?" Michael demanded. "I'm obviously not the most welcome person on earth in your apartment," he said as he followed her in. "But I didn't come up here thinking I was dangerous."

She gave him a withering stare. "You really are something. You have no right to defend yourself as far as I'm concerned, so don't even try. Don't even bother. I don't know if I'm angrier at you for scaring Darcy off or for coming here in the first place. Damn it, Michael—" She turned from him, knowing that every moment she spent looking into those deep dark eyes was a moment in which her anger was deflected.

"Lisa, I'm sorry," he said, coming around behind her and taking her by the shoulders. "What more can I say?"

She yanked out of his grasp and stalked to the other side of the room. She whirled around. "Nothing, obviously. You've already come here and you've already scared Darcy off. There's nothing you *can* say. But that doesn't make it any better."

"Was wanting to see you that terrible?" he asked softly. His eyes were dark and soft, deep and gentle as she remembered them. Damn him and his black eyes. "Was it?" he repeated.

She said nothing, love fighting with anger.

"Lisa, I'm sorry about what happened. I'm sorry I did something you didn't like when I spoke with Candace. But I'm not sorry I came up here. Because

I know that's the only way I can talk with you. And that's all I care about." He came forward, and as he came closer she kept trying to think of all the reasons she was angry, all the reasons she had been angry at him over the past few days. But instead, unasked and unwanted, memories took over—memories of how softly and gently he held her after making love, how he had reached her so deeply, how he had radiated such happiness when he had shown her the places he loved at the inn. He had been so happy bringing her into his world.

"Lisa, I am sorry. Really. But I want to tell you one thing," he murmured as he reached her.

She looked at him questioningly, still at war with herself, at war with her feelings.

"I love you, Lisa. I know this is the worst time to tell you, and I know you're angry with me, but I can't leave—I can't walk out of here—without telling you."

"Oh, Michael," she said softly, and she began to smile. "You rat." She laughed. "*Now* how do you expect me to stay angry at you?"

He laughed, affection shining in his deep dark eyes. "Tell me you're not, then." He put his warm, strong hands at her waist and held her tight. "And darling, I want you to remember what I said. I do love you and I'll love you no matter what happens. Maybe it's too soon for you; maybe your feelings aren't as strong as mine; but I just had to let you know."

She smiled, tears brimming in her clear gray eyes. "I'm so glad. But Michael, it isn't—it isn't too soon. I love you too. I was just so angry." She gazed into his eyes. "And nothing has changed, really, except

. . ." Her voice trailed off uncertainly. Nothing *had* changed in terms of external factors. She couldn't change the fact that he had spoken to Candace. But wasn't that just the point? She couldn't change that fact; it was over and done with; and he loved her. That was so much more important than everything else—everything else in the world.

"Come," he murmured, leading her down the hall. "I want to make love with you, Lisa. We can make it all right again."

Part of her rebelled at this idea; she had always done this with Keith—making love even when they were angry, thinking it would solve everything. And it hadn't; it had only dragged out a marriage that should have ended long before. You couldn't erase what was done, and it was silly to pretend you could, and she resented the fact that Michael thought you could. But then she made a decision. She would stop picking and finding fault. She loved Michael; she wasn't going to give him up because of a minor incident.

Michael sighed as he led her down the hallway and into the bedroom. The slight resistance he could feel in Lisa made him unbearably depressed. Hell, he had just told her he loved her, something he had been wanting to do for days. And while he hadn't expected her to go wild with joy, he had hoped she would be happy. And she was still angry.

"Lisa, why don't we forget this for now," he suddenly suggested.

She whirled to face him. "What?"

He shrugged. "I can feel your anger when I take your hand. I'm not here to force you to do anything."

"I know that," she said softly. "*You're* the one

who doesn't really know that. I was angry, but that isn't important right now."

He studied her eyes. Was she telling the truth? She was so precious to him; and he knew that inevitably, he was going to make mistakes in the future. But he wanted them to be as few and far between as possible. "I love you so much," he said softly. "I wanted this to be a night of—oh, it sounds too corny."

She smiled. "Tell me."

"Well, a night we could both remember."

"Oh, Michael," she murmured. "Just love me."

And love her he did. As he took off each piece of her clothing, sliding her silk dress over her head, gently removing her bra, he kissed the skin he had exposed, running his wet lips in trails that burst into flame. She felt as if every part of her were tingling, needing him, coming alive for him. He slowly slid her panties off, and his fingers against her skin were rough and warm, tender and provocative.

"God, you are so beautiful, Lisa," he said huskily, gazing down at her with fiery eyes. "So beautiful."

She loved the way he was looking at her with such obvious pleasure, and as his warm hands reached for her, trailing hotly over her breasts, across her stomach, over the curve of her hips, she reached for him but he shook his head.

"Wait," he whispered.

His hands moved lower then, growing more urgent, more coaxing as he grasped her buttocks and moved over her thighs, teased her inner thighs with their heated message. Then his touch grew more intimate as he stroked her deeply and she was awash with pleasure, liquefying under the magic of his movements. "Michael," she whispered as he lowered his head to her stomach.

He kissed her navel, circling it and entering it with his tongue, and then he trailed his wet lips downward, making her cry out as he nipped the sensitive skin between her hipbones and soothed it with gentle kisses. Then he grasped her hips and brought his lips to her softness, and his tongue coaxed and stroked, melted and teased her, bringing her to a trembling pitch. "Oh, Michael," she moaned, clutching at him, grasping his shoulders, his hair. "Michael, I want you," she whispered.

He looked up at her, amazed that this beautiful woman he had dreamed of so often was real, that she responded to him as hungrily as she did. In moments he had torn off his clothes, and when he laid her back against the bed and lay down along the length of her, a thigh slung across her hips, he couldn't believe how smooth and warm her skin was, how soft and ready and perfect she was for him.

And then he took possession of her hips and made them one in a burst of thrilling passion, a merging of moans and graspings as he rocked her to the core. They quickened immediately, her need taking over their rhythm, and as he moved inside her, she felt as if she were made only of pleasure, a smoldering ember that was growing with every stroke, every whispered "I love you," every "Yes, Lisa, yes."

And then she was aware only of inexpressible joy, waves of bliss that overtook her, made her one with Michael as a few moments later he shivered with pleasure, shouting with passion and love.

As Lisa relaxed in his arms, very slowly coming back to a time and place that had been all but forgotten, she felt so much love for Michael that she was nearly overcome. She loved making love with him, and had known it would be wonderful. But now that she knew—really knew—that he loved her, that he was willing to say it and do all that went along with saying it, it made a difference. She had always felt loved by him. But he had taken that leap that said "I want you to know how I feel about you." And she was very, very happy.

"Oh, God," she sighed, smiling and stretching lazily. "I can't believe I almost kicked you out."

He laughed warmly. "I'd say you were pretty close."

"I was."

He shifted so he was facing her and gently stroked her cheek. "Tell me about this Darcy you were with, Lisa. What was that all about?"

"Damn," she said softly. "I totally forgot."

"What happened? Who is she?"

"Doesn't she look familiar?"

He shook his head. "No. Should she?"

"Well, she was at the ball the other night. But, oh, you had already left, hadn't you?" For a moment she plunged back into anger, remembering how smoothly he had led Candace across the dance floor, how easily he had laughed with her. But that was then; that night was over; right now, he was in her arms. And he loved her. "Uh, anyway," she continued, forcing herself back on track, "I had thought you might have seen her around. At parties in the city or whatever."

"Why? Who is she?"

Lisa sighed. "Well, actually, she's Richard's girlfriend. Or was, anyway."

160

"Richard? Hollingworth?"

"Yes." For a moment she debated whether she should tell him about Darcy's predicament or not. Darcy had, after all, run when she saw Michael. But that was because she thought Michael had a connection with Richard that he didn't in fact have. And she trusted Michael in this situation. Maybe he would even have some ideas. "Well, actually, Michael, she happens to be pregnant with Richard's baby."

"What?"

"Well, you don't have to look that shocked," she said irritably. "It does happen, you know." She wasn't sure why she was so annoyed, but his gasping surprise was very irritating to her.

"I'm not 'that surprised,' Lisa. Just surprised. Surprised that Richard would let that sort of thing happen."

She looked at him in disbelief. "That *Richard* would let it happen? Look. I'm a very firm believer in both sexes taking responsibility for things like birth control. But you make it sound as if—I don't know, as if Richard were some kind of god. Whereas he strikes me as just the sort of man who doesn't concern himself in the slightest with that sort of thing until it happens, and then he can't understand how or why it did!"

"What are you getting mad at me for? I didn't do anything."

"Well, I don't like your attitude, Michael. It just sounded as if you thought Richard were a lot better than he is. And as if Darcy didn't really enter into the equation at all." She sighed. "I don't know how or why neither of them did anything, but that sort of

161

thing does happen. And now she's in a very vulnerable, really horrible position. Richard is being a complete bastard about it."

"You mean she wants to keep the baby?"

"Yes, she wants to keep the baby," she snapped. "I don't know why that's so hard to understand."

Gently, he held his palm to her cheek and looked into her eyes with deep concern. "Darling, what's wrong?" he asked softly. "I like the fact that you're concerned about Darcy, but I don't understand why you seem to be angry at me."

She sighed. She was angry at him, and she suddenly knew why. She was frightened—frightened of the love she felt for him because she knew it couldn't last, threatened by the fact that someone like Darcy could blithely—or perhaps with a great deal of pain —decide to keep a baby fathered by a man who at this point didn't even want to know her. Lisa had been thinking a lot lately about relationships—especially about her friend, Patricia, who was having a baby literally on her own, through artificial insemination, without any knowledge of who the father even was. And Lisa realized she had a lot of conflicting feelings about her friend's pregnancy.

When she had first heard about Patricia's plan, she had applauded it on general principles. Then she had wondered if it was really fair to the child to start his or her life with an automatic hardship. But when she had looked deeper, she had found to her surprise that what was really at the bottom of all her feelings— positive and negative both—was envy and uncertainty. For as she pictured Patricia with a baby, she realized she wanted one, and that she had completely hidden this feeling from herself. She had been so certain she could never have a lasting relationship with a man, and so certain that she wanted to keep things light, that she had pretended a very deep desire simply didn't exist. And she had pretended so well that she had fooled even herself.

And now, with Darcy's predicament, her feelings were getting stirred up all over again.

"Lisa? What's the matter? I wish you would just tell me," he said gently.

"Oh, it's nothing," she said quietly, deciding she wasn't ready to talk about it. After all, if she wasn't even sure of her feelings, how could she talk to Michael about them? Aside from the fact that it was absolutely the wrong time to discuss something like this. Suddenly she felt horribly like Jay, and she knew how he had felt when he had realized how deeply he cared for her, known it was too soon to talk about, and had told her anyway, unable to stop himself. He had asked her to marry him; she had said no; and she'd never forget the look in his eyes for as long as she lived.

She had too much willpower in every area of her life to spill feelings she didn't want to reveal. But she did have a new understanding of what it was like to want something and be unable to tell anyone—and she didn't like it. She wanted more from Michael than she had thought. And she was sure she wanted more than he'd be able to give.

"Well, I know it's something," Michael said softly. "But I know you'll tell me when the time is right."

She looked away from him, and he could tell she was deeply bothered by what they had just been talking about. But why? There were so many things that could have touched her off. He wished so much that he knew what it was. "Do you know Darcy well?" he asked, making a stab in the dark.

"What? Oh, no, not at all. I met her for the first time tonight, actually."

"Really?"

"Well, it's a little odd. I came home from work, and there she was in my lobby, waiting for me."

"I don't understand."

"She knew who I was because she saw me at the ball and I guess she asked around, and then when she went to Richard's office today and had that awful experience—" She shivered, and Michael held her closer. "It's so awful to think about. I can just see his pale, beady little eyes as he said he didn't want to have anything to do with it. Ugh. He was a real prince after she told him about it. He demanded that she leave, she refused, which I can understand, and he threatened to call Security, and she dared him to go ahead. Which naturally he didn't, and he left her in the office because I guess he didn't want to spend any more time with her. She said he had a meeting, but I don't believe it. He's a very strange guy, Michael, from what I've seen. Anyway, she, uh—" Lisa suddenly stopped. She had been about to say that Darcy had gone through Richard's files, but some instinct, some inner voice, told her not to. As it stood now, she had already revealed a confidence she wasn't entirely comfortable having revealed. But mentioning the files would mean treading into a trouble area for Lisa and Michael, and Lisa decided to say nothing for the moment. "She, uh, found my address in the Rolodex," Lisa continued, "and she found me when I came home."

"But why?" Michael asked, a little impatiently, she felt.

Lisa smiled at the memory. Darcy was so naive, it was touching. "She thought I was seeing Richard and she wanted to ask me to stop."

"Good Lord," Michael said. "How old is she?"

"Hey, come on! She was upset. And you can't possibly know how you'd react in a situation like that. She was scared. Now, unfortunately, she's even more scared, because something about your being here frightened her."

"But why?"

Lisa shrugged. "I don't know. She must know you were married to Candace, or that you know Richard. I just don't know, Michael. Maybe Richard told her some weird things about you."

He frowned. "Like what?"

"I don't know, Michael. I told you."

He sighed. "I really don't understand you. I think you're involving yourself in a situation that could get very, very touchy. I understand why you'd be tempted to get involved—I think you have a natural empathy for people that goes directly against the kind of work you do. But you have to realize this is a very messy situation, right off the bat."

"Just what situation are you referring to?" she asked testily, ignoring his comment about her work but letting it annoy her nevertheless. "My talking to her, or what?"

"Well, what did you have in mind until I came in and made her run off? What do you have in mind now?"

"Helping her, obviously."

"Helping her and hurting Richard, in other words."

"Hurting Richard? Do you hear yourself? Who's pregnant, Michael? Which one of them doesn't have anyone in the world to turn to? And which one is being a total bastard, with more money than he knows what to do with?"

"Lisa, you're getting angry at me again. I'm not Richard."

"But you're siding with him!" she blazed. "So you might as well be Richard! And when I think about it, it seems to me that all you're ever doing is siding with the Hollingworths. You chose not to believe me when I told you about Richard's plans for the inn, and then you chose to go and tell Candace what I thought. I don't know what came of that, but—"

"That's because you haven't let me tell you," he cut in. "And I'll tell you: nothing came of it, because there's no plan, no plot, no conspiracy."

"Right," she said sarcastically. "Sure. Because Candace Hollingworth said so."

He looked into her eyes. "Lisa, don't. Please, don't."

"Please don't what?" she snapped.

"Please don't do this. To me. To us." He reached out and ran a finger along her cheek so smooth and soft he could hardly believe it. "I love you. I don't want you to forget that and I don't want to fight."

She looked at him unwillingly, knowing he was doing what he had done before, and not quite sure where she stood.

"You have a way of using your not inconsiderable charms, you know," she said, "at the most opportune of moments. For you, that is."

"What do you mean?"

"Well, you know what we're like when we're making love. Everything dissolves in pleasure, and whatever we've been talking about just disappears. But it doesn't disappear, Michael. It comes right back the minute our lovemaking is over." An unwelcome thought suddenly occurred to her. She had said almost the exact words to Keith years ago.

"Would you want to wait until everything was perfect?" he asked. "Until the weather was perfect and everyone in the world was happy and every single thing in your life was just right? That's not going to happen, you know."

"I know," she said quietly. His tone had been tender and concerned, and she felt that perhaps she was just being negative because he was reminding her of Keith at that moment.

And when he slid his warm hands over her buttocks and said, "I just can't help wanting you, Lisa," she wanted him too. He was already fully aroused again as she reached out and touched him.

"Oh, Lisa," he whispered. "Oh, yes."

She loved his responsiveness, the thought that she could give him pleasure in so many ways, that he was so turned on to her that he was nearly always ready at the mere thought of making love with her. He reached for her and brought his masterful hand between her thighs, melting her under his fiery fingers.

And she wanted to wait no more. She swung astride him, and he thrust into her with urgent strength that took them on a quick, deep path. He clutched at her hips and her buttocks, played with her nipples, and gazed up at her in wonder, and she thrilled to the pleasure that was burning deep inside, branding her as his forever.

"Oh, yes," he cried. "Yes, Lisa." And together their moans became cries of joy, release that brought them together in a frenzy of deep and coursing ecstasy.

She collapsed on top of him, his chest wet and hot against her own, and as he held her close, together they drifted off into half sleep, half dreamy contentment.

Michael loved the way she felt in his arms. Making love with Lisa tonight had been special for both of them, and he was sure that one reason was that he had told her he loved her, and she had told him. He smiled at the thought. She really loved him. He had fallen for her the first time he had seen her, and had dreamed about her in incredibly arousing fantasies. She had seemed too perfect in his dreams to be true, too rigid in real life to be someone he could ever love. But the dream woman had turned out to be real, and the real woman better than in his dreams. And even though he knew he had to go slowly—she seemed like such an unbeliever, such a cynic when it came to relationships—he wanted to know what was bothering her. She seemed testy, wary. And she had been so set off by that Darcy business. Why?

"Lisa?" he said softly, as she shifted and happily sighed.

"Mmm." She was half asleep.

"I want to ask you something."

"Ask away," she murmured.

"Did you want to have children when you were married?"

Her eyes flew open. "Why do you ask that?"

He shifted so he could see her face, her eyes. She was all alertness, all wariness. "What's wrong? I don't want to pry into something you don't want to talk about. I just thought . . ."

"That's okay," she said, propping herself up on an elbow. She looked down, avoiding his gaze, and he just couldn't get over how beautiful her long dark lashes were against her pale skin. But he also knew that he had touched a raw nerve, and he was sorry.

"There's really no need to apologize, Michael. It's not a difficult subject for me." She hesitated. That wasn't quite the truth. But there was no point in explaining something even she barely understood, was there? "And no, I really didn't. Strangely enough, we never even talked about it. And I mean never."

"That is strange."

"Yes, well. But why do you ask? Did you and Candace talk about it?"

"Lots. She never wanted them. Or rather she said she didn't, but she was very, very ambivalent. I think that deep down she sincerely wanted them. But the one form of rebellion against her parents that she could ever take was in not having children. You may have noticed, by the way, that there are no heirs to the Hollingworth fortune. At least not yet."

"Not including Darcy's baby," Lisa said.

"God, yes. I forgot. Well, that's to be determined way in the future, if ever," he said. "But with Candace it was a question of whether to please Daddy or not. Complicated further by the fact that she couldn't really be Daddy's little girl if she had a baby. So it was a matter of damned if she did and damned if she didn't, and in the end it never happened. But

169

I always wanted kids." He sighed. "And divorce and all, I still—well, it's silly to speculate," he said uncertainly. "But what about you? Why wasn't it an issue with you and Keith?"

"I don't know. I guess because the marriage was so impossible. I mean, we fought so much that there just wasn't any question about it. And I had always thought that one of the prerequisites of having a child was having a good marriage. I guess that's not really true anymore though," she said musingly. "Who knows though?" She shrugged. "I just feel sorry for someone like Darcy, that's all. I don't know what's going to happen to her, obviously, but if she does keep the baby, and if she stays on her own, she's going to have a hard time of it no matter what people might say."

He looked confused. "I would assume that, yes. Who says differently?"

"Oh, I have for one. I really try to support my friends who do things in a new or different way. And a lot of times, people can get misled. All their friends say, 'Oh, yes, that sounds great. We'll all help you.' But take my friend, Patricia, the one who's having a baby on her own. We all *say* we'll be there to help. But I'm not so sure we will be. Who's going to be there at three in the morning for her when the baby's sick? Or when the baby's not sick but she just needs some emotional support?"

Michael reached out and stroked her hair. "You sound as if you've been thinking of doing the same thing."

"Me? No, I couldn't do that sort of thing without thinking of it as some sort of admission of defeat, as a last resort."

He looked into her eyes. "But do you want children eventually?" he asked softly.

"Well, yes," she answered cautiously. "Eventually, yes."

He smiled. "Don't look so nervous. I was just curious, that's all."

"Thanks a lot!"

His smile broadened. "Would you rather I was asking you because I wanted to?"

She could feel the blood rush to her cheeks, could feel her heart quicken as she looked into his eyes. "I would rather we talked about something else actually," she said softly. For the discussion had brought up unwelcome feelings, old uncertainties that said Lisa would never have a successful relationship, that she wasn't cut out for anything long-lasting. And she didn't want to have any sort of face-to-face discussion about anything as serious as the future.

Michael spent the night, and he and Lisa talked and made love, whispered and laughed, and finally slept, until morning came too quickly for both of them.

When Lisa awakened she was blissfully happy seeing Michael and remembering the night they had spent together. But then she remembered Darcy, and the report Richard expected. Damn that man, who was at the root of both problems!

Michael seemed to be sleeping soundly, so she slipped out of bed carefully and managed not to awaken him. She went into the kitchen and made herself a pot of tea, and by the time Michael came stumbling in, looking endearingly sleepy and charming in the oversize terry robe she had left on the bed

171

for him, she knew what she would do about the report. And she knew, too, that she wouldn't tell Michael about it until she was ready—in a day, perhaps. Perhaps more. She didn't want to hear the discouragement she was certain he'd express; and she didn't want to get slowed down by her own nagging doubts. She would be taking a risk—a grave risk. But suddenly she felt she had no other choice.

Michael rubbed his eyes and came over and kissed her, then slid onto the chair next to hers at the butcher block table that faced the window. "Early," he mumbled, pouring out some tea for himself.

She smiled. "I thought all you outdoor types got up at the crack of dawn."

He tried to muster as much of a voice as he could through his fatigue. "Again?" he complained with a smile. "The very first day you came up to the inn you called me Mr. Universe. And it's been downhill ever since!"

"I never called you Mr. Universe," she teased. "You're such a liar. An outright liar."

"But a liar who loves you," he said, smiling. "And I'd be a liar if I told you I wasn't interested in who this robe belongs to."

She smiled. "Oh, really! Maybe I shouldn't tell you. You'll probably infer all sorts of meaning that isn't there."

"Oh, really!" he mimicked her. "Why is that?"

"Oh, instinct," she said. "It's no big deal, really. It belongs to my ex-husband. Or almost did, once. I bought it for him before we separated, and I just never gave it to him."

He nodded, silent. Finally he said, "I wish that sometime you would tell me what happened between

172

the two of you. I feel I'm fighting something without even really knowing what it is."

She shrugged. "Oh, there isn't that much to know, really. It had to do with power, I guess. I held it and he wanted it, only he kept giving it back to me."

"I don't understand. What sort of power?"

"Well, it started with money—or maybe it didn't start there, but that was the problem area that was easiest to recognize. You know that the problems you might have with someone tend to crop up in a lot of different areas." She shrugged. "Anyway, Keith was an entrepreneur, someone with a lot of ideas and very few business skills. I was put in charge of making us 'get rich.' And it didn't happen. And each time it didn't happen, he'd resent me more. Yet the very next day he'd rope me in again. And the tension just drove us apart."

Michael looked into her lovely gray eyes. "It's strange to hear about what drives two people apart. When you hear something about someone else, it's always so hard to understand. My reaction is always, 'Really? *That* drove you apart?' But I guess what you describe could be very destructive to a relationship."

"Yes, it can be," she said quietly. And silently, to herself, she said she wouldn't let that happen with her and Michael. She wasn't going to let external problems have any effect, if she could help it, on a relationship she deeply wanted to keep alive.

And so, when she said good-bye to Michael later that morning, she didn't tell him she had a plan that would blow Richard Hollingworth's treachery—at least in one area of his life—sky high.

CHAPTER SEVEN

That evening, as Lisa was hard at work on her plan, the phone rang.

"Hello?" she said, scribbling off one last thought on her legal pad.

"I just wanted to hear your voice," Michael said. "How're you doing?"

She smiled. "Great. I'm glad you called."

"I miss you already."

"I miss you too," she said, smiling.

"So come up."

She took a deep breath. "Actually," she said, "I *will* be coming up to the inn to show you what I've done. When it's finished."

"What you've done? With what?"

"With the report. You may or may not be pleased, but I'm sure you'll be surprised."

There was a silence, and she dreaded the thought of more arguments. The issue of the report had never been settled between them; and somehow, every time it came up, it dragged to the surface all sorts of other problems Lisa had never thought about. She was tired of fighting. But she refused to compromise herself in this new job. Perhaps, miracle of miracles, she'd even convince Michael that her plan was a good one.

"When can you get here?" he finally asked.

"Well, I have to stop in at the office tomorrow morning to finish up some other work, and I can probably get away tomorrow afternoon. If not, I'll call you."

"Great. Then I'll see you or hear from you in the afternoon. And Lisa—"

"Yes?"

"Don't forget how much I love you."

She smiled. "I love you too."

"And you'll stay the weekend?"

"We'll see," she hedged, instinctively cautious. For she was almost certain he wouldn't be happy with what she was doing. What she was planning could perhaps affect Candace very directly and very negatively.

At the office the next day Lisa passed Richard Hollingworth in the hall, and he seemed more abstracted than ever, hardly noticing Lisa at all. When she got back to her office, Grace handed her a memo from Richard.

TO: Lisa Bennett

FROM: Richard Hollingworth

RE: Inn Evaluation

I still have not received a draft of your revised evaluation. I told you to do it right, but I had no idea it would take as long as it has. I expect to see the draft on my desk by Monday morning at the latest. If for any reason you find this impossible, please be good enough to let me know in advance.

I'm sorry your first few weeks at Eastland haven't been as promising as I—and no doubt you—expected. I trust your work will improve in the very near future.

Lisa put down the memo and swore quietly. Now she knew she had been a fool to believe him when he had said she should take her time. She knew his type and should have spotted it earlier. He wanted all of his employees lulled into a false sense of security so that he could rip the footing out from under them any time he wanted. It gave him incalculable psychological advantages at every stage of the game. And Lisa had seen half a dozen other supervisors use the same technique.

Which just made her more determined than ever to expose Richard Hollingworth for what he was. He thought he had all the power he needed at Eastland, but clearly he didn't. For if he did have it, he wouldn't need to pull the wool over anyone else's eyes. He could just say "Let's sell the inn" and have done with it.

Of course, there was a chance that she would show him up for what he was, and that nobody would care. But there was an equally good chance that she could topple his empire if she worked carefully and calmly.

And she wanted Michael's support for what she was doing.

She worked for the rest of the day, and she also tried to reach Darcy. But Darcy wasn't listed in the phone book or with Information, and Lisa had apparently reached a quick dead-end.

Reports in hand, she left early that evening, joining the crowded Friday-night exodus from the city but not caring much. She couldn't wait to walk through the cool night air, to smell that forest-damp freshness, to hear the birds sing at dawn. And she couldn't wait to fall into Michael's arms, to forget if only for an hour or so all the problems she had to face.

Michael was at the main lodge when she arrived. He was deep in a chess game in a corner by the fire, talking softly with the old man who was his opponent.

But as Lisa began walking across the room, as if by magic he sensed she was there, and he looked up and smiled, not at all surprised he had been right.

He stood and kissed her lightly on the lips, and at the first hint of his scent, the first brushing of his rough cheek against hers, she felt a rush of pleasure.

"Just let me finish up this game, Lisa, okay?"

As she glanced at the board and saw they were probably near the end of the game, the old man looked up. "Go ahead, Jamison," he said with a smile. "I can go to sleep knowing for sure I would have beaten you."

Michael's face lit up with amusement. "What? Not a chance!"

The old man's eyes sparkled. "What's your next move?"

Michael looked imploringly at Lisa. "Do you mind?"

"Not at all. Go ahead."

He eagerly sat down, and a few moments later made a move that brought a shout from the old man. "Hah!" he cried. "Just as I thought!"

Michael jokingly swore at him, and watched in amazement as the old man deftly moved a bishop into place and very quietly said, "Checkmate."

"I don't believe it," Michael murmured.

The old man laughed. "I've never seen you play so badly, Michael. You were distracted right from the beginning. But now I see why," he said, smiling at Lisa. "Now I see why."

Michael stood and introduced Lisa to the old man. "And beautiful as she is, there's no excuse for what just happened. Rematch tomorrow night?"

"I'm ready if you're ready," the man said.

"Great."

Michael took Lisa's bags, and together they walked out into the woods and to his cabin. Lisa loved it more than any other building at the inn. It was wonderfully cozy, with a stone fireplace, a brass bed, trapper blankets everywhere, and a wonderful hickory smell.

Michael took her in his arms and kissed her, and then gazed into her eyes. "Did you notice how beautiful it was out there?"

"Yes. Warm. And a million stars."

"How about a walk?"

"Great. It's a little warm in here anyway."

They walked out through the woods, talking about the past week but scrupulously and tacitly avoiding the subject of the inn and Lisa's reports. They walked

178

far in the warm night air, through the meadows near the bridge and back into the woods. Michael took Lisa's hand as he shined a flashlight for both of them, but the light was almost unnecessary. There was a full moon above, and the forest was bathed in its clear bright glow.

Soon Lisa heard what sounded like rushing water quite close, and a few moments later they were standing at the edge of a spectacular-looking waterfall, absolutely beautiful in the nighttime light. It was a very protected spot, with great pines and spruces nearly obscuring it from view, yet, as if designed for people's pleasure, there was a deep, lovely swimming hole just past the base of the falls, as Michael had once promised.

"How beautiful," Lisa cried. "Really, that's just lovely."

He smiled. "Care for a swim?"

"Absolutely. I may not be the warmest person in the world in a few minutes, but I can't resist. I haven't swum in anything but chlorinated water in years!"

They undressed in the quiet of the forest, and Lisa, naked first, smiled and stood back as she watched Michael undress.

He must have sensed her scrutiny, for he stopped as he was about to pull off his briefs, and he turned to Lisa. He was battling his own smile as he said, "What are you smiling at? Is something wrong?"

She laughed. "Hardly. I'm just admiring you."

He smiled. "Good. I thought maybe I was wearing these backward or something."

She narrowed her eyes. "That would be pretty difficult, wouldn't it?" She had come forward, and she reached down and trailed a hand along the line of hair at the center of his stomach, then went just inside the waistband of his briefs. Seeing him like this had made her want him, and her touch grew more intimate as she let her fingers trail down.

"Lisa," he whispered.

She leaned down and took a nipple in her mouth, playing with the other between her thumb and middle finger and bringing both to hardened peaks. Then she knelt lower and kissed the warm skin of his stomach, ran her fingers along the lean path to his hips. She loved the way he was all muscle, fine hair covering warm skin she wanted to know every inch of.

And he was ready for her, wanting her as much as she wanted him.

"I've missed you so much," he murmured huskily.

"Then show me," she whispered to him.

And he tore off his briefs, guided Lisa down to the soft blanket of grass nearby, and suddenly he couldn't wait any longer, didn't want to wait.

He moved on top of her and claimed her with his lips, and he brought them together quickly, with a passion that was deep and right for both of them, undoing the time they had spent apart with velvet strokes that filled her with rapture, filled her with love that seemed endless. She bit at him, raking her hands over his damp back, clutching at his hips with urgent fingers. And then she was his, forgetting everything but the rolling bursts of fire he was filling her with, the waves of pleasure that reached deep within her and exploded in ecstasy. He followed quickly, convulsively, crying out his pleasure and love and satisfaction.

And then there was only the sound of the waterfall, thundering though neither Lisa nor Michael had been the slightest bit aware of it.

Lisa sighed and absently trailed a hand down his wet back. "God, Michael. I just can't believe how wonderful it always is with you."

He looked at her then, his eyes as bright as the moon above. And he reached out and gently brushed the sweat-dampened hair back from her face. "It's wonderful because it's the two of us, Lisa. The two of us together." He smiled. "Now, how about a swim?"

"That sounds great. I'm drenched."

The water was ice cold, and Lisa was just gingerly dipping her toes in when she felt Michael sweep her into his arms from behind, and she laughed and screamed. "Hey, wait!"

"Too late!" He plunged them both into the water, and the shock was delicious and painful at the same time, refreshing and amazingly icy.

"I don't believe how cold this water is, Michael. You rat!"

He laughed. "You said you wanted to swim. I don't want us to get eaten alive out here. For what we just had, though, I think I'd go through anything."

She smiled, and tried to remember whether she had ever felt this good with anyone else. As she swam out into the cool deep, she could remember loving making love with Keith, and certainly with Jay. But had she felt like this?

She was sure she had asked herself the same questions. Could something this wonderful last? Didn't it have to end sometime? Wouldn't her love and desire

181

for this man disappear at some point? Wouldn't his for her?

At those times she had always thought it was impossible that the love would fade, that the pleasure would ebb. But the inevitable always happened. Wasn't it inevitable that the same thing would happen with Michael?

From somewhere quite close, an owl hooted, and Lisa widened her eyes and smiled. "What a great sound," she whispered.

She followed as Michael climbed out of the water. It was too cold to stay in for any length of time. He handed her her shirt and slung his own on, and lay back down on the grass.

"I know," he said. "That's the kind of thing—hearing the birds outside my window every morning, seeing the sun rise and set every day, hearing an owl or coyote or a mourning dove—that makes all of this worthwhile." He looked into her eyes as she settled next to him. "You probably think that sounds corny, don't you?"

"Not at all. Don't forget I was a country girl originally. It's in my blood."

"But you left."

She looked down and pulled up a blade of grass, and thought of the taste of its end—sweet, tender, usually tasted on a sun-drenched day in the middle of a field, with the grass blowing in the breeze and its sweetness gently touching everything. Life, too, had been sweet back home, until they had lost everything. And then everything had changed.

"I had to make money," she said musingly. "I wanted to become invincible, to get the power my family never had. Money is a tremendous freedom—

more powerful than any other freedom on earth, I think."

"It can be," he said carefully. "But it can be a trap too. I was making a lot more money when I was in banking than I make now. But I wasn't living the kind of life I wanted to live. I just can't tell you how much it meant the first time Candace and I came up here and I realized there was a whole other world I could live in, a whole other rhythm of life I really responded to."

"But you hadn't spent all your life in cities; you had come to places like this before."

He shrugged. "I know. The time was right though. I was thirty-five, I had achieved the kind of financial success I had been aiming for, and . . . well, it had a lot to do with the kind of life Candace and I were leading—parties every night, auctions at Sotheby's and Christie's, weekends in the Hamptons and Kent that were so filled with the trappings of that class we were in that we might as well have stayed in the city."

"But you don't have any freedom," Lisa suddenly said. "Don't you feel insecure, knowing you're just an employee of Eastland? Don't you want to have your own place? That would be real freedom."

"I'd love to," he said. "But I don't have that kind of money yet. This place is worth several million dollars, as you know. Anyway, I was an employee of the bank too. There was no more security there. At least I'm happy here—doing what I want."

She sighed. He seemed so unconcerned, so relaxed. Too relaxed, she felt. "Michael," she began cautiously.

"Hmm? Look up—quickly."

She looked up at the blanket of stars above, so bright they were like thousands of little moons lighting up the sky. "It's so beautiful," she sighed.

"But you missed it. A shooting star, all the way across there," he said, pointing. "That's lucky, you know."

She smiled.

"I can tell you don't believe me. You're not superstitious?"

"Not really."

"You don't believe that something brought us together? Some kind of providence? Or do you just think it was coincidence that we met and I dreamed of you for a month, and that finally I met you?"

She smiled. "I don't know. It's an interesting thought. But listen, I do have to talk to you about something, shooting stars or no shooting stars."

He searched her eyes. "You're lucky I'm not too sensitive," he mused. "Do you know that you are one of the most practical, no-nonsense people I've ever met in my life?" His eyes sparkled. "And if I said that to anyone else, it wouldn't be a compliment."

"Thanks a lot."

"Well, admit it. Here I am trying to charm you with the moonlight and shooting stars and the most beautiful swimming hole on earth, and you want to talk to me about something that sounds suspiciously like business."

"Why do you say that?"

"The look in your eyes. Your voice."

She sighed. "Well, you're right. But I'm getting eaten alive out here anyway with these bugs."

He smiled. "Then let's go back."

She was glad she hadn't said anything about Eastland yet. It didn't seem right to discuss something as unpleasant as that under the shining beauty of the stars. Talk of lies and schemes didn't mix with the chirping of the crickets; and angry words didn't belong in the forest.

But as they got dressed and made their way back through the woods and meadows, along paths lit by the glow of the moon and the stars, Lisa thought that maybe—just maybe—Michael wouldn't object to the plan. How could he go against a plan that would help keep him in charge of the inn? It was a plan that went against all he was against, exposed the sort of corruption he despised. And it was a plan that would be implemented by the woman he said he loved.

When they got back to Michael's cabin, Lisa felt wonderfully cozy and confident of Michael's support as he bustled them both into bed with brandy.

"All right, Lisa," he said. "Let's hear it."

She smiled. He did know her rather well. "Okay, I've come up with a plan, and I didn't want to discuss it with you before because I didn't want to hear you object to it. But now I'm not so sure you will."

"Go on," he said carefully.

"All right, this is the plan. Richard wants me to show him a draft of the report I wrote—the one *he* wants. The negative one, in other words."

"The one you *think* he wants," Michael cut in.

"The one he wants," she said firmly. "I've written that report." She ignored the flash of surprise in Michael's eyes and went on. "I've also kept the original report, Michael—the honest one that he didn't like. And I intend to present both reports to all the members of the board."

"You what?" he exploded. "Lisa, that's professional suicide."

"I doubt it," she said. "I've researched the files on the inn at Eastland's offices, Michael. I've read hundreds of letters that Scribner Hollingworth wrote when he took a larger interest in the place. I know how he feels about it, and I know he'd want to know what Richard is doing. Anyone would want to know that someone's scrambling in order to pull the wool over their eyes."

Michael rubbed the bridge of his nose with his fingers and said nothing. When he finally looked up, his eyes gleamed anger. "I don't understand you, Lisa. Every time we talk about your job and what you want out of life, you impress me as very single-minded, very sure of yourself in terms of your goals. You have a job you really like, and one that apparently pays very well. And now, for a reason I can't even begin to fathom, you want to throw it away." He quickly shook his head. "I just can't understand that at all."

"For reasons you can't fathom?" she demanded. "Are you serious?"

"Yes, very."

"Try you and all the people who work here, for one. All these jobs—including yours, Michael—are on the line."

"In your opinion."

"In my informed opinion!" she blazed. "I *know* what I'm talking about, damn it."

"And I don't want you losing your job on my account," he snapped. "Not too long ago you told me about you and your ex-husband, Lisa. He'd put you in charge and then resent you, and you resented him

186

for the roles he expected you to play. Well, I don't want to play out the same scenario, Lisa. We're too damned good together to get torn up by reruns of old patterns."

"Old patterns? What are you talking about?"

"Your 'sacrifice'—and a damned big one too. Why in hell you're throwing away your job for me is just beyond me."

"All right, look. I made a mistake saying that first. You are not the main reason I'm doing this. I'm doing this, Michael, because I won't ever be able to work in that environment—not as it stands now. If Richard hired me to be a mouthpiece for him, it isn't a job I even want. And I plan to start looking for another job as soon as I get back to the city. But if Scribner Hollingworth and the other members of the family find out what Richard's been doing, they might kick him out of his position. Or at least try to make sure he's more honest with them in the future."

He stared. "You really think your sending both reports to the family will have any effect on the Hollingworths?"

"Yes, I do," she put in, but he was already talking again.

"You're nothing to them, Lisa. Nothing."

"I think you're wrong," she said, but she saw too that she wasn't going to convince him.

"You're going to lose your job," he said quietly.

"Maybe." She met his gaze. "Look, Michael, I've given this a lot of thought, hard as that is for you to believe. I've gotten to know Richard. I see how he operates in public, and I see how he operates in private, and I know I can't work that way. If he's going to expect me to doctor my reports every time he opens his mouth, forget it—it's not even a job I want."

"You sound like a college freshman, Lisa. Grow up. Jobs don't come along every day."

"Why don't *you* grow up?" she snapped. "You ran out on a life-style that admittedly may not have been very romantic, but it *was* responsible. You could have carried that responsibility to this job, but you didn't do that. Now I'm trying to help."

"And I told you I don't need or want your help. And I told you days ago that you were wrong about your theories anyway. You're going to make a fool of yourself."

"Ah. I see. We're back to the central issue, then, aren't we?"

"What? What central issue?"

"Whether you believe me or Candace. That's really what it comes down to."

"I don't see why you say that," he said flatly, turning away and pouring himself some more brandy.

At that moment she hated the sight of his back, for in his voice she had heard something she had never heard from him before—defensiveness, hostility, a coldness that was chilling. He didn't want to know what she thought, didn't even care why she thought certain things.

He turned back to her but didn't meet her gaze. "Why do you think it's a question of you or Candace?"

"It has been all along," she said quietly, as much to herself as to him. "At first you didn't think I could be right because Candace would have told you. Then you went ahead and asked her about it after I specifically asked you not to—that was very important to me, and for God knows what reason, you went to her."

"I told you. I was trying to help."

"And I told you I didn't need that kind of help, Michael. And now, now is the worst instance. I had thought you might, that you just might, support me at a really difficult time. You're right that it's risky. That's why I need you. And now you're telling me I'll just make a fool of myself and that the reason I'm wrong is that Candace told you so. That's just great, Michael. Just great."

He said nothing, looking at her with near-black eyes that gave out no clues. "Tell me something," he finally said. "Would you be taking this step if I weren't involved? If the manager of the inn were some Joe Shmo you hardly knew?"

She shrugged irritably. "I don't know. How can I answer that? I really don't know. I feel very passionate about this, and maybe it's because of you, but maybe it's just because I really despise seeing this kind of thing happen. Don't you see how it reminds me of what happened to my family? To my father? Here's this snake—this bastard, Richard Hollingworth—who's decided he wants to convince everyone to sell the inn. And he's going to do it through lying and manipulating and doing whatever he has to. And he's going to get away with it too! And if you can forget about yourself for one moment, Michael, think about the people who work for you. What about Tim? What about all these kids who have been so loyal to you all these years? Do you know what they say about you? They're crazy about you. What about old Murph? What would happen to him? He's lived at the inn for over fifty years!"

Michael was silent. Finally he said, "You can't look out for everybody, Lisa. If you do, you spread yourself too thin and you end up not being able to help anyone."

"I'm not spreading myself too thin, Michael. I'm doing one thing—taking one action—which is my only choice if I want to work at a job I can live with." She paused, searching his eyes. "I just can't believe you're not with me on this."

"And I can't believe you're proceeding so rashly."

"I've given it a lot of thought."

He reached out for her, but she turned away. "Lisa?"

She closed her eyes. "Don't," she said quietly. She didn't want him to touch her, to dissipate the mood or distract her from something that was so important. "Just promise me one thing," she finally said.

"All right."

She turned. "Don't say all right until you know what it is, Michael! You broke your promise already by telling Can—"

"Hey, how old are we here?" he demanded. "Come on, Lisa."

"You don't think that was important to me? Don't make me a promise you can't keep, Michael."

"All right. Tell me what the promise is."

"I'm going ahead with this plan, Michael. Unless something changes between now and then, I'm doing what I told you I was going to do. And I want to know I can trust you not to tell Candace."

"You can trust me."

"That didn't take very long. Why don't you try thinking about it before you answer?"

He looked at her with exasperation. "What's the point? If I decide to tell her—if there's a reason to tell her, as I thought there was before, then I will."

"No matter what you promise."

"Lisa, I—"

"No matter what you promise," she repeated.

"Yes, if I think it's the right thing to do."

"That's just great," she said, getting out of bed and facing him. "I'm really glad I came up here tonight. Really glad, Michael, because I've learned a lot."

"Lisa, please." He held out a hand.

She shook her head.

As he looked into her eyes he saw only a hint of the love he had seen only an hour before, a shadow of the wonderful feeling that had seemed to envelop them both. Why was she pushing like this? he wondered. Maybe he had said some things he didn't mean—for instance that he'd tell Candace if he felt like it. But Lisa had made him angry. Now he saw clearly, for the first time, how her marriage had gone so wrong. She was intent on helping as many people as she could when she thought a wrong could be righted; but once she set out on that course, she had to have everything her way. You had to accept her help even if you didn't want it. And he didn't want it.

"You're very stubborn, you know," he said quietly, watching as she pulled on her jeans. "You want everything your way, and it doesn't always work that way. You can't expect people to do what you want all the time. Even outside of business—with your personal life—you ask people to accept things they don't necessarily want to accept. Like the fact that you can't stay interested in any one person for any length of time. It's all the same—you want things your way in every area."

"Oh, come on," she snapped. "That's awfully easy for you to say. I don't see any big incentives to change coming my way. You say I can't stay with one person, which is pretty much true. I was the one who told you that. But what have you done? Run to your ex-wife every time you have a problem. And as far as I'm concerned, there are still sparks there. Believe me, I know all about it."

"I see," he said. "Between you and Keith, you mean."

"Yes, between me and Keith. I'm sure there are marriages where once they're over they're over for good, but there are just as many where there's still a lot of passion left over. All it takes is one kiss, one night, even one phone call."

"You seem to be very well acquainted with this post-divorce syndrome," he said acidly. "Exactly how long has it been since you've seen Keith?"

"I don't have to tell you and I don't have to argue, Michael. I don't run to him every time I have a problem."

His eyes darkened. "Candace is a member of the Eastland board, Lisa. It's perfectly natural for me to consult with her."

"Ah. I see. Okay, fine. Look. I'd really rather not stay here tonight, Michael. I'm sure you understand. I'll wake up Tim and have him find me another room." She smiled ironically. "We both know there are plenty of those available, right?"

"Lisa—"

"I'll talk to you tomorrow," she said without looking at him. She gathered up her things, and when she reached the door, she hesitated, half expecting him to say more. But he said nothing, and she quietly stepped out into the cool night air, the chirping of the crickets the only sound she was aware of.

The freshness of the woods was some comfort, enveloping her in its cool, scented breeze. But by the time she got to the main lodge, she realized she didn't want to get another room and she didn't want to be back in Michael's cabin. She wanted to be alone with her thoughts, to think about what had happened without worrying about how she would react to Michael the next day. There was no need and no reason, after all, to stay. She had come up to see Michael and show him her plans. And she had done both things.

And so, instead of waking up Tim and settling into another room, she got back into her car and drove.

The highway was cool and dark and empty, and Lisa drove quickly, only occasionally passing another car.

It was only when she let herself into her apartment back in the city, two hours later that she allowed herself to think about what Michael had said. And she wondered whether he had been right or wrong.

He had said she wanted everything her own way, that she was trying to make their relationship the same as the one she had had with Keith. She had told him so much about her lack of stability in relationships that she appeared to have finally convinced him she couldn't be counted on. He had brought up things she didn't want to think about, raised questions she didn't want to answer.

But he had ignored his own faults, his own problems. Where was he now that she needed him? And what she had said was true—he did go running to Candace every time he had a problem. Why didn't he see that it was a real slap in the face when he supported Candace over her every single time? And why couldn't he see that he was throwing away his chance to take a stand on the inn, even if that chance just meant supporting her? He was trapped in romantic notions about the goodness and honesty of Candace, the inviolateness of the inn. And this last belief was new—perhaps a reaction to her position. For she remembered that when she had first met Michael, he was suspicious of her and her motives. Now he seemed to be taking a position just to go against what she believed.

And what had he said about her and Keith? That she was trying to turn the relationship into the same one she had had with Keith, in which she took charge and then tried to hand the power back. Was that true?

She didn't think so. It wasn't her doing that Michael refused to see the truth, that Michael would lose the inn if it weren't for her intervention. Of course, maybe he still would lose the inn; there was no guarantee her plan would work. But at least she was trying.

She sighed as she got into bed and remembered the comfort of Michael's wonderful bed at the inn. She had been so happy with him. And ironically, what she had worried about most—that her interest in him would fade—hadn't happened. She was angry at him, but she still loved him, and she knew that would never change.

CHAPTER EIGHT

Michael couldn't reach Lisa all weekend. When he had first found out that she didn't have a room, he had panicked. Had something happened to her in the woods between his cabin and the main lodge? But her car was gone. And he knew she was angry.

Hell, he was angry too. He felt pushed. She constantly accused him of sitting back and taking no action. But she didn't want him to act on his own, to do anything she didn't agree with. He had taken action, anyway. He had spoken to Candace. And if the Hollingworths were going to do anything to the inn, he was prepared to fight. Calmly. There was no need for a suicide mission, which was what Lisa was on.

He had called her three times and left three messages, but she hadn't called him back. And now he was angry. She was just being childish by not calling him back. Stubborn. Because he wasn't doing everything the way she wanted. Because he didn't agree with her. Which wouldn't have bothered him all that much if the issues were minor. But Lisa probably felt that his not acting as she wanted was a major flaw. What, after all, had she said about Keith?

Damn. He didn't want to call her again. He'd just have to wait. But when would she call? It was already Sunday night.

Late Monday morning, Richard and Candace Hollingworth sat in Richard's office, each with a copy of Lisa's new report.

"What *is* the matter with you?" Candace demanded. "You're barely here, Richard. And you look dreadful."

He smiled sarcastically. "Thanks so much."

"Seriously, Richard, is anything actually wrong with you? Physically, I mean?"

"I'm just fine," he said quietly. Lord, Candace was the last person he wanted to know about Darcy. Strange how she hadn't called. No phone calls, no letters, no messages of any kind. He even missed her when he put her predicament out of his mind. Just certain things about her—her smile, her eyes, how she had seemed to really love him in bed.

He had hurt her, obviously. But he'd had to

. . .

"Yes or no?" Candace was saying.

"What?"

"Yes or no?" she demanded. "Do you or do you not agree that Lisa Bennett should be fired?"

"What? Why?"

Candace rolled her eyes. "Honestly, Richard. Haven't you heard a word I've said?"

"Obviously not. Why should Lisa Bennett be fired?"

"Fired or laid off, actually," she added. "Because she's served her purpose. You got a very damning report out of a very capable operations manager and I really don't think you want her around to let it slip that you steered her very firmly in the right direction."

He looked into his sister's eyes. "You're beginning to think like me," he said musingly. "That's a very, very good point, Candy." And for a moment he felt so good that he almost forgot his other problems.

Darcy Bonner lit a cigarette and took a long, slow drag—as long and slow as she could make it without inhaling, anyway. She had already dialed the number once and messed it up. She had to do it right this time or it would mean fate was telling her she was wrong. And she was pretty sure she was right. Not *sure* sure, but pretty sure. And the tapes had been pretty clear.

She rested her cigarette in the ashtray, and suddenly remembered that Richard had given it to her, which was a bad sign, maybe like an omen. But maybe not, she felt. She dialed the number, and she dialed it right because the next thing she heard was "HHQ Pharmacies Incorporated," and she knew that was where Scott Hollingworth worked.

"I'd like to speak to Scott, um, Hollingworth, please."

"One moment. Who's calling, please?"

"Darcy Bonner. I'm, um, a friend of his brother's."

"One moment."

Darcy took another drag, coughed, and waited.

* * *

Lisa couldn't get through to Richard all day Monday. She called once in the morning, when he was "in a meeting." And then, figuring she shouldn't call again but that maybe his frazzled-sounding temp had forgotten to give him the message, she called again in the afternoon. He was still "in a meeting."

Lisa didn't like the feeling. She had put her report in his IN box at nine that morning, and his secretary had sworn later on that she had given it to him. Lisa's first thought was that he had found something wrong with it. Or worse yet, that he had somehow seen through her plans. After all, the report she had given him today was almost too perfect, too much of what he wanted—very negative about the inn and its prospects for the future, even very negative about Michael's management style. Maybe he had figured her plan out. It was unlikely, but it was possible.

She tried to concentrate on other work as the day dragged on, but it was nearly impossible. She kept thinking about Michael, kept wondering what was keeping her from resolving things one way or the other.

But how could she? Whenever she thought of his lack of support, his clear preference for Candace when it came to sharing his problems, she felt hurt and angry all over again. And here she was, waiting on tenterhooks for word about a plan she was very unsure of, and Michael wasn't even backing her up emotionally. In a way, she felt it was perfectly fitting that she was down in the city at the Eastland offices, biting her nails and worrying, while he was probably —what? Fishing. Or leading guests on some crazy hike. It was perfectly fitting and perfectly depressing,

198

an echo of her marriage, a reminder of problems she wanted to put behind her.

At the end of the day, having accomplished just enough to justify her salary, Lisa was getting ready to leave when her intercom buzzed.

"Yes, Grace."

"An envelope just came for you, Lisa. I know you'll want to see it." Her voice was quavering.

"Okay. Come on in, Grace."

A moment later Grace, looking as if she had just aged five years, stepped in carrying a thin gray Eastland envelope. "Here it is," she said in the same frightened voice. "Richard Hollingworth's temp just brought it over."

Lisa looked at it. PERSONAL AND CONFIDENTIAL, it said, typed in red letters. And beneath that, LISA BENNETT.

Lisa took a deep breath and opened it. Good news, she knew, rarely came at 5:00 P.M. And it rarely came unexpectedly. Bad news was what—

She began reading.

TO: Lisa Bennett

FROM: Richard S. Hollingworth

SUBJECT: Your employment

It is my rather unpleasant duty, Lisa, to inform you that your services and talents are no longer required by Eastland Industries/Domestic or any other division of Eastland Industries.

You have, in the end, done a fine job after a somewhat slow start. Unfortunately for you, however, I've decided to redistribute all responsibilities and functions that had fallen under your aegis. Henceforth, certain associates and I will function as an operations team. I feel this will be a more efficient use of Eastland's already fine resources, and will allow various divisions of Eastland/Domestic to interface more effectively.

In lieu of the customary two weeks' notice, we are extending two weeks' extra pay to you. Naturally, no severance is forthcoming.

I trust you will feel free to come to me for a recommendation if one is needed in the future. Though your start here was, as I said, slow, I felt that you showed great promise at the end of your brief tenure at Eastland. The fine report you turned in this morning is just one example.

Lisa looked up from the sheet of paper. "Well, I've been fired."

"What?"

"Well, laid off, technically, but it seems pretty clear."

Grace sank into a chair. "Oh, dear. I'm so sorry, Lisa."

"Funny," Lisa mused. "I hadn't thought it would come so soon."

A few minutes later Lisa was trying to get through to Richard, again to no avail. She couldn't believe what had happened: Laid off, and no one to tell her in person? It was too late to call Personnel—they all left at five on the dot. So there was nothing left to do, really, but to leave.

Lisa thought about what she would take out of the

office. She had been there such a short time she hadn't even moved any prints or photographs in. She was babbling on about all of this to Grace, who was still in something of a daze herself, when it suddenly hit her: She had lost her job.

She had been so concerned with the details—Where was Richard? What did Personnel have to say about her position? What would she take home?—that she had utterly blocked out the horrible truth of the matter: She was out of a job.

Before she could react, she decided to leave quickly, because that was the only way. She asked Grace to pack up whatever few things were hers and send them on when she could. Then she left, more angry than anything else because now she wouldn't have the chance to go through with her plan.

All the way home she kept wondering: Had Candace had anything to do with the "layoff"? And did that mean Michael—indirectly—had been involved? Had he revealed her theories about Richard's motivations and her plan to send the reports? Was that what was at the root of Richard's actions?

She couldn't bear to think about it. She didn't want to be angry at Michael, not now. She felt vulnerable, alone, afraid, and what she wanted more than anything was to have him hold her close, just to be with him and know that *that* was what was important—more important, even, than a job. Hadn't she planned to quit anyway?

But she couldn't shake her anger.

She tried to get some perspective: the job hadn't been her dream job of all times, after all. But it had paid well, damn it.

When she got home there was a message from

Patricia, her friend who was having a baby. Her voice sounded trembly and uncertain on the tape, and though she said she hadn't called for any special reason, Lisa could read the tone: she needed company.

Though going out to dinner was the last thing Lisa wanted to do, she knew Patricia was upset, and they arranged to meet at a restaurant they both liked. When Lisa arrived and saw her friend, she was glad she had geared herself up and called Patricia back. The woman looked terrible—pale, tear-stained, rigid in her seat in the glassed-in café section of the restaurant.

Patricia tried to smile when Lisa approached, but it was clearly an effort. "Thanks for coming," she said. "You seem to be the only friend I have who isn't away on some great vacation."

"Yes. Well," Lisa said, figuring she shouldn't talk about her situation just yet. "How's it going?"

Patricia looked down at the tablecloth, obviously trying to stop herself from crying. Lisa knew the feeling well, from times she had just been managing to hold herself together, and then someone would say a kind word, and she'd collapse into helpless tears. Patricia was a beautiful woman, just slightly older than Lisa, with black hair, dark blue eyes and lovely fair skin. She was the type of woman you'd expect to see happily married. But after dozens of disappointments, too many men who wanted either too little or too much, she had decided she was going to have at least part of the family she had always wanted—and the man who fathered the baby was going to be someone she didn't even know—a forever-anonymous donor. Lisa admired Patricia enormously—at times like this, even more so. She had the courage to call a friend and say, "I need you," the courage to take a risk and see what happened.

"I know I look like a wreck," Patricia said after they had ordered their meal. "I really feel like one." She forced a smile. "The joys of the second month of pregnancy seem to have passed me by." She shrugged. "I just needed some company, actually."

"I'm glad you called," Lisa said.

"What about you? You look a little shaky yourself."

"Oh. Well." Lisa didn't know how to get out of it. "I lost my job."

Patricia stared. "You're kidding. The one you just got?"

"A 'reorganization,' they said. But everyone knows you don't get laid off in a reorganization after just a few weeks. I was fired."

"When?"

"Today."

Patricia shook her head. "Well, *we're* quite a pair. I'd say this called for champagne except that I'm not drinking these days. What happened?"

"Oh, it's too complicated to go into. And not very cheering. One nice thing, though, was that I did meet a man through the job, and that's something that's developed on its own."

"Does he know you've gotten canned?"

Lisa shook her head. "We've had a fight. It turns out he's a lot like Keith."

"Uh-oh." Patricia sighed. "There are probably worse things though. As I remember from college, you were always looking for perfection, Lisa. One false move and a guy was off your list before he knew what had hit him."

Lisa shrugged. "I never believed in settling back then. I still don't."

"I don't either," Patricia said. "But I know no one's going to come along who's perfect in every way. I know what's important to me and what isn't. And if he's great in the really important areas, what does it matter if he—I don't know—if he snores or whatever?"

"Well, I wasn't talking about that sort of thing," Lisa said. "Michael has some real problems, among them an ex-wife who seems to be in the picture more than I am."

"Do you love him?"

"Yes, yes I do. Which infuriates me because I just ... I didn't want to jump into another relationship. He's ... he's really great when he's not being a jerk."

Patricia laughed. "I'll tell you something," she said, stirring the lime in her Perrier. "I don't want to get maudlin or anything, but I just think you should know—" She hesitated. "I'm not sorry about what I've done. I believe in all that 'life is what you make it' business. But I've been looking back a lot, at relationships and mistakes I've made. And there's a lot I regret, in terms of not having tried harder, not trying to fix things that could be fixed. I'm even thinking about calling up some of those old boyfriends I threw over so blithely. And not out of desperation, Lisa. I see potential I never saw before. I think I'm—I don't know, it sounds corny, but I'm a lot more mature."

"Well. Some things you just can't change," Lisa said abstractedly. She was thinking about Michael.

Thinking about him and missing him, remembering times that had seemed so easy, laughter that had come so quickly, lovemaking that had been so blissful.

"Lisa?"

"Hmm?"

"You know what one of the biggest things in my life is right now? Trying not to feel sorry for myself. I really don't—at least most of the time. But every time I meet someone and I tell them I'm having a baby and they say 'Oh, when did you get married?' or 'Oh, you and your husband must be so happy.' I have to tell myself over and over again that this was my decision." She sighed. "I don't know how serious it is between you and this guy. And I don't believe that it's necessarily better to be with someone so-so than no one at all. But you say you love him. Don't mess it up."

Lisa slowly twirled her wineglass around. "A lot of it is up to him, Patricia. We'll just have to see."

By the time the food came they were onto happier topics, and at the end of the evening both felt more relaxed. Lisa had to promise Patricia half a dozen times that she didn't think Patricia was maudlin or self-pitying, and Patricia urged Lisa to call Michael.

When Lisa got home there was a message from him on her answering machine: "Lisa, I'm up at the inn. Please call me no matter how late you get in. Even if you don't want to talk, please—just call."

She sat down and dialed the number of his cabin, and he answered on the first ring. His voice was soft but urgent and anxious.

"Michael, hi."

"Lisa. I'm so sorry."

"I'm just so angry," she said. "Do you know *how* Richard did it? Through a memo. A memo! Granted I wasn't exactly a fifty-year employee, but still. And there's nothing I can do either. You can't fight decisions like that and it would just look worse if I did."

He sighed. "Look. Maybe this isn't the time to say this, but you did say you weren't happy with the way things were going."

"It isn't a good time to say that, Michael. I've lost a job. Now, I don't know how much money you have. You obviously have enough to afford to keep an apartment in New York, where you don't even live anymore. I don't have that kind of money. And for me, every job represents everything I've ever fought for, everything I've ever worked for . . ." She took a deep breath. "And who knows why I was even fired, Michael? I just wonder—" She hesitated.

"Wonder what?"

"I just wonder if Candace had something to do with it, that's all."

"I know she didn't."

"How do you know?"

"I just talked to her."

Lisa closed her eyes. He had just talked to her, and for some reason he believed everything the woman said.

"Michael, I'm really tired, and I—I just don't want to talk anymore, all right?"

"I'm coming down tomorrow."

"Why?"

"To see you."

She sighed. "Look, don't, okay? I don't think you have any idea of how upset I am."

"Why do you think I want to come down?"

"I don't need someone feeling sorry for me, Michael, and I don't need to hear your theories about how innocent Candace is in all this."

There was a silence. Then: "All right. I wanted to help. I'm sorry I can't." And he hung up.

Lisa listened to the dial tone for a moment, and then hung up. And then the tears began. Why had she said all that about Candace? She didn't know for a fact that Candace was involved. And even if she did know, was Candace Michael's responsibility? He didn't have to answer for all of his ex-wife's actions. No, he had to answer for his own. And suddenly an image of walking through the woods with him in the moonlight and under the glow of the stars came to her, and she wanted to be with him, wanted him just to hold her close, to shut out the rest of the world for just one night, one precious night.

And she remembered Patricia's words, too, about not messing things up. Had she done that already? Was she driving him away?

She wiped away her tears, picked up the phone, and dialed the number of Michael's cabin.

"Yes?" His voice was curt.

"Hi. It's me. Listen. I'm sorry. I know you're not responsible for Candace." He didn't say anything. "Maybe—I don't know. Maybe I've been too critical." Her throat began to close over her voice as she remembered the fight they had had the other day. She had been screaming at him, telling him he was irresponsible, haranguing him, telling him he was still involved with Candace when she didn't even know that was true. "I just . . . maybe we can start over or put some things behind us, now that I'm not involved with Eastland anymore."

207

"I think that sounds wonderful," he said. "Really, Lisa, I think the Eastland business . . . well, let's hope some good can come out of what's happened to you. And listen—I'm going to wrap some things up up here, and then I'm coming down, all right?"

She smiled. "That sounds nice."

And after talking for a few more minutes, they hung up.

Lisa was just getting into bed when the phone rang. She looked at her watch. It was already past midnight.

"Hello?" she answered warily.

"Lisa."

She closed her eyes. It was Jay. "Jay, hi."

"Sorry it's so late. Were you asleep?"

"No, no. Just getting into bed." It was difficult listening to him. He was so kind, and he'd been a good friend. Had she done the right thing by breaking the relationship off so abruptly, so completely?

"Do you know what's coming on TV at twelve thirty?" he asked.

"No, what?"

"*The Thin Man.*"

She smiled. One of the first things they had discovered about each other was that they were both crazy about old movies, *The Thin Man* and old romantic comedies in particular. "What channel?" she asked, sitting down on the bed.

"Uh, nine, I think. Nine or eleven." He paused. "How is everything, Lisa?"

"Oh, so-so."

"I miss you."

She swallowed. "I miss you too." But she winced at her words. Had that been the right thing to say?

208

She did miss him, but that didn't mean she wanted to see him again. Especially for him, it would be like slicing open a healing wound, breaking apart something that had just begun to grow together.

"Are you seeing anyone?" he asked quietly.

"Yes, yes I am."

Silence. Finally: "I'll talk to you some other time, all right? I shouldn't have called." And he hung up before she could say another word.

He had sounded so sad, so torn up. She was sad too, and guilty, which was why she was always afraid of hurting someone at the end of a relationship.

But there was something different with Michael. She couldn't imagine his calling as Jay just had. Michael seemed concerned that she not see other people, possessive in a kind of old-fashioned way. But he wasn't insecure. No, she had more cause to worry than he; he was still seeing his ex-wife in one way or another. She, on the other hand, hadn't even thought about another man since she had first met Michael.

Over the next week, though, Michael made Lisa forget all her worries about the relationship. Though she was out of work and bothered deeply by her situation, the week was one of the happiest she had ever spent, because she felt Michael's love and support so clearly she felt as if she could do anything. Every morning he made her breakfast, went over interview strategies, took her mind off her problems with jokes and some of the silliest stories she had ever heard. He was lover, manager and friend, adviser, confidant and coach, and she saw sides of him she had never even glimpsed before.

On the first day he was there, he made her call

209

anyone and everyone she could, telling her what she had already told to countless friends but had never done herself: that anyone, even the corner grocer, might know of a job, and that her odds were much better the more people she told. It was an unpleasant task, but she knew it made sense, and with Michael's encouragement, it wasn't all that awful. And happily, some good came out of it: an old friend from the company she had worked for before Eastland knew of a job with a construction company in the area. Lisa called and they couldn't see her until the end of the week, but it was certainly a lead, and the job sounded interesting.

Lisa contacted Ellis-McGee, the main agency that specialized in real estate management positions, and before her interview there, Michael coached her until she was ready to scream.

"Michael, *I'm* the one who knows real estate!" she had cried when he had objected to an answer to one of his questions.

"But I'm the interviewer, Lisa. And there was nothing wrong with what you said; it sounded great to me. It was the way you said it that was wrong."

"Why was it wrong? I know what I'm talking about and I think I showed that."

He smiled. "But do you have to look so sexy when you're making your point?"

She looked at him incredulously. "What?"

"I mean it."

She smiled. "Should I show up in a sack? Or not smile?"

He looked at her assessingly, battling an affectionate smile. "Well, both of those would probably help. Maybe I should come along too."

She laughed. "Right. That would be just great. 'Here's Michael Jamison, by the way. He goes wherever I go.'"

His eyes sparkled. "I'd like to, you know."

Smiling, they looked into each other's eyes, and the moment was charged with emotion. For Lisa wished he had said "forever," that at some point they would begin talking about what they meant to each other. She knew she had steered him away from this sort of discussion before, that she had even hinted that she'd never be interested in a serious relationship. But all that had changed. And she was nervous about bringing the subject up herself.

During the week Michael called his own contacts, too, about Lisa, and Lisa did have one interview with a friend of Michael's, a man who didn't have any openings at his company but who conceivably might in the future.

Once again Michael was a relentless coach, quizzing Lisa on every question his friend could possibly ever ask. With someone else Lisa might have been annoyed by this almost Svengali-like approach to her job-hunting efforts, but she looked at it with good humor instead, for Michael was clearly doing what he was doing out of love.

And the week, one that should have been one of the worst of Lisa's life, flew by. One day when she came home her apartment was filled with flowers, each bouquet with a note. One, tucked into a bunch of daffodils, said, "I love you too much to see you frown. Smile!" And when she had turned around she couldn't help smiling, for Michael had sneaked up behind her and dared her not to, just by the sparks in his beautiful dark eyes.

Another said, "This note entitles bearer (you) to one steak dinner at Gleason's. (I just burned ours—sorry.)" And she had laughed again.

On another day, she had come home to a drawn bubble bath with Michael in it, ready and waiting to make her forget the rotten afternoon she had had.

Each time she came home something else made her happy, and her troubles faded—temporarily, at least—to the back of her mind.

Lisa was pleased by Michael's desire to be with her during this difficult time, but she couldn't help worrying about the inn. Michael had promised he had left the inn in Tim's very capable hands, and that he had tied up the loose ends. And he spoke with Tim over the phone every day anyway, so there was nothing to worry about.

"But what about my report?" Lisa had said. "Don't you see that that's the very good reason Richard laid me off? He had what he wanted from me; he didn't want me around anymore. Which seems to be a pattern of his."

"What do you mean?"

"Well, with Darcy for example. I still worry about her, you know. There doesn't seem to be any way of finding her."

Michael looked up at her. "I think she'd be findable if she wanted to be found, Lisa. Maybe she just doesn't want to be. By you, at least, since she obviously doesn't trust you anymore."

"But that's what's too bad. She was so wrong."

"I think you have other things to worry about," he said gently. "Like finding a job. And don't spend your time worrying about that report. I promise I can take care of myself."

"You keep saying that!" she said in exasperation.

"You just concentrate on getting yourself a job," he said, holding her face in his warm hands.

All she could do was look into his eyes and hope his confidence was justified.

On Friday Lisa went for her interview at Castelli-Marconi Construction, and met with Pete Castelli, his chief administrator, and the director of personnel. She was honest about losing the job at Eastland; the information had just slipped out and then she had to explain herself, but Pete Castelli apparently liked her honesty. Something similar had happened to his grandniece, and he understood that things like that happened all the time. What was important was whether she could deal with the men in his yards and the architects equally well, whether she was experienced at cost projections and smoothing complicated disputes and soothing frayed tempers.

And she must have impressed him, for by the end of the morning she had a job, as field liaison for Castelli-Marconi—not her dream job, but one that paid well and one she could learn from.

On the way home Lisa stopped at a gourmet deli. Tonight she and Michael could feast together in bed and celebrate.

She opened the door to her apartment and happily called out "Michael," but didn't hear any answer. She put the bag of groceries down on the counter in the kitchen and walked to the living room, but when she came to the doorway of the room, she stopped in her tracks.

Michael was sitting at her desk by the window, with his back to her, his head in his hands.

"Michael?"

He turned around very slowly. "I just spoke with Tim up at the inn," he said quietly. "Half my staff has been fired."

CHAPTER NINE

Richard Hollingworth's purge had been sudden but thorough. Tim had received one week's notice, with two weeks of compensation pay. His friends had been given the same notice as Lisa had: They were to leave the premises immediately and would get two weeks' extra pay in the mail.

Old Murph was to receive exactly one month's extra pay. He had never had any kind of formal contract with Eastland, and he was now out in the cold, at age sixty-nine.

Lisa watched in pain as Michael called Scribner Hollingworth and learned that the old patriarch had nothing against his son's actions. As chief executive officer of Eastland Industries/Domestic, Richard had the right to make a move like that, and Scribner felt it was about time someone did.

"I hadn't realized the inn was in such bad shape," he said to Michael. "I'd thought I'd left it in capable hands."

"And you did," Michael said.

Scribner said nothing. Finally, quietly, he said, "You know I've always liked you, Michael. Even when Candy didn't want me to, I said yes because I thought you'd be a damned good manager. And after the divorce I saw no reason to change anything. But a damned good manager knows cutbacks are often necessary. No pain, no gain."

"No gain for Eastland in the long run, Scrib. We were operating with the bare minimum. With a skeleton crew. How much do you think Eastland will save by this move? A hundred thousand a year? A hundred twenty?"

"Around that amount, yes, Michael."

"With no help left at the inn, Scrib, you'll lose that—eventually—several times over in lost business." He paused, realizing he wasn't getting anywhere. Scribner Hollingworth had always been stubborn, a tough and impulsive man who had made a great fortune and never let you forget it. But he and Michael, until now, had always gotten along. "I'd like to come and see you, Scrib. We can talk this over then."

"No need to talk, no need to ask about it," Scribner said. "When I handed the reins over to Richard this year, I didn't think he'd be able to make a move without me. Now that he finally has, I can promise you I'll be the last to step in."

"You're making a very big mistake, Scrib. I really think—"

"Talk to Richard if you're so sure of yourself. He hasn't laid *you* off; talk to him."

"Yeah, sure, I'll do that," Michael growled, and hung up.

"I'm so sorry," Lisa said quietly, coming up behind him and putting her hands on his shoulders. He reached up and covered her hands with his.

"I didn't know you were still in here," he said. "I don't like it when you see me like this, Lisa."

"Like what?"

"Down. Beaten."

She came around and sat down and faced him. "You're not beaten, Michael. You can fight this."

"Oh, I know. I know. I plan to. But I can't stand to have you see me like this; I haven't won yet."

"Oh, just stop. Come on. This is just something that happened; you'll take care of it."

He studied her eyes. "I don't remind you of anyone?"

She thought about it, but no one came to mind, and she shook her head. "No. Why?"

"How about your ex-husband?"

She stared. She hadn't even thought of him. After all this time, all these days of comparing Michael to Keith. But lately she hadn't felt that the comparison fit. "That hadn't even occurred to me," she said. "And you should stop judging yourself, Michael. You're obviously going to do something about this— I don't know what, but I know you'll do something." *Maybe,* she thought, *he'll see now I was right about Richard and Candace.* She only hoped it wasn't too late.

"Yes," he said musingly. "I do plan to do *something.*" Suddenly there was a new light in his eyes, a spirit she knew meant he was up to something good. He looked at his watch. "This is just great. Four thirty on a Friday afternoon: who's even going to be in the city?"

"What are you going to do?" she asked.

"Something I should have done a long time ago," he said, shaking his head. "I'm going to round up a group of investors and I'm going to buy that damned inn right out from under them."

At HHQ Pharmacies Incorporated, Darcy Bonner was led into Scott Hollingworth's office by a secretary she figured was about her age. Twenty and free. Maybe poor or not very rich, but free.

God, she had made a big mistake. And maybe she was about to make another one—a giant one. Scott Hollingworth had sounded very nice over the phone, though, and now that she saw him, she felt she had made the right decision. He was cute, with Richard's nice blue eyes and blond hair, but he had a moustache, and he looked a lot less sharklike. Plus he wasn't as skinny, which was always nice. Now that she wasn't going with Richard anymore, she could admit that he had bones that stuck into you and hurt.

But this Scott was cute, and he looked just right about seeing her—not too happy, not too friendly, but curious. Just right.

"Miss Bonner?"

"Hi," she said, shaking his hand. It was nice and warm without being clammy. Richard's was clammy, she remembered from the day she had met him.

"Why don't you sit down," Scott said, indicating a chair.

"Okay, thanks." She smiled. "I'm really glad that we finally got together, you know. I kind of started remembering all the things Richard used to say about you, and I figured if you didn't want to see all this stuff, no one would." He didn't look all that

218

interested—kind of blank, actually—but she went on. "I hope you don't think I'm some kind of angel of vengeance or anything like that. I'm really not. But I don't like to see people cheated and I know that when Richard gets involved in things, sometimes people get hurt."

He nodded slowly, and she thought she saw a slight smile trying to come through. "Well," he said quietly. "Let's see what you have there."

During the next few weeks Lisa and Michael hardly saw each other but spoke often on the phone. He was busy going back and forth between the inn and New York City, alternately trying to smooth things out and gather together private investors. But there was little he could do at the inn. In the city he had confronted a stubborn and smug Richard Hollingworth, who had declared he wasn't going to back down, and for the employees who had been laid off, Michael showed up for emotional support more than anything else. He rehired old Murph with a salary that would come out of his own pocket, but he wondered how long the arrangement could last. More important to Murph than money was where he lived —the home he had made for himself near the vegetable gardens. Michael had decided to look the other way, naturally, but knew that at some point Eastland would force Murph to go. Unless Michael could make an offer that Richard and the other Hollingworths would accept.

But rounding up investors was difficult. The task was made that much more difficult, too, by the recession in the economy and the fact that the inn had in fact lost money over the past eighteen months, and he began to get discouraged. Where were the hale days of his banking years? Where were all the investors who had always wanted to make a killing in real estate? Of course, some were still around, but he didn't want that kind of investor. He was going to choose his partners very carefully.

Lisa, meanwhile, began her new job, and found it hectic but unusually satisfying. The commute up to the site she had to visit most often was relatively painless, since it was north of the city and in the opposite direction from 99 percent of the area's daily commuters. The job was a challenge too. The union had just resumed work after a strike and everyone on the site was particularly touchy about demands. But Lisa was assertive and confident, determined to hold on to the job for as long as she wanted it. She wasn't going to make any mistakes.

Her evenings with Michael, now that they were both so busy and could see each other only once or twice a week, were passionate and intense, times in which they shut out the rest of the world and concentrated only on each other.

One evening, after they had made love, Lisa and Michael lay silent on her bed, the rustling of some papers on the bureau the only sound in the cool, breezy bedroom. The lovemaking had been good, but Lisa had felt something was missing—a warmth, a connectedness she usually felt very strongly. She was used to feeling totally enveloped in Michael's love, and tonight something had been different. And now that she thought about it, he hadn't told her lately that he loved her. And she was frightened.

When she had first started seeing Michael, she had been sure she'd feel trapped within a few weeks. She always had, and she had figured sadly that she always would. But it hadn't turned out that way. And now that she was just beginning to be sure of her love, sure that she wanted to try to make something real and deep and lasting out of the relationship, she was no longer sure of *his* love. All her thoughts about family and children, all these feeling she had suppressed for years, were beginning to come to the surface. And she was perhaps losing the love of the man who was making it all happen, this wonderful man who had once whispered words of love that made her heart soar.

She looked back on the early part of their relationship, and in it she saw a lot of bickering and complaining on her part. Had she driven him away? Had she unconsciously turned it into what all her other relationships had been?

She turned onto her side and gently ran her fingers through the hair on his chest, and he smiled and clasped her hand.

"Michael?" she said, uncertainty and fear beginning to steal her voice.

"Mmm?" He shifted so he was facing her.

"I have a question," she began, totally unsure of what she was going to say. How could she ask if he still loved her when there was a chance he'd hesitate, and in his eyes she'd see an answer she wished she could change? He wasn't the type to be harsh—ever —in response to a question like that. But his eyes never lied. And she was afraid.

"Lisa? What is it?" he asked tenderly.

She sighed and swallowed, her mouth suddenly unbearably dry. "Is something . . . different between us? I mean, has something happened that I don't know about?"

He studied her eyes, his own dark and caring and concerned. "Why?" he asked.

She shrugged. "You seem different. Less . . . interested, maybe."

He gathered her up in his arms and held her close. "Darling," he whispered. "Don't ever think that. Ever."

"But you seem so distant. I thought—"

"Don't think anything but that I love you." He sighed. "Maybe I have been a little distant lately. I'm just so wrapped up in the business." He raised her head and looked into her eyes. "Have you felt this way for a long time, Lisa? I'm really sorry if you have."

She shook her head. "No, no. Just lately. And tonight most of all."

"Well, I've just been working so hard. I promise that's all it is."

She smiled, but she didn't feel all that much better. There was still something. . . . "Here," she said, running her hand along his side. "Let me give you a backrub. That'll relax you."

"Great," he said, turning over onto his stomach.

She began massaging his shoulders, but her mind was already elsewhere. Lately, in addition to not being all that affectionate except during lovemaking, Michael had been very close-mouthed about everything in his life. Candace's name had come up only once or twice since Lisa had been laid off; Michael didn't talk much about the inn or his plans; they were growing apart, whether he admitted it or not. And Lisa didn't know what to do.

"Michael?"

"Mm. Don't stop."

She ran her fingers down his spine and began massaging each vertebra. "How come you haven't told me more about your plans, about what you're doing and what's happening with the inn?"

He turned and looked up at her. "Is that really what you want to spend our time doing? We see each other so little these days."

"Well, I think it's important to talk. I don't even really know what you're doing lately."

"I'm trying to do something on my own, Lisa. You once said I reminded you of Keith, and I don't want that to be true."

She sighed. "But we can share in the experience, in the struggle."

"I'd rather do it my way," he said quietly. And to himself, he silently added, *You wouldn't like it if I told you what I was doing. And I'm going to hold off telling you until the time is right.*

Of course, he reminded himself, nothing was definite yet. Candace had called him just this morning. She had heard that he was trying to round up investors—a fact that annoyed him because the whole plan was very confidential and someone had evidently let it slip. But the fact was that she had heard. And she wanted to talk about becoming a major partner in the project.

He had been shocked at first; the inn, as far as he knew, represented much of what Candace hated—the outdoors, the spell it had cast over Michael. She blamed it for having started the chain of events that eventually broke up their marriage. She didn't even seem to like any of the people who worked for Michael. And now she wanted to invest in it with her own money rather than Eastland's.

It was an intriguing proposition. Her interest meant that she thought it was likely or at least possible that Eastland would sell the inn. And she certainly had reason to know.

She would be an interesting partner too. He had always pictured his banking friends—male banking friends—as silent partners. But Candace—that was an entirely different proposition.

Yes, it was an intriguing idea. But he didn't feel comfortable discussing it with Lisa, especially if it wasn't definite. He was meeting with Candace tomorrow. Then maybe, if all went well, he'd tell Lisa about it.

And for now he meant what he had said about doing something on his own. He had always wished he had come to know Lisa in another context. It was too bad that she had lost her job at Eastland, but at least it had given them a chance for a new start. He had always been his own man, and a successful one, yet when Lisa had met him he had been at his lowest in every way. Now he'd have a chance to show her that he could run his life successfully, smoothly, profitably. And if he acted a bit distant for a while, that was the price they would both have to pay.

Scott and Darcy walked out onto Scott's terrace and looked out at the view. It was early evening, a purple dusk that promised a cool, breezy night. Darcy couldn't get over the view—all the way east to islands she didn't even know the name of, plus downtown—even the Empire State Building. And

224

Scott was so nice and so cute, kind of the opposite of Richard now that she thought about it.

He had been great too. He didn't move so fast you didn't know what was happening. When he finally kissed her, she had been hoping for hours that he would, and he even asked if it was okay. Afterward, he had seemed pretty depressed, and she had asked him what the matter was because it was the right thing to do. Polite and everything. But she hadn't thought he'd actually tell her! Richard had almost never confided in her!

When he told her he was upset because he already had a girlfriend, a woman he was serious about, she had felt like a boiling geyser inside. These Hollingworths! Did they treat everyone like dirt? But it turned out that wasn't what Scott planned. "I really like you," he had said, and she had felt tears coming to her eyes even though she knew they would make her look too emotional. "And I've met you at the worst time in my life," he had continued softly, gently holding her hand. "I've been on the verge of being engaged to a woman for the past six months or so."

"Why haven't you been? Engaged, I mean," she had asked.

He had smiled to cover up a hurt. "Oh, she wasn't interested."

Darcy frowned. "I sure know what that's about." She looked into his eyes. Suddenly they seemed much nicer than Richard's ever had. "I'm glad I met you. Even if it was just for vengeance at first. I really like you, Scott." She had been scared to say those words, just to come out and say them as if she had said, "It's a nice day, isn't it." So many times with Richard she had told him something private or per-

225

sonal, and he had acted as if she were dumb or worse. "Too emotional," he had always said.

But Scott wasn't like that.

And now, as she stood with him on his terrace and felt him edge a little closer to her, she couldn't get over how gentle he was. Richard had been all over her with his sharp knees and elbows and hipbones practically the first second they had met!

"I'm sorry I've put off listening to the tapes," Scott said as he looked down into Darcy's green eyes. "But I just haven't felt like it."

"I brought all the notes that go with them," she said.

He smiled. "I'm sure you did. It just seems wrong somehow."

"But if you heard what he said about—"

He shook his head. "That's not what I meant. Being with you these last few days has been very special to me, Darcy. And it seems so strange—so strange to me that we met because of Richard."

She shrugged. "It's not such a big deal. People meet in lots of ways."

"Yes," he mused, "that's certainly true enough. But I'm sure that anyone who looked at us would assume I was with you for one reason."

"What do you mean?" she asked quietly.

"Well, aside from your obvious assets, Darcy, people would assume I've come to like you so quickly because of some sort of sibling rivalry. Revenge and all that—thy brother's wife, you know."

"But we weren't married. You know that."

He smiled. "I just meant 'thy brother's wife' in terms of an idea, Darcy. You didn't have to be literally married to him for the idea to fit."

"Oh," she said, disappointed over what he was saying.

"But I don't think that's why I've fallen for you," he said softly, turning her to face him. "I honestly think I would have fallen for you the first time I met you."

"Oh, Scott," she whispered, looking up into his eyes, "But doesn't it bother you?"

"Doesn't what bother me, darling?"

"You know."

"You mean the baby?"

She nodded.

"I think you're beautiful and wonderful in every way, Darcy. In every way."

She smiled, and when he kissed her, she thanked fate for having told her to take those tapes and notes from Richard's office. She was almost sure she liked Scott for himself, not because he was maybe going to help her get revenge. She really liked him, and he seemed to like her.

Candace signaled for the waiter and ordered another Perrier as Michael looked through the folder she had given him. He wasn't concentrating on what he was reading though. For he realized the scene was almost an exact repeat of one they had shared years ago, before they were married. They had met in the same place—the Palm Court at the Plaza—because Candace had been coming here since she was a little girl and it was her "favorite place on earth," as she put it. Then, as now, Michael was going through a folder listing stock holdings she owned under various corporate names as well as her own.

Back then, however, he had been intent on impressing this beautiful woman who seemed to have been blessed with everything life had to offer. She had asked for his advice, and he remembered pretending he knew more than he in fact did.

But now—now he had to examine her investments with a keen, discriminating, dispassionate eye. She wanted to buy a staggeringly large chunk of the inn with her own money, and he had to be sure he advised her correctly about selling her investments. He still couldn't believe she was interested though. And she had barely told him anything on the phone.

He looked up from the folder. "Candy, tell me something."

She smiled. "Anything, darling."

He ignored the "darling." "Tell me why you're doing this—why you want to buy the inn."

For a minute she said nothing. She had thought of this moment many times since she had made her decision, countless times and in countless variations. In her favorite one he asked why she wanted to buy the inn, and she said, "To be with you." And that old light came into his eyes, he brought her into his arms, and whispered, "Darling, at last," or something equally corny but equally wonderful. In another, he simply came out and said he hoped they would be spending more time together now that they were partners. In yet another, she was coy, only hinting at the truth.

But the truth—that this was the only way she was going to have another chance with Michael now that Richard was putting his plans to sell the inn into motion—was impossible to tell. She had initially— foolishly, she now realized—been optimistic about Richard's plans. He would convince Scott and

Scribner to sell, he'd sink the several million dollars they'd get from the inn's sale into the faltering disk-drive company he wanted to acquire, and she'd have a good shot at Michael once he was forced to come back to the city, disillusioned with his Man of Nature routine. But since Richard had made Michael so furious about the firings, Michael had put a kink into the plans—he wanted to buy the inn. And this was fine with Richard; all he cared about was getting the money for the new acquisition. But Candace was going to be left out in the cold. Left out, that is, if she hadn't thought of her own plan.

She still wasn't completely thrilled with the idea. She couldn't bear the inn and those cold rains, those long winters, those interminable, hot summers. But who was going to insist that she be there twenty-four hours a day, seven days a week? No, she had a much more pleasing, much more romantic vision of midnight meetings in the city, long drives to the inn when the time apart had been too long, passionate reunions that made long-ago love deepen and flame.

He had loved her once, and together they had made mistakes. She had learned, though, and she wanted him back. She wanted his kisses, that unleashed passion that now warmed her night thoughts, those husky words of love he had breathed and urged and whispered. And she knew, deep in her bones, that this was the way.

"Candace, why?" he asked. "It's important that I know."

"I'd like to make some money on my own, Michael," she finally said. "With Richard at the helm of Eastland and me never really doing anything substantive at the company, I don't have all that much

229

faith in the security of the company. He plays a lot of games, Michael, and I need to know I have a major enterprise that I can count on."

He searched her eyes. What she had said didn't sound quite right. There were so many other possibilities for her to invest in. As a matter of fact, her non-Eastland money was financially secure in very lucrative holdings. "You know as well as I do that the inn is hardly a blue-chip surefire investment, Candy. I'd consider it something of a risk."

She arched a delicate brow. "You're some salesman."

"I have to be honest with you."

"Oh, Michael, I feel I owe you too."

He looked up sharply. "Owe me? Why?"

She paused and took a sip of Perrier. "Are we on for the inn?"

"Candace, that's a big decision. I don't know if it's the best thing for you to do with your money—"

"But if I decide it is?" she interrupted.

He looked into her eyes. He wanted the inn so damned much. With Candace, it would be his. He had two or three other men who could kick in whatever he needed, but the important part was that Candy would be providing the big money, with his own money second in line but in a rather different league. And he could deal with her; he knew her; he knew how to reason with her. But he still couldn't make the decision on the spot. There were still so many questions, not the least of which was the price.

"Yes or no?" she prodded.

"Look, Candy. I was glad when you called and I'm very, very optimistic about all of this. But I'm certainly not giving you a yes right now."

Her pale eyes flashed, but she looked away for a moment, and he could see she was trying to rein herself in as she took a sip of her Perrier. "All right," she said quietly. "I understand," she added, but he wasn't at all sure she did.

He reached out and gently brushed a strand of blond hair back from her face. When the gesture was over, he wondered what had possessed him to even make it. Was he using her? Was he growing closer to her? And if that was true, was that just because he wanted something from her? "Tell me," he said, unable to shake this strange feeling. "Why do you owe me?"

She looked into the middle distance, lost in thought. "Let's . . . leave that for a while," she said abstractedly. "It really isn't all that important."

Candace and Michael ended up extending cocktails into dinner, dinner into after-dinner brandy, a mixture of easy conversation and increasingly inspired talk about possibilities for the inn. Candace made it clear she'd be a relatively silent partner, concerning herself with decorating, advertising, and other matters that could be basically handled from the city. More interesting to Michael than that, though, was the news that Candace felt she and Michael could get a very good price for the inn.

"Naturally," she said, "my name would have to be kept out of this. If Daddy and Scott knew I was buying the inn, they would certainly have questions and qualms about selling. We'd have to form a corporation beforehand and my name would have to be kept out of it entirely. But the fact remains that I know Richard is interested in selling. I certainly am, which means we just need one more person—Scott or Daddy."

"But that doesn't explain why you think we'd get a low price."

She smiled. "You don't know Richard as well as I thought you did. When you come dangling even a relatively attractive offer, he'll bite."

"What about the others?"

"I don't know. Scott could go either way. He's never taken an interest in Eastland and he's not all that bright when it comes to finance. Father's the one I'd be worried about, of course." She sighed. "Discovering what I was doing and all that."

He studied her eyes and wondered how she could be so dishonest with her own family. Even if they didn't find out eventually, which they almost certainly would, wouldn't she feel guilty? How could she sit in on a board meeting and recommend selling to a corporation of which she was the major part, without telling them what was going on?

Michael's questions gave him some real doubts about teaming up with Candace. He knew that if a friend were to tell him that he planned to form a partnership with his ex-wife, he would tell him right off the bat that he was making a serious mistake. Why, then, couldn't he take his own advice?

But the answer was obvious and inescapable. He wanted the inn and he wasn't going to find another investor like Candace—not quickly, anyway. And she was a known quantity, one he could deal with.

He thought about how wonderful it would be to surprise Lisa with the news that the inn was his. What a wonderful ending to a situation that had been fraught with difficulties for both of them since the beginning. After all, she had once asked him why he didn't want to own the inn, and he had replied—probably infuriatingly passively—that he didn't have the money, and he'd left it at that. Now, he—and Lisa eventually, he hoped—would be the owners of a magnificent tract of land, a solid, lasting, secure property that would have to serve for Lisa as some compensation for what had been ripped so cruelly from her family's grasp back home.

And as for Candace, well, she had said she'd want to be a relatively silent partner and he'd see to that in the corporation papers. In the meantime he'd keep that wonderful future a secret from Lisa until it was more fully worked out. She'd see him as strong, capable, inventive. She'd be so happy.

CHAPTER TEN

Michael called Lisa that night but didn't see her. He had spent hours with Candace, and it didn't seem right to see Lisa at that point. She would ask him all about his day and evening; she would mind if she found out what he had been doing; and he didn't want to lie. No, he wanted to keep everything simple, and then he would surprise her.

He remembered other deals he had made when he was younger—really great stock-market buys especially—and the thrill that had gone along with making a decision he knew was risky but right. That thrill, oddly enough, was missing. He wasn't sure that signing with Candace was better than waiting. But damn it, he didn't want to wait.

The next night, when Lisa came to his apartment, she seemed in a particularly good mood. Her day at work had been exciting, she said, and she was feeling great.

"Let me make you a drink," he said, pleased she

seemed so happy. He wanted so much to tell her about the inn. But first there was something else. . . .

"Okay, great," she said, sinking into the soft cushions of the living room couch and tucking her feet up under herself. She looked more beautiful than he had ever seen her—absolutely exhilarated, with a glow to her lovely skin and a sparkle in her eyes he had never seen. "How about a vodka martini?" she said, spreading her arms across the back cushions of the couch. "I worked really hard today, and I think I'm ready to play really hard."

He smiled. "Sounds good to me," he called over his shoulder as he made a pitcher of martinis.

When he came and sat down, she ran a cool hand down his cheek and looked into his eyes. "You look as good as I feel," she murmured.

His smile broadened. "Seeing you is a pretty nice way to end the day," he said. The look in her eyes told him to go ahead, that now was the right time. "As a matter of fact, Lisa. . ." He paused, trying to find the best words, perhaps words she would remember for a lifetime. If he were lucky. But he was lost; all he could say was what was on his mind.

"Yes?" she asked softly.

He took her hand and held it against his cheek, drinking in the pleasure of her touch and the scent he loved so much. "I've been thinking a lot lately about how it would be to come home to you every night," he said quietly. "Every time I go back to the inn, I'm no good for anything because I'm just thinking of you. Every time I come back to my apartment, too, I wonder why I'm here and not with you."

She smiled. "I've wondered the same thing," she murmured.

He gazed into her eyes and saw so much love there, he had all the encouragement he'd ever need. "Lisa, I've been making a lot of plans, as you know. I wasn't going to tell you about this until it was all set, but—well, it looks as if I'm going to make a bid for the inn. And when that happens—"

"You're really doing it?" she interrupted, smiling with joy. "Michael, that's *so great*! I'm so happy for you!" At last he would be free, she thought. Free of that terrible family, free of the need to answer to an irrational boss. She was sure that much of what she had initially seen as his irresponsibility was just a reaction to Richard Hollingworth, a need to do the opposite of whatever he asked just to be contrary. But if he were his own boss, there would be no stopping him.

He smiled and took a sip of his martini. "I'll be happier when all the details are smoothed out, but it looks very promising."

"Well, what happened between yesterday and today that you're so definite all of a sudden? Did you finally get enough small investors, or—"

"No, no," he said quickly, shaking his head. "One major one, actually."

Her eyes widened. "But that's great! That will make things so much easier! Who is it?"

He hesitated. Now that the moment to tell her about Candace had finally come, he wished he had saved it for another time. Certainly he had to tell Lisa sometime. But now was the worst of times. Yet, it was too late to put her off. He could hardly say never mind. She had been very sensitive last night about his not confiding in her.

"Michael? Who is it?"

She looked into his eyes, and he watched as her expression changed from one of curiosity, to wonder, to horror. She looked away and took a sip of her martini, and then, so quietly he could barely hear her voice, she said, "Why do I have the horrible feeling that your major investor is Candace? Tell me I'm wrong, Michael."

He shook his head, and for a moment of wild hope she thought that meant she *was* wrong. But then he said, "I can't. It *is* Candace."

She stared. "I don't believe it. I just don't believe you did that. It isn't a fait accompli, though, right? I mean, you haven't made it definite."

"I haven't yet, but I'm going to."

Her heart began to pound, and she felt dizzy, as if she were going to be sick. She looked at him, took a deep breath, still couldn't find her voice, and took a gulp of her drink. "Tell me how it's going to work," she said quietly. "What will her involvement be?"

"Oh, minimal, really. You know she doesn't like the inn."

"I see," Lisa said sarcastically. "Which doesn't exactly explain why she wants to go in on it with you, does it?"

"What is that supposed to mean?"

"Why is she going in on it with you?" Lisa pressed. "Seriously, Michael. She's never done anything like this before. You yourself have said she doesn't like the inn. And as far as I can tell, she knows nothing about that sort of thing."

"What are you saying?"

She rolled her eyes. "God, Michael, you really are something. Are you pretending not to know or do you really not know? What do you think I'm saying? I'm saying that Candace is going to use this to get you back."

At first he said nothing. Then: "You sound very sure of yourself."

She sighed. "Look. I don't know. You know Candace, and I don't. Maybe I'm wrong, Michael. But I honestly think that's the reason."

"So? What if it is? I'm not interested."

She studied his eyes. How could she be sure? "I just don't see why you have to pick Candace," she said. "It just seems like asking for trouble, Michael. That family is nothing but trouble as far as I can see. Nothing but trouble and scheming. And I don't see why you need that. Here you have a chance to get out from under the thumb of one Hollingworth, a man who has done everything he could to hurt you and nothing to help you. And now you want to team up with his sister?"

"It's absurd to lump them together like that."

"I don't think so," she retorted. "As far as I can tell, the two of them have the exact same value system—something I would have thought you'd want to escape. I really can't believe you're going to be so foolish."

He finished his drink. "Look," he said hoarsely, "you said it before. This is my chance, Lisa, and I'm not going to miss it. You once complained that I wasn't supporting you in your plans. I'm sorry if that was the case. But I had hoped you'd be able to support me in this. And your unwillingness makes me wonder if all you said about Keith is true."

Her grip on the glass tightened. "What do you mean?"

"Well, I think you once said it yourself—that maybe in some way you wanted to hold Keith down, to hold him back."

"And you think I'm trying to hold you back?"

"I think you should think about that."

She stared at him in amazement. "I don't have to think about it. I know damned well why I don't want you teaming up with Candace and it has nothing to do with holding you back. You know as well as I do that there are other investors you could get, Michael."

He poured a generous slosh of the martini mix into his glass and went over to get some ice at the bar. He was suddenly dying of thirst; his throat was like parchment. And he knew another drink would only make him thirstier. But he wanted it; he needed something to calm him down.

When he came back to the couch, he took a long sip and then looked at Lisa. "I want you to think about something," he said quietly.

"All right," she said warily. "What?"

"When we first made love, I told you you would have to change your ways, and you basically laughed my comment off."

For a moment she remembered that wonderful night. How impossible it would have been back then to be with another man!

"I decided to trust you," he continued, "because I knew that trying to hem you in would get me nowhere. I didn't want to be another Jay with you. I trusted you, and I think I was right to. It was the only way we could have come this far. I had faith,

Lisa, in you and in our relationship. And I don't see why you can't have that faith in me."

She sighed. He was partially right. It was important to trust, to have faith. But some deep, inner instinct had always told her not to trust Candace on a personal level. And she believed this instinct; she always had. Just as important, hadn't Michael learned anything from dealing with Richard Hollingworth? True, you couldn't blame a sister for a brother's actions, but couldn't he see that Candace was up to something? And couldn't he respect her opinion enough to see that, or at least examine it as a possibility?

"Michael."

He turned and looked into her eyes, and she was frightened by what she saw. They were so dark. Dark and dull and defensive. "Michael, I do trust you—in areas that don't have to do with Candace. And I agree that trust is important. But what about being flexible?" She hesitated. "I just can't fathom why you're doing what you're doing. It seems so crazy."

"What do you suggest?" he asked. His voice was flat, hollow. "You're asking me to choose between you and the inn, Lisa."

"No, I'm not," she answered, a void in the pit of her stomach growing with sickening speed. "I'm asking you to get another investor, Michael, not to give up on your idea. I think it's a great idea. Just get another investor."

"I can't do that," he said quietly. "And I'm not going to do that, Lisa."

For a moment she was silent, the weight of his words sinking in. "Then I don't think we have any more to talk about," she said sadly. She rose and looked down at him. "I'm sorry, Michael. I really am."

She picked up her purse and ran from the room. A moment later he heard the front door slam shut.

Lisa was hardly aware of going home. She walked, she finally got into a cab, and she was driven to her door in what seemed like thirty seconds. When she got back to her apartment, she collapsed on her bed, but sleep was the last thing she was ready to do. Her mind was racing, going over what Michael had said, what she had said, what she wished each had said differently.

She couldn't believe that the inn was still at the root of their problems, that she was having the same sort of argument with Michael that she used to have with Keith. But it was worse. Where Keith had been weak, Michael was strong. Where Keith had been petulant, Michael was simply stubborn. And it wasn't simply an argument. It was much more. To him this move meant everything—a change in the opposite direction, a decision that represented an amalgamation of all his strengths. And she respected that. But he was making a mistake—a terrible mistake. And while she couldn't cite any specific facts to plead her case, couldn't he see how much the situation bothered her? Couldn't he compromise?

Something had stopped him though. Something had made him refuse. She could see it in his eyes, hear it in his voice, hear his tone curdle in defensive hostility. He had pushed back the minute she had started to push, and there had been no turning back. And that had hurt. He had taken offense at what she had said, turned rigid in the face of her comments and questions.

He wanted to run the inn with Candace, and that was that.

She tried to think about possibilities. Maybe he would change his mind. Maybe he would realize he was wrong. But even as she thought about it, she knew that wouldn't happen. And then a new thought struck—she had been acting as if he were the innocent, as if he were naively going back to the lion's den of Hollingworth territory, and that he'd fall victim to both financial trickery and Candace's charms. But maybe he wanted to be with Candace for—oh, God, maybe this was just his way . . .

But then another thought struck. Before they had gotten onto the subject of the inn, he had talked about missing her, wanting to be with her, wanting to come home to her every night. Those words hadn't come from a man who really wanted to be with Candace, had they? No, it had sounded as if he had been planning to ask her to marry him. And, oh, Lord, she would have said yes if all the rest hadn't happened.

And now, what would happen? She was the one who had walked out, but what was going to change? She couldn't compromise about Candace. And even if there had been a chance that Michael might have compromised before, there was almost certainly no chance now. She had pushed him into a corner. He saw this as the opportunity of a lifetime and he wasn't going to give it up.

Slowly, in one of the worst heat waves in decades, the days passed. July dragged into August; the city

242

sank into a humid, smoggy haze that made everybody feel trapped and irritable, sweaty and snappish, that made Lisa long for the clean, clear air of her home state. On top of missing Michael, she missed the inn too. It had been the first place since she had moved east that had held any meaning for her, that had reminded her of home. And she knew this wasn't because of geography, because of mountains or meadows or the way the grass smelled in a warm breeze. It was because she had been happy there. And that happiness had existed because of Michael.

Each day, then each week, she expected him to call. Each day part of her heart froze as she realized the rift might be permanent, and she realized she had assumed that something would happen to bring back the magic that had enveloped her while she was with Michael.

She felt lonelier than she had ever felt in her life, cut off from everyone because she was trapped in a lethargy she couldn't control. Jay had called again, but he had caught her at a bad time and she had been unfriendly. And even though she meant to call back and apologize, something held her back.

Keith, too, called—this time from Chicago, where he had just bought into a restaurant with money he had made from his last venture. Strangely enough, he was the one person she enjoyed talking to during this period. He sounded genuinely happy—finally—and that made her feel good, and it made it easier to remember the good times they had had at the beginning. But she resented both Keith and Jay for even existing. They weren't Michael. She had unconsciously adopted certain attitudes and habits when she had been involved with them and she blamed them for what had happened with Michael.

She missed Michael; that was all there was to it. And while her job was exciting, she was aware almost every minute of the day, even when she was busy, that she was fighting a deep sadness, a deep disappointment.

She tried to think about what she could do. Michael had loved her, had wanted to be with her, possibly even marry her, and there had to be a way to get that happiness back, to undo what had happened. But how? He certainly wasn't ready to talk again. If he were, he would have called. And she didn't want to call him unless she had something new to say. For she didn't want to call and hear him say he was still going through with the plan, that nothing she could say would stop him.

And so the days passed, and Lisa grew more angry and less sad, furious that Michael was so stubborn and so blind. Couldn't he see that the fact that they were meant for each other was the most important thing in the world? More important than the inn and Candace?

One day, a little more than a month after Lisa had had the fight with Michael, the phone rang and a vaguely familiar voice said, "Is this Lisa Bennett?"

"Yes," she said warily. "Who's this?" It was a voice she hadn't liked much.

"Uh, you don't know me, but my name's Scott Hollingworth."

So that was why the voice was familiar! He sounded like Richard.

"Oh, yes, Richard and Candace's brother."

"Yes. And I'm sure you're wondering why I'm calling."

"Well, yes."

"Actually, I'd like to talk to you. Do you think it would be possible to meet somewhere?"

"Gee, I really don't. . ." She paused. She was curious. Why not meet him? "Well, okay. Why not?"

"Great. I'll be with Darcy. Do you remember her?"

"Darcy Bonner? Of course. Is she all right? How is—"

"She's fine," he said, and she thought she could hear him smiling. "She's just fine. And we have something we both think you'll be interested in. A plan."

She frowned. How strange. "Well, all right."

They arranged to meet at a restaurant on Second Avenue, and half an hour later Lisa walked in, trying to hold her hopes in check. Since Scott had called, all sorts of fantasies had bloomed. Michael had gone in on the deal with Candace and now regretted it deeply, and needed her. But what could come next? What did Michael have to do with Scott *or* Darcy? No, she'd have to resign herself to the fact that what they wanted to talk to her about probably had nothing to do with Michael.

Darcy looked beautiful and happy when she walked in. Her green eyes were clear, her skin was rosy and smooth, and she was glowing with joy. She was also on the arm of Scott Hollingworth. Strange.

Lisa had never seen the man, but she would have been able to easily pick him out of a crowd as Richard and Candace's brother. They all shared the same blond coloring, and their blue eyes and full mouths were so similar it was striking. But even at a glance, he looked warmer, happier, nicer. Friendlier. And when Darcy pointed Lisa out and the two came over to the booth she had settled into, he seemed surprised and happy Lisa had come.

He guided Darcy into the booth and then extended his hand as he sat down. "Good to meet you," he said. "I apologize for all the mystery. And please don't think I'm paranoid like Richard. I just like to talk to people face to face. Especially about things that are, well, a little delicate."

"Yes, well, I can see that. But what is it that you wanted to see me about? And Darcy, how are you?"

Darcy beamed. "Just great. Really great. And I'm sorry I ran out that day. I was real nervous, that's all. And I didn't really understand who Michael was."

"You had me worried," Lisa said. "But as long as you're okay."

Scott hugged Darcy close and kissed her on the nose. "She's just great, as she said. Anyway, let's order some food for Darcy and drinks for ourselves —have you eaten, by the way?"

"No."

"Then please, dinner on me. Then we can get down to business."

They ordered steakburgers, french fries, and beer, and then Scott leaned forward and set his hands on the table. "We'd like your help," he said simply. "And I think you might be interested in what we're doing."

"Go on," she said, curious and impatient. He wasn't a fast talker like his brother.

"Richard has called a board meeting," he said.

The words hit Lisa hard, as she anticipated what this meant.

"The subject of the board meeting, as you might have guessed, is the sale of the inn," he continued. "The *possible* sale of the inn, I should say." He was silent as the waiter set down their drinks, and went on only after the waiter was well out of earshot. "Anyway, Darcy tells me that she's already told you all about Richard, and about the fact that Richard left her alone in the office. What she didn't tell you was that she took some tapes—"

"A whole bunch," Darcy interrupted. "Like five or six."

"Five," Scott said. "And some old-looking files that had been stuffed into a drawer."

"What sort of tapes?" Lisa asked, confused.

Darcy's face lit up. "Let *me* tell, Scott." She edged forward in her seat. "Richard never told me things I wanted him to tell me. He never told me how he felt, he never told me I looked pretty, he never told me things a girl really likes to hear. But he used to talk to me during a period of maybe two or three months. He was afraid he was going to die because of the headaches he kept getting, and he'd tell me things, just hold me at night in the darkness and talk about what he was afraid of. That was when he was nicest. Then he turned rotten again. But what he told me one of those nights was that he had a lot of fears about things happening. People trying to double-cross him and stuff like that. So he taped everything —all his phone conversations on this special machine, all the conversations in his office that were supposedly confidential. Little stuff and big stuff, everything that went on."

Lisa listened eagerly, her mind racing to all the implications of what Darcy was saying.

"So just to get back at him, I took some of them. I don't know, I wanted to take something that would really bother him, but not something he'd notice right away, like that brass paperweight or those real fancy bookends. If I had taken those, he probably would have sent two giant guys over to my apartment. I wouldn't put that past him at all. Anyway, I took them." She shrugged, and her face began to flush. "And then I got to thinking—"

"Which was when she called *me*," Scott interrupted. "And we decided to call you when Richard called the board meeting. Up until then I had thought the plans might not go through. But it's all going, well, as Richard and Candace have planned it." He paused, taking a sip of his beer and then staring into space for a few moments. When he looked back at Lisa, his blue eyes were sad. "I've really never been a fighter, Lisa. May I call you Lisa, by the way?"

"Of course."

"Anyway, Lisa, I've never been a fighter. I was always considered the weak kid in the family, by everyone, including my own mother." He turned and looked at Darcy, and Lisa could tell they were in a world all their own. In love. Something she missed so much. "Now I have something to fight for," he said quietly, happily. "I don't care what anyone thinks about our situation, about the fact that Darcy is carrying Richard's baby. I've decided to take a stand, though, because I have more reason than ever to want to hold on to what's mine and to try to make it grow. And my father has the right to know that Richard wants to sell the inn so he can sink the money into that disk-drive company that's on the verge of collapsing. I can't let him throw my money away on a losing proposition and I won't let Richard, Candace, and to some extent Michael Jamison defraud me out of what's rightfully mine. I'm not sure about Michael, but he's been spending so much time with Candace I think he must be in on it."

"Look, I want to know everything you know, including what role you think I have in all this. But first, my understanding was that each of you owns twenty-five percent of the shares of Eastland stock. You vote against selling the inn, and—"

"That still leaves my father."

"And the negative report I wrote so well," she filled in.

"Exactly," he said. "I can vote against selling the inn and I can put my two cents in as far as Father is concerned, but he's always listened to Richard and Candace more than he has to me, and if he thinks the inn is going to continue to be a drain on our capital, which is what he'll think, he's going to vote with Richard and Candace. But I'm getting ahead of myself."

The waiter brought their burgers and fries, and once again Scott was silent until the man had left. Then he continued. "I wouldn't have known about any of this unless Darcy had contacted me. I'm ashamed to say that, but it's true. Until now, I've never paid much attention to what went on at Eastland. Anyway, as I understand it from what I can piece together from the tapes, Richard asked you to write the report in a certain way. Is that right?"

"Well, it wasn't quite that simple. I suppose at first that he did hint about what he wanted, and I just didn't pick up on it. So I went up to the inn, saw a lot of things wrong, but also saw great potential and great possibilities, and I came back and wrote a very glowing report—realistic and critical, but glowing in terms of the future."

Scott smiled. "Richard must have loved *that*."

Darcy laughed. "Yeah."

"You can imagine," Lisa said. "So I was sent back. He asked me to include more comments from the employees, too, at that point. And the comments were unanimously wonderful. All I could figure out about *that*—because I think Richard is pretty smart —is that he must have known that would be the case, and he felt that a report in which all the employees were wild about Michael would reflect badly on Michael's management style."

"Oh, it would," Scott observed. "To my father, at least. He doesn't think a manager should be well-liked by his employees—not to the extent you describe, anyway. So you went up, you came back, and you wrote another report."

"Yes, I gather a perfect report, given what happened. My theory is that Richard had all he needed from me, so he fired me."

"Well, we'll get to that in a minute," Scott said quietly. "That's something I *do* know about, from the tapes."

"Really?" It was such a strange feeling to be discussing something she had never imagined discussing with virtual strangers before—certainly not with a member of the Hollingworth family.

"First I want to ask you something," Scott said.

"Okay. Shoot."

"Why were you so cooperative with my brother?"

he asked, frowning. "From what I understand, you had a personal relationship, if you will, with Michael Jamison. I gather you liked him. He's a very likeable guy. What made you just turn around and do my brother's bidding? Was it that you felt you had no choice?"

"Well, I saw that I had two choices. To cooperate with Richard and possibly spend years doing the same thing over and over again, or pretending to do what he wanted and exposing his scheme later to all the members of the family. Which was what I was going to do."

Scott slowly shook his head. "That's amazing. That would have taken a lot of guts."

"Well, I didn't have all that much to lose at that point. But if I had known I'd be fired before I could pull something like that off, I certainly wouldn't have written the report. All I did was give Richard the ammunition he needed."

"Which was why you were fired," Darcy chimed in. "Candace told Richard—he hadn't even *thought* of this, Lisa—that he should get rid of you because you had done all he needed. And it would be stupid to keep you around."

"Candace said that?"

"Uh-huh," Darcy said, nodding. "A real sneak. *I* think."

Scott slung an arm around Darcy's shoulder. "We're not being totally aboveboard ourselves, Darcy."

"But we're *right*," Darcy cried. "They're doing something rotten and they should be stopped. It's the only right thing to do."

"Just what did you have in mind?" Lisa asked.

"Well, it's really very simple," Scott said.

But it wasn't simple. If Lisa did what they wanted, she would be a major part of a plan in which she went directly against Michael, directly against something that was very important to him.

She was so disturbed by the thought, that she actually felt dizzy as she tried to decide what to do. Emotionally, the idea was totally repugnant. She was going to ruin his dream. But what was the alternative? Sitting back and letting him go into business with a snake—a woman who had had her fired—and having him tie up his money and future for who knew how long?

For a moment she thought of what Michael would say if he knew she was doing this. He'd be furious, yelling that she was trying once again to be the power holder, the one who got what she wanted and didn't care if other people felt undercut or hurt. And in a way it was true; she *was* going to wrest power from Michael. But she knew that what he was doing was going to hurt him in the end.

And then she thought about Michael and Candace. Perhaps, after all, he had gone back to her.

Tentatively, she asked Scott if he knew anything about it. He didn't think anything new was going on. All he knew was that they were spending a lot of time together, and he had made the assumption that Michael was going to be one of the partners.

But even if Michael and Candace weren't together now, wouldn't Lisa's actions surely drive him to Candace? By trying to help, wouldn't she inevitably be pushing him toward the woman she wanted most to keep him away from?

The truth was that if she tried to save him, there was a very good chance that she'd lose him.

She was caught. Trapped. At a complete standstill.

She took a sip of beer and looked from Darcy to Scott. "I'll really have to think about this," she said quietly.

"But—" Darcy began.

"Darcy, quiet," Scott said gently but firmly. "I think that makes sense, Lisa. But I'll need to know soon. The board meeting is this Wednesday, and there's a chance I could do what I want to do without your help, but I'd like to know that in advance. And your account of what happened—and what you think the future holds for the inn—would be even more powerful than the tapes we have. They're really quite spotty. I don't want to pressure you, but that *is* the truth."

"I understand," she said. "There isn't any chance Michael will be there, is there?"

"Absolutely not," Scott said. "This is a family-only meeting to determine the advisability of selling the inn. As far as Candace and Richard are presenting it, the purpose of the meeting will be to discuss an offer for the inn from a corporation called Innesco, Inc.—a corporation that no one is supposed to know is principally owned by Candace and others. So, no, there isn't a chance that Michael will be there."

"Well, good," she said. "That makes a big difference. I really couldn't do it if Michael were going to be there."

"And I wouldn't expect you to," Scott said.

"But tell me," she said. "How do you know Innesco is Candace?"

"Oh, I've gotten a lot wiser in the past few days," Scott said. "I've learned to listen and ask a lot of questions and call in favors people thought I'd never call in. It's time I had a say in how my money is invested."

They finished up the meal with more talk of the inn and their plans. They all felt so passionately— each for different reasons—that it was impossible to talk about anything else.

At the end of the meal Scott handed Lisa his card and asked her to call as soon as she had made up her mind. "And I do thank you, Lisa. Really. Just for even considering the idea."

"Oh, that's all right," she said, standing up. "Believe me, if I decide to do this, it will be because I want to, Scott."

He looked into her eyes. "That's the way it should be. I hope you decide it *is* the right thing to do. And if not, thanks for listening and considering it. I'll be in touch even if your answer is no."

"And I will too," Darcy said.

Lisa smiled. "Good. Well, I *will* be in touch, and thanks for the dinner."

The process of making a decision was agonizing. It was so hard to separate her feelings. If she did what Scott wanted, would that really be because she wanted to help Michael? Wasn't there just a little bit—or a lot—of anger behind her actions? Michael still hadn't called. That meant he was still angry, still as stubborn as ever. From Lisa's perspective, it was *his* fault that the relationship had crumbled, his fault because of his blindness, his obstinacy. There was a chance he was now romantically linked to Candace, the woman who was responsible for her having been fired. And she was angry about all of it; she couldn't pretend her motives were purely altruistic.

Yet she felt, too, that she had to help him, that she had to save him. She still loved him. And as long as there was a chance they'd get back together sometime, she wanted to help. And so, the very next morning, she called Scott and told him she would do what he had asked.

Over the next few days, as Lisa waited for the endless time before the board meeting to pass, she was tempted to call Michael to say "Look, I'm about to blow your plans into the water; get out while you can and have done with it." But that would have only created a needless fight, perhaps a deep rift that could never be mended. If she was going to do it, she had to stand behind what she was doing, to believe in it and follow through on it with conviction. Otherwise the whole action would be pointless.

Lisa cleared taking the morning off with Pete Castelli. She was high enough up in the organization that she was basically entitled to take off essential time when she needed it, and she had made sure in advance that the people in both the architects' office and at the construction site would be gone, but she checked nevertheless. This was her new job, and she wanted to keep it.

Finally, the morning of the board meeting arrived. Lisa awakened at 4:15 with a start, cold fear making her body rigid, her heart pounding as if it were going to jump right out of her chest. Today was the day. She would stand up in front of Scribner, Candace, Richard, and Scott Hollingworth, and she would blow apart Michael's dreams in order to save him. There would be questions, recriminations, accusations, shocked disbelief. She was going to go into a family meeting and tell that family that one of its members—Richard Hollingworth—was a liar. And she would be helping to show that Candace was one as well.

And she still didn't know if she was doing the right thing.

CHAPTER ELEVEN

Lisa caught a glimpse of herself in the mirrored walls of the Eastland lobby, and she was shocked by her appearance. She had been so tense this morning, so conflicted about what she was about to do, that she had done a remarkable job—unconsciously—of disguising herself. The young woman who looked warily back at her from the mirror was heavily made up, and was wearing a seersucker suit she had never donned in her life because she had always felt it was too severe. Her hair was up in a bun, a hairstyle Lisa hadn't sported in years, and her shoes were the kind that mothers always called "sensible"—something else she had always avoided.

But her eyes were the same gray eyes, filled today with tension, anger, fear.

It was time to do what she had promised.

She looked at her watch: 9:48. Scott and Darcy were supposed to meet her at 9:45, and the board meeting was scheduled for 10:30. The plan was to meet, go out and have coffee, and then split up. Scott would go up to the meeting on the twenty-second floor as scheduled. Darcy and Lisa would follow soon after, and would be ready in the reception area for Scott to call them as his surprise witnesses when the time was right. The important thing was that no one see Lisa or Darcy before the meeting.

But damn it, where were Scott and Darcy? The last thing Lisa wanted to do was stand around the lobby and risk being seen by Candace or Richard.

Though her suit was lightweight, and she was wearing a cotton man-tailored shirt, she felt suddenly drenched in sweat, hot and confined in her clothes and this damned airless building. And she began to have serious second thoughts. Had Scott made some kind of side deal? Was he going to leave her out in the cold? Had he reconsidered? His actions were probably going to take a great deal out of him if he actually did what he was planning. If what he had told Lisa was true, he had been the family weakling and scapegoat for over thirty years. That was a heavy burden to throw over in a single morning.

Suddenly she saw Darcy and then Scott coming through the revolving door. They both looked as nervous as she felt, and even from a distance she could see that Scott's face was shining with sweat.

"Sorry we're late," he said breathlessly as he came trotting up to Lisa, leaving Darcy behind for the moment. "Let's get out of here before we're seen. It was a dumb place to meet."

"I agree," Lisa said as they all hurried out of the lobby and out onto Park Avenue. "And the fact that none of us thought of it doesn't really fill me with confidence in terms of the rest of the day."

"Don't worry," he said quickly. "Really. I'm as nervous as I've ever been in my life, but I know it's going to work."

"He really does," Darcy offered. "I can tell. And I do too."

Lisa forced a smile. "Well, that makes two of you. I hope you're right."

They went to a small coffee shop on Lexington Avenue and drank sour, greasy coffee for half an hour. No one was able to eat—least of all Darcy, who turned green when she smelled the coffee. But the time passed, then Scott was standing up and saying good-bye, and Lisa knew the plan was in motion. She couldn't turn back now.

She and Darcy lingered at the coffee shop, and at 10:25, began walking back toward Park. Darcy talked nonstop and Lisa only half listened, too nervous to do anything but nod and say "mmm-hmm" and imagine variation after variation of what could happen at the Eastland offices. She had panicked back at the coffee shop when she thought she had forgotten her reports, and she wanted to try not to panic again, but it was difficult to hold it back. The fear had shot so much adrenaline through her veins that her heart was still pounding. What if she had stood up and begun her speech, only to find that one of her most important pieces of evidence was gone?

But thank God she hadn't forgotten it. And maybe it would all be all right.

When Lisa and Darcy got off the elevator at the twenty-second floor, Lisa felt a little skip of her heart. The same thick beige carpeting hugged the floors, the same muted ceiling fixtures cast just enough light to allow a person to see, the same hush made the hallways seem charged with expectation. Only she didn't work here anymore. She was here for a different reason now.

Lisa turned toward the smoked-glass doors that said Eastland Industries, took a deep breath, and said, "Come on. Let's go." She looked at her watch. Ten thirty on the dot.

Lisa was glad to see there was a new receptionist at the front desk. It was easier not to be recognized, and when she gave her and Darcy's names, there wasn't even a slight flicker of recognition in the young woman's eyes.

"Mr. Scott Hollingworth is in a board meeting," she said. "And he doesn't even have an office here—"

"We know," Lisa cut in. "And we'll wait, thank you. He *is* expecting us."

And just at that moment Scott came through the doors that led to the inner offices.

His face was sheet-white, pasty and pale and sticky-looking. Lisa's heart went out to him; she just hoped he could continue to hold himself together.

"Well, it's time," he croaked, his voice strangled and barely audible.

Darcy looked as panicked as Lisa felt, and Scott guided her back to the couch and put a hand on her shoulder. "I want you to wait out here, okay, Darcy?"

"But why? I thought—"

"I know," he said gently. "But it's very, very tense in there right now. I made an announcement that I was making a presentation, and they went into shock. And I don't want to put a strain on you. I think we can make it through the meeting without you. And I promise I'll come out for you if we do need you."

She looked disappointed but relieved as well, and a few moments later, as Lisa preceded Scott down the familiar hallway, she wished she had been given the same sort of reprieve. She wasn't at all relishing the experience. She was swept by uncertainty, convinced she would stand up and lose her voice, forget everything she could possibly say.

When they reached the closed board-room doors, Scott leaped forward and held one open for Lisa. And the first person she saw as she stepped into the room was Candace.

Candace's pale blue eyes widened in amazement, and she turned first to her father, then to Richard, then to Scott. "What could Lisa Bennett possibly have to do with this discussion?" she demanded. But her voice was unsure, sharp in its uncertainty.

"You'll see," Scott said. "You'll see, Candy."

At that moment Lisa was so aware of the enormity of what Scott was doing by standing up to his family that she was suddenly filled with determination. He needed her; he didn't think he could do what he wanted without her help. And damn it, she'd give more than he had even hoped for.

Lisa glanced at Scribner Hollingworth as she sat down next to Scott. Hollingworth was a dour-looking man, with thinning white hair, a pale, skeleton-thin face, high cheekbones that sank into deep, drawn hollows beneath. He was wearing a dark suit, and Lisa guessed that he probably never wore anything else—a conservative, traditional man. But with one exception: His glasses were thick-framed and heavy-looking, totally out of proportion to his face

261

and bone structure. No eyeglass salesman in his right mind would have recommended such frames for such a diminutive man, but Lisa knew well that Scribner Hollingworth wasn't the type to ask the advice of anyone—certainly not an eyeglass salesman. And she suspected he wore the glasses in order to intimidate, perhaps to shock, to unsettle the uncertain observer.

Now he had lowered them down his nose, and was looking at Lisa across the table as if looking at a large bug that had just crawled up onto the table.

"Scott, you're well aware of the fact that this is a *board* meeting, and that this Lisa Bennett is quite obviously *not* a member of our board." He fixed his son with his pale blue eyes. "Explain yourself, please."

"I will," Scott said.

Lisa winced; his voice had actually cracked when he had spoken, as if he were thirteen years old and had just been called on in school.

"This is ridiculous," Richard cried. "I *will* not discuss board business while an outsider is here. Especially an outsider who is a dismissed ex-employee of this company."

"I'm not asking you to discuss board business," Scott said much more firmly than before, Lisa was glad to note. "You can listen," Scott continued. "All of you. I promise you won't be bored."

Lisa didn't look at any of them. There was venom in the air, in their voices, in their very gazes. Better to keep her mind on what Scott was saying and on what she was planning to say.

And she listened carefully as Scott began to speak, his voice growing steadier with each angry sentence.

"Father, I'd say most of this is going to be for your benefit. For perhaps the first time in our lives, everyone in this room knows more about what's going on than you do. Now, there are so many issues here—so many really nasty deceptions and games—that I could probably keep all of you here all day and keep at least you, Father, in a state of amazement. But I realize we all have other business to attend to. Father, I know you, for instance, have an afternoon meeting. And I'm sure you two have something planned," he said, looking at Richard and Candace. "You always do. So I'm going to keep this relatively short, because I want to highlight the most interesting points—the ones that you, especially, Father, will be interested in."

Lisa was growing nervous again. Scott was wandering from the point; his introduction had been too long; and while Richard and Candace both looked rigid with apprehension, Scribner Hollingworth was beginning to look bored. She was tempted to kick Scott under the table, but he'd probably shout in pain and crumple into a heap. No, she just had to hope he'd improve as he went along.

He pulled a cassette recorder out of his briefcase and placed it on the conference table, and Richard groaned and twisted in his chair.

"Come on!" he whined. "You're not even involved with the company, much less the inn, Scott. What could you possibly have to say about any of this?"

Scott smiled a strange, mirthless smile. "Oh, it's not what I have to say about the inn, Richard. It's what you and Candace had to say about the inn that will interest Father in particular."

He pressed a button on the recorder, turned beet

263

red as he realized he had pressed the wrong one, pressed another one, and Lisa cringed in her seat until finally, miraculously, Candace's voice was coming through loud and clear.

"Tell me about Lisa Bennett," Candace said from the tape.

"What's to tell that you haven't read in the folder?" Richard asked.

Lisa looked past Richard as the tape continued to run. He was pale as a ghost, completely immobile, his jaw clenched in what had to be painful tension. As everyone in the room listened to his reasons why Lisa was going to find problems with the inn, he seemed paralyzed, as if all the will had been sucked right out of him.

But not Candace. "Where did you get that tape?" she demanded, her voice shrill and strident. "*There was no tape recorder in that office.* You must have—you must have forged it somehow."

"Forged it? Hardly," Scott said. He stopped the tape, rewound it for a moment, and played it again so that everyone could hear what Candace had hidden by talking.

"And you think she'll find problems with Michael's operation," she was saying on tape.

"She'll have to," Richard said.

"But she won't make Michael look bad?"

They all listened in silence. Lisa was beginning to think Scott should have cut it when she heard some more interesting statements, this time from Richard: "This year, I intend to be a victor rather than a victim, Candy, and nothing's going to stop me. Including you."

"I could always tell Father," she said.

"We're on the same side, Candy. Interested in the same things. Why don't we try to keep it that way?"

As the tape continued, Scott rifled through the other cassettes. Lisa was annoyed because he was making such a clatter that Candace's and Richard's voices were being obscured. But the temporary interruption had been worth it, for the next tape was even more damaging.

"What about Scott?" Candace's voice again.

"Scott? What does he know?" Richard scoffed. "He won't know what's going on. The important thing is that the report will clearly state—clearly, so even Scott can understand—that there isn't a chance the inn will ever make money again without enormous reorganization and capital improvements."

"And you think Father will go along with it?"

Silence. Then: "As long as one of them does, it doesn't really matter, does it? Even if Father votes against it, so what?"

"I've heard enough!" Scribner Hollingworth bellowed. His face was shockingly flushed after his earlier pallor, and a vein was bulging on his forehead.

"But there's more," Scott put in, and Lisa wished once again that she had some way of signaling him. He was ahead; he didn't have to push.

"Father," Richard said, "I have some serious objections to—"

Hollingworth's hand slammed down so hard on the table everyone was stunned into silence.

"You will sit here and be quiet until I tell you to speak," Hollingworth said through his teeth. "And if that takes forever, that's your loss." He looked at Candace, then looked quickly away. So much pain flashed in his eyes that Lisa felt very sorry for him.

265

It had to be extremely difficult to have heard what he had.

Then he turned to Scott and very quietly said, "I apologize for interrupting, son. I think it's very important that we hear all there is to here." He glanced at Lisa. "But I don't understand what she's doing here."

Some manners, Lisa thought. He was very, very upset, but still . . .

"Ms. Bennett is the one who wrote the reports," Scott said, "and I thought you'd want to know how those reports were written, as well as—"

"Reports?" Hollingworth interrupted. "I only saw one report."

Scott turned to Lisa. "Lisa? Do you want to explain what happened?"

"Sure, Scott," she said, trying to sound calm. But her voice had been breathy and weak. There was so much tension in the room that it was difficult to breathe.

She began, nervously at first and then more confidently, by explaining what Richard had done—that he had rejected her first and honest report, and that he made it very clear what he wanted in the revised version. Scott apparently didn't have a tape of that conversation, but at this point Lisa felt it was unnecessary. No tapes could do any more damage than had already been done.

Scribner Hollingworth listened to Lisa in rapt attention, taking in every word with a concentration that bordered on the ferocious. He was hungry for information now, and he was going to get it out of everyone he could.

"That's *your* opinion," Richard finally interrupted, unable to hold in his anger any longer. "Father, for your information, Miss Bennett was dismissed by Eastland several weeks ago."

"Laid off," she corrected quickly, angrily. "And for *your* information, I have a memo from you that states it was because of reorganization."

"I was being polite," Richard snapped. "You were dismissed, Miss Bennett."

"*I* will be the judge of that," Hollingworth rumbled. "Now, please go on, Miss Bennett." He wouldn't even look at Richard.

"Well, as I said, Richard wanted a very different kind of report. And he made it clear that I had no choice in the matter, that I was simply to fulfill his request. The understanding was that I would then move on to other areas at Eastland. But it was very clear there was no choice in the matter. Very clear."

Hollingworth narrowed his eyes. "Do you have that report?" he demanded.

"Of course. Right here," she said, and for a moment she had another wave of panic as she thought it was missing. But it was at the top of the folder, where she had put it in the coffee shop, and she handed the clipped sheath of papers to Mr. Hollingworth.

His anger was clearly visible as he scanned the papers. His face darkened to a deep red again, and his breathing grew heavy. When he looked up, his eyes were pale specks. "This is intolerable," he said hoarsely. Still he wouldn't look at his children. He leveled his gaze on Lisa. "And your opinion is that the inn can make money?"

"No question about it. I outlined several plans for possible improvements, in the report you're holding, and there were a few more I went over with Michael Jamison that I didn't feel were quite appropriate for inclusion in the report. But they're definitely all feasible."

"Jamison," Hollingworth snapped. "And what exactly is his role in all of this. Is he Innesco? What the hell is it all about, damn it?"

"Why don't you ask Candace?" Scott said. "She knows as much as Richard does."

Scott sounded childish, like a little boy accusing his sister of stealing his building blocks. But Lisa could see that it would be easy to slip into that vein. Whenever she went home to Iowa, she invariably regressed, especially when her brothers were around.

"Candace?" Hollingworth said quietly. "Candy. Tell me."

Candace swallowed and brushed her hair back from her face with both hands. "I—"

But at that moment there was a knock at the door. For a moment no one moved or made a sound, and Lisa guessed this was because no one knew who should answer the door. No one knew whether answering the door would seem powerful or powerless, and they were all so concerned with that sort of thing that they were paralyzed.

Finally Richard jumped out of his chair and swung the door open.

Standing there was the receptionist from the front desk, looking shaky and nervous. She was holding an envelope in her hand. "There's a man at the front desk who just dropped this off with me, and he said something about his resignation. Mrs. Merino stopped him and she wanted me to come tell you he's still here. She's holding him there," she added in wonder. "He said he'd see you, Mr. Hollingworth, if you wanted."

Scribner extended his hand. "Give me that," he ordered, and impatiently waved his hand as she ran around the conference table and finally handed him the envelope.

He tore it open and then stared. "It's Jamison," he sputtered. "Get him in here!" he demanded.

The receptionist was out the door in less than a moment, and a few seconds later Michael strode in. "Scrib, I—"

But then he saw Lisa. For a few moments it was as if they were the only two people in the room, staring at each other as if alone. He looked exhausted, with dark circles under his dark eyes, and he looked thinner. Really worn out. And angry.

He turned to Scribner, and a chill passed through Lisa, as she had the horrible feeling that that had been the last time Michael was ever going to look at her again.

"Scrib, I had no intention of breaking up this meeting or even seeing you." He looked at the roughly opened envelope on the table. "The letter is self-explanatory, obviously. I'll stay on for a couple of weeks if you'd like. But I'm finished."

At first Scribner Hollingworth said nothing. Then he yelled, "What the *hell* is the meaning of this? Jamison, you've missed an interesting meeting. I've just discovered that my children—possibly with the exception of Scott, although I haven't discovered what his motives are in all of this—have been plotting against me. *Plotting*, Jamison. And the implication so far is that you had some hand in this too."

"I wanted to make an offer for the inn, as you know or should know. That offer is now withdrawn."

"What?"

"It's withdrawn effective immediately." He glanced at Candace. "And I'd rather not say anything more about it, Scrib. This is a family meeting and I think you have enough to discuss without me." He glanced icily at Lisa and turned and walked out the door, letting it swing shut behind him without looking back.

Michael walked down the carpeted hallway to the elevators in such a state of shock he barely knew where he was. Lisa had been there. At the board meeting that had been scheduled to discuss the sale of the inn.

He had been caught so off-guard, had been so stunned, that he didn't know whether he had stared at her for ten seconds or ten minutes. All he knew was that in that time, his feelings had coursed from love to hate to—what? He didn't know how he felt beyond one overwhelming, all-powerful emotion—anger.

For she had clearly been there for one reason and one reason only. Scrib had said he had just discovered Richard and Candace had been plotting against him. Scott had obviously exposed them, though Michael had no idea how. Or why, for that matter. But Lisa had clearly played a part in the exposure. She had been sitting next to Scott, who had a tape recorder on the table in front of him, and the first report she had ever written about the inn was on the conference table.

Had she been right all along when she had said Richard was forcing her to write a certain kind of report? When Candace had come to him, he had assumed she had come only because she had heard he was trying to round up investors, and he'd assumed her actions had nothing to do with anything that had happened earlier. But now . . . maybe Lisa *had* been right, and had been telling Scribner of her experiences.

Which meant she had turned on him, done something that was directly hostile, directly harmful to his plans.

And he couldn't believe it.

He had loved her so much. She had never been able to accept his plans, had felt strangely hostile and negative about what he was doing. She had never understood how important it was for him to do something like bid for the inn; and he had decided she'd never be able to accept him as he really was.

She seemed to require some sort of power in every relationship she had and it was usually economic power, sometimes sexual power, sometimes both. She fought against this, suffered because of it, but did it over and over again nevertheless. And he had nothing against it. He certainly didn't expect her to be weak. What he did expect was for her to be able to accept when he changed roles, no matter who else that involved.

In the end, of course, he had realized he had done the wrong thing. He had decided to resign and cancel his arrangement with Candace because it was simply too dishonest. It smacked of fraud, of dishonesty that would taint the entire future of the inn. He hadn't wanted to hurt Candace, and thus hadn't made any big speeches in the meeting about their arrangement or what had happened. But he had decided he wanted out, and he had followed through.

Unfortunately, he saw now that Lisa had been right to an extent. She had felt—as he did now—that Candace's willingness to lie now boded ill for the future, and Lisa had told him there were other inns, other pieces of property he could acquire, even other investors if he was going to insist on bidding on the inn. And he hadn't listened. It was something he had planned on his own.

But the fact that Lisa had been right didn't excuse any of the wrong things she had done. She had deserted him at a time when he had needed emotional support, and today—today she had done something that truly shocked him. She had gone up in front of Scribner and the rest of the Hollingworths, and she had deliberately, with what he had to consider malice, done all she could to ruin his plans. And for that, he couldn't forgive her.

As he walked up Park Avenue, blisteringly hot under the August sun and smog, he remembered—unwillingly—some of the times they had shared. He remembered throwing her into the swimming hole, walking through the forest at night, laughing as she had tried to tell him a joke, which she was terrible at. He remembered that first night they had been together, when she had been so honest, so forthright, so straightforward. He had loved her honesty, her sincerity. Where had those qualities gone? And why —why had she betrayed him like this? He remembered how they had argued at first, how she had driven him crazy with what he thought of as her operations-manager/efficiency-expert mentality. She had only been trying to do her job then, and she had given him some great suggestions. But today hadn't had anything to do with her job. She had another job, and she didn't need her Eastland one back. Today had been vengeance, and he didn't understand why.

CHAPTER TWELVE

The meeting at Eastland didn't last too much longer
after Michael had left. At least Lisa's role in it didn't
last. Scribner Hollingworth had asked her to leave,
telling her he'd be in touch, and Scott had thanked
her and walked her to the door.

Irrationally, she had thought Michael might be
waiting. From the look in his eyes, of course, it was
extremely unlikely. He had looked as if he never
wanted to set eyes on her again. But she had still
hoped. . . . For even if he was furious at her, didn't
he at least have questions?

Deep down, though, she knew the answer. There
were certain things he couldn't accept, certain places
where he drew the line and then wouldn't cross.
When she had fought with him about his going in on
the inn with Candace, she had thought they'd speak
again. She would have called him herself, except she
knew that if he wanted to speak to her, he would call.
And he hadn't.

And today, she suspected, was worse. Never had she seen such anger—possibly even hatred—in his eyes.

Now it was over, unless he forgave her. And she knew that would never come to pass.

Damn! She had had such qualms about appearing at the board meeting. She had wondered whether it was the right thing to do, whether doing it would drive him into Candace's arms or alienate him at the very least. She had done it to save him, but she had lost him forever.

That night Lisa spoke with Scott over the phone. The Hollingworth family was in utter chaos. The only thing anyone knew was that the inn was no longer up for sale. And that Richard was no longer CEO.

"Well, that's one good thing that came out of it," Lisa said disconsolately. "I wouldn't want to think I did all of that for nothing."

"You're really upset about Michael, aren't you? I saw what went on between you when he first came in."

"I guess nobody missed that. Yes, I'm very upset. Naturally. It was something I had worried about, and I guess if I hadn't felt so strongly about stopping the deal, I would never have done what I did. It was a stupid risk. I hadn't really thought our relationship was over at that point. And obviously now there's no question."

Scott sighed. "I'm so sorry, Lisa. After all you've done for me and Darcy." He paused. "We're getting married, by the way."

"Really?" Lisa smiled her first smile of the day. "That's really wonderful, Scott. I'm very happy for you. And I admire you too. You've done a lot of strong things lately, taken a lot of strong actions other people would have been afraid to take."

He laughed. "Yeah, well, not too many people would marry a girl who's pregnant with their brother's baby. But I love her too much. Love at first sight, I guess. And it looks as if Father's going to offer me Richard's spot at the company."

"Really? That's wonderful!"

"Well, yes and no. I really don't think I want it, to tell you the truth. I like my work, and as long as I can know that my Eastland money is safe, I'm not obsessed with the idea of running the company. I just don't want my money drained or abused, that's all. Anyway, we're even thinking of leaving the city. Darcy likes it, but she's homesick, too, and I thought we might move somewhere closer to Iowa so she could go home more easily."

Strangely and annoyingly, Lisa suddenly had tears in her eyes. Darcy and Scott had suddenly become such a fairy-tale couple. And the mention of Iowa had made her homesick too. Everything that had happened to her lately—since the breakup with Michael—had been so rotten.

"Oh, and Candace is leaving for Europe tomorrow. She can't deal with what happened at all."

"But what about Michael?"

"Who knows? I doubt if he's exactly enamored of her at the moment, Lisa. You could see how fed up he was at the meeting. Something made him change his mind. And while he tried to spare Candace, he didn't go that far out of his way."

"Yes, I suppose that's true," she said musingly.

276

"Listen, when do you two think you're going to move? And what about your business?"

"We'll set up out there," he said happily. "Darcy says now that she's been a model she can at least say she's done it. She doesn't care all that much anymore. She wants to see some cows, she said. And blue sky. And I want to go where she wants to go."

Suddenly Lisa couldn't bear to talk to him anymore. She was jealous—happy for them, but jealous and sad and disappointed over the way things had turned out for her. For a time everything had seemed so wonderful. She had finally met a man who meant the world to her, someone she knew she'd love forever, someone she wanted to spend the rest of her life with. And now what did she have? A job that was interesting but not thrilling, an apartment she liked but which seemed as lonely as a tomb, a colorless autumn in the city to look forward to. And how many more after that? "I have to go," she said quietly. "But I really wish you the best, Scott, and we'll keep in touch, okay? I want to hear everything that happens."

"Sure thing," he said. "And best from Darcy. She'd talk but she feels kind of sick right now. Her morning sickness turned into all-day sickness today."

"Gee, I hope she's okay." Lisa said. "I didn't see her when I left the meeting and I was so distracted I didn't notice that she wasn't feeling well."

"Well, she was in the ladies' room. Anyway, talk to you soon. Bye-bye."

Lisa hung up, and tears she had suppressed for a long time suddenly sprang forth. She lay down on the couch and cried, washed her face, and cried some more.

Her life seemed so empty. She had never felt a man was totally necessary, had always believed deeply that there were other things in life besides marriage and all the traditional milestones one was supposed to reach. And she still did believe this. But she was lonely, and she missed Michael, and she felt an emptiness that didn't seem as if it would ever go away.

And she knew she had never felt this way before.

She thought about calling Michael. Perhaps they could talk things through. She could explain what had led her to do what she did, and they could talk about everything they had fought about, everything they had disagreed about.

But she knew it wouldn't work. What had bothered Michael most, no matter what they were fighting about, was that she insisted on getting her way, that she insisted on holding the power and making the decisions in the relationship. Maybe, in fact, he had done certain things just to show he was independent, that he could make decisions that flew in the face of her own, and that he could succeed. And he had been so driven to do this that he had been blinded to the dangers of the course he was choosing. She knew he had been a very successful man once. All of a sudden he had begun to make unwise moves —very unwise moves that had culminated in his resignation. Maybe he had done all of that because of her, because she had tried too hard to shape things for him.

And now, if she called and suggested they get together, maybe he would resent that as well.

She simply didn't know. She wanted to call him,

but she was afraid. The memory of the look in his eyes instantly killed whatever courage she had.

And so she didn't call, and the days passed and her loneliness didn't shrink. It grew, in fact, as she went to work each day and joined in a camaraderie she suddenly didn't feel part of. And it grew as she came home each day to her empty apartment.

She got together with friends she hadn't seen in a long time, and on those evenings she was much happier. But still, deep inside, the pit of loneliness was growing.

Patricia had a miscarriage and was heartbroken for weeks, and then she turned bitter, deciding everything in life was a gyp and a fraud, that there was no winning.

And Lisa didn't want to end up like that. She firmly believed a person could recover from anything, no matter how difficult.

And so she worked at cheering up as if it were a project, filling her days and nights as well and as compulsively as she could. And it began to work. She'd snap out of her funk eventually, and she was coming through already, if only in tiny steps.

A new project at work suddenly made her days twice as frantic, and Lisa was exhausted but much happier.

One of her brothers came to visit for the first time, and Lisa had great fun showing him the sights of New York and just reminiscing about old times. It made her homesick but happy, and she recognized she was coming further and further out of her depression.

And then, on a blistering-hot day at the end of September, when the construction crew was sweating oceans and Lisa could hardly bear to stand out in the sun for even a second, she saw a familiar-looking figure walking across the construction yard, the sunlight shimmering his silhouette into a dream-like vision.

It was Michael.

As he came forward, past the bulldozers and jack-hammers, past the girders and I-beams, her heart began to pound, and Lisa leaned against the trailer door for support.

She had thought of seeing him again so many times. But she hadn't known how deeply—and physically—the mere sight of him would touch her.

He was wearing all white—a T-shirt and jeans and sneakers—and his hair looked jet-black in contrast, his skin dark and shadowed.

When he saw her, his step hesitated, and she smiled. It meant she reached him, that the sight of her could affect him as the sight of him affected her, that he was nervous, hesitant, uncertain.

She didn't know what stance she was supposed to take. Was she supposed to be casual? Wave as if they hadn't seen each other for a day or two? As he came closer she stared, but she was unable to move. And by the time he reached her she still hadn't moved.

He smiled when he came up to her, and it was an uncertain smile, touchingly honest. "I've been trying to think of what I should say," he yelled over the noise. "Can we go somewhere?"

She turned and led him into the trailer, almost as hot as outdoors, but a bit quieter. She closed the door after he had stepped in, and she faced him.

"Well," she began. But she didn't know what to say. He looked so wonderful, so handsome.

He smiled again. "For two people who shared some really great times together, we're not all that quick." His smile faded. "I've missed you so much," he said softly.

She looked at him warily. "You didn't call."

He sighed. "I needed time, Lisa. A lot of time to figure out why you did what you did. I talked to Scott about it, I thought about it day and night, I wanted to understand, but I just couldn't. And before that, when you were so against my buying the inn, I was so hurt that you didn't have faith—" He shook his head. "What bothers me most is that I let it go on so long. I wish I *had* called. Now that I'm here."

"What do you think now? I mean about what happened."

He sighed. "I think I understand so well that I hate myself for having been so blind."

"Why? What did you decide?"

He smiled. "You sound as if I'm a judge, as if I had a right to judge. I didn't have that right, Lisa. But I was so hurt that I couldn't get past my self-righteousness." He shrugged. "Maybe I'm wrong too. But I saw something that made a lot of sense, and I'm just so sorry." He pulled out a chair for each of them, and they sat down. "The thing I couldn't understand was why you had so little faith in me in terms of the inn and Candace. I had always thought I was the one who had to worry about fidelity, because of everything you had told me. And I had been in banking long enough to feel I knew what I was doing. A mistake, but that wasn't something I saw at the time. But the other night there was a program on television about farming—how farmers are losing their land, how the small farm is going out of existence, how a whole culture is disappearing from this country."

She smiled. "I saw it too."

"Well, I started thinking. It reminded me so much of what you had told me about your family. And I suddenly realized: No wonder you were protective and suspicious and pessimistic. You had watched as the farm your family had owned for generations was taken away. You had watched your father turn into a broken man. I think the whole experience reached you a lot more deeply than you may realize. I don't know, but . . ." He shrugged. "Maybe this is silly."

She smiled. "I don't think so. I just realized something myself. I never could understand the absolute passion that was making me crazy about your getting the inn. I knew it was a bad idea, but I was obsessed with it. And maybe that was because it reminded me that the same thing that happened to my family could happen to you."

He nodded slowly. "That's what I finally realized. But the reason I wanted to understand, Lisa, is that I love you so much. I've missed you so much. I wanted to find some reason—something I could understand."

"Oh, Michael, I've missed you so much. It was so awful." She sighed. "There's something, though, that I have to know."

"What's that?"

"Well, I kept trying to figure out what had gone wrong—why you had taken such offense, why you wouldn't call. And you're saying—now—that you didn't understand why I wouldn't support you. But when I was thinking about all of this, I kept coming up with the idea that you couldn't stand for me to be strong. That maybe some of what you had said was true. I don't know. How can we reconcile the fact that—"

"Don't," he interrupted softly. "Don't think that. I said some things that weren't true. You did have a right to disagree with me, whether I thought you did or not. I was hurt by what you did. That doesn't mean you were wrong." He took a long, deep breath. "What kept breaking my heart, Lisa, was that I had been planning to ask you to marry me before we fought." He hesitated. "A lot of things have happened to me since we last talked. I got another group of investors together—*real* silent partners this time —and we bought some property near the inn—"

"Really? Oh, Michael—"

He laughed. "Don't be excited until you know the details. No, it really *is* a good deal, and I was careful as hell with it. I realized I really could do what you had said—get some other people involved—which I probably knew before, but I just refused to see it because I was so angry. Anyway, I saw something much more important in all of this, Lisa."

"What's that?"

He sighed. "There's nothing more important than love, than being with the person you love, the person you were meant for. I've always felt that we were meant for each other—and I mean that. Our relationship was just so different from anything I've ever had. And when I lost you, I lost everything. Even if I had gone ahead with the inn and everything had worked out, I would have lost the most important part of my life. And I want to change that—I want to marry you, Lisa, if—"

"I'd love to," she interrupted, laughing and rising

from her chair. She threw her arms around him and he stood, and they held each other close, each amazed they had been apart for so long. Tears came to Lisa's eyes as she hugged Michael, tears came to Michael's eyes as he held Lisa in his arms, and he knew that whatever happened in the future, he would never forget this moment. And he would never forget that love—the love he felt for this marvelous woman—was more important than anything in the world.

He kissed her long and deeply, and when he drew back and looked into her eyes, she was smiling.

"I can't wait to see the place you bought," she said. "And it's so wonderful to imagine—land that will be ours!"

He stroked her hair back from her face. "Does that really appeal to you? I was worried about living at the new inn in terms of your work and all."

She shrugged. "I don't see why that should be a problem. My job is north of the city anyway. But can't we split our time between the city and the country?"

He grinned. "That was exactly what I had in mind."

She wrapped her arms more tightly around him and rested her head on his chest, and he held her close, lovingly stroking her back.

"It just amazes me that we could have been separated for so long," she sighed. She looked up into his deep, dark eyes. "It bothers me that I didn't call though. To think I almost lost you."

"I wouldn't have let that happen," he whispered.

But deep inside she came to a realization she kept to herself—that she had always run or turned away

284

from what meant most to her, whether it was a life-style and a home she had loved and lost or a man she felt she was getting too close to or even the idea of a deep and long-lasting relationship. She had been trying so hard to control everyone and everything for so many years that she had lost all she loved in the process. She hadn't even been home as often as she really wanted and she was sure this was because she still felt the pain of her loss.

But she would try never to run again.

And as Michael drew her chin up and kissed her again, she knew that she'd love him forever, that together they could live the kind of life she had dreamed of long, long ago, before she had become convinced that dreams couldn't come true.

Now, for the first time in her life, she knew that they could.

LOOK FOR NEXT MONTH'S
CANDLELIGHT ECSTASY SUPREMES

$2.50 each

At your local bookstore or use this handy coupon for ordering:

 DELL BOOKS   B123A
P.O. BOX 1000, PINE BROOK, N.J. 07058-1000

Please send me the books I have checked above. I am enclosing $ _____ (please add 75c per copy to cover postage and handling). Send check or money order—no cash or C.O.D.'s. Please allow up to 8 weeks for shipment.

Name _____

Address _____

City _____ State Zip _____

Rebels and outcasts, they fled halfway across the earth to settle the harsh Australian wastelands. Decades later—ennobled by love and strengthened by tragedy—they had transformed a wilderness into fertile land. And themselves into

The Australians

WILLIAM STUART LONG

THE EXILES, #1	12374-7-12	$3.95
THE SETTLERS, #2	17929-7-45	$3.95
THE TRAITORS, #3	18131-3-21	$3.95
THE EXPLORERS, #4	12391-7-11	$3.50
THE ADVENTURERS, #5	10330-4-40	$3.95